JUDGE DREDD
BLACK ATLANTIC

"Dredd! Six o'clock!"

At Vix's alarm, Dredd whipped about and put a three-shot burst of execution rounds into another Warchild's chest. He heard it shriek and saw it go down, its camouflage flashing crazily. Then the first one was on him again, blades whirling. One went diagonally through the dead comms operator's skull, shearing most of his head off. Anther sliced into a control board, sending up a spray of brilliant sparks.

Dredd hurled himself away. There was no way to block those blades – from the way they went through metal and bone with such ease, they must have been edged with monomolecular fibres. He heard a blade sing through the air again and the comms operator's chair fell away in two pieces. The corpse did too.

D1598357

Judge Dredd from Black Flame

#1: DREDD vs DEATH
Gordon Rennie

#2: BAD MOON RISING
David Bishop

#3: BLACK ATLANTIC
Simon Jowett & Peter J Evans

More 2000 AD action

ABC Warriors

#1: THE MEDUSA WAR
Pat Mills & Alan Mitchell

Strontium Dog

#1: BAD TIMING
Rebecca Levene

Judge Dredd created by **John Wagner**
& Carlos Ezquerra.

Chief Judge Hershey created by **John Wagner**
& Brian Bolland.

JUDGE DREDD

BLACK ATLANTIC

SIMON JOWETT
AND PETER J EVANS

BLACK FLAME

A Black Flame Publication
www.blackflame.com

First published in 2004 by BL Publishing, Games Workshop Ltd.,
Willow Road, Nottingham NG7 2WS, UK.

Distributed in the US by Simon & Schuster, 1230 Avenue of the
Americas, New York,. NY 10020, USA.

10 9 8 7 6 5 4 3 2 1

Cover illustration by Dylan Teague

ISBN 1 84416 108 0

A CIP record for this book is available from the British Library.

Printed in the UK by Bookmarque, Surrey, UK.

MEGA-CITY ONE, 2130

1. DUST BUST

"Careful with that, you barely-sentient gimp!"

The woman's shout was so loud, so unexpected, that Arnold Crobetti almost dropped the canister a second time. He started, the mech-splint around his left leg whining and stiffening reflexively, and only just managed to pass the canister to the next man in line before it slid out of his fingers. Drokk it, the things were *heavy*!

Crobetti turned back to grab the next drum from the man behind, and saw the woman striding towards him, her long lab coat flapping. There was an expression on her sharp features that he didn't like the look of at all. "Aw c'mon," he whined. "I had my foot under it when it came down, honest. Barely scratched the paint…"

The woman stopped in front of him, glaring. "Listen to me, you throwback," she snapped, poking him in the chest. "Every one of these canisters is worth more than you are. More than your family, your friends, their friends and their pets put together!" One of the other men in the chain sniggered and the woman looked up and fixed him with that awful glare. The snigger trailed off into silence.

"That goes for all of you. Remember that your boss is paying for this. If the equipment gets damaged, so do you." And with that, she turned her back on the lot of them and stormed off.

Crobetti swallowed. "Man, is that any way for a professor to talk?" He took hold of the next drum – carefully – and handed it on.

Little Petey, the next man in the chain, lifted it out of his grasp without trying. "Doctor," he singsonged. "She's a doctor. I heard one of the tekkies call her doctor."

Oh brother. Crobetti's eyes went up. There were twenty guys in the chain, passing the heavy drums one to the next, all the way from the freezer wagon on the factory's loading ramp to the building itself. Twenty of Big Jimmy's finest, and he had to be next to Little Petey Steene.

Little Petey was a head taller than Crobetti, but there wasn't much inside that head to speak of. He could squash shell casings flat between his finger and thumb, but he had trouble counting past four and once he started talking it was difficult to get him to shut up. He'd just keep saying the same thing, over and over and over, with a grin on his face so wide it looked as though his jaw was about to fall off. Big Jimmy only kept him on as part of the MegEast Mob because he could pull people's noses off with his bare hands.

There was a small scar on Petey's left temple, and Crobetti wondered if maybe a bullet had gone in there one time and scrambled things up a little.

Not that Crobetti was exactly a stranger to bullets himself. The mech-splint holding his leg together was enough evidence of that. The wound he'd got from last month's rumble with those MegCentral sneckers hadn't healed yet, and the splint was old and needed tuning. It made him limp, and it had made him drop one of Doctor grud-face Hellermann's precious canisters.

"'Yes, Doctor Hellermann. Right away, Doctor Hellermann.' That's what he said," Petey was still chanting. Crobetti grimaced and hauled another drum around for him.

"Yeah, okay, Petey. Thanks for clearing that up. Now grab." Anything to stop him getting into a rhythm. Crobetti limped round to take another item of Hellermann's equipment – some kind of armoured crate, this time – and pass it on to Little Petey. He looked longingly at the pile of weapons he and the boys had brought with them from MegEast, expecting that the job would involve using them on members of the MegSouth mob. Not acting like a gang of baggage-bots at Grissom Spaceport.

"If I don't see another one of these things as long as I live, I'll be a happy man," Arnold muttered as he limped back to move yet another of the canisters down the line.

"I'm a happy man," Little Petey chimed in. "I've always been a happy man. Can't remember a time when I wasn't happy. Happy, happy, happy. That's Little Petey…"

Arnold Crobetti sighed. It was going to be a long night.

Tek-Judge Gleick was having a long night too. He had been watching MegEast mobsters haul drums about for far too long, and Little Petey's singsong ramblings were making the job almost intolerable. Still, annoying or not, these scum were certainly going to be a worthy catch for the ground team. Not only did most of them have a rap sheet as long as the proverbial Judge's arm, but the canisters they were manhandling from the truck were plastered with biohazard stickers – not something one would normally expect to find being driven about in a Sunshine Synthifoods freezer wagon.

But then, when Elize Hellermann was involved, nothing was normal.

Gleick was running a public surveillance workstation, situated in the Statue of Judgement in MegEast, not far from Big Jimmy's home turf. It was kilometres from the supposedly abandoned factory where Jimmy's boys were unloading, but the link between Gleick's workstation and the spy-in-the-sky camera he was controlling was close to perfect. He sent the insect-sized camera darting away from the chain of mobsters, past the wagon with its cheery logo of happy farm animals and up to a higher vantage point overlooking the factory.

Why farm animals? Cows, pigs, chickens – what kind of a futsie would enjoy the thought of eating extinct species?

Gleich shrugged, and as the big mobster's voice faded he selected a reserved channel and opened it. "PSU 767 to Ground Team One, over."

"Receiving you, PSU." The answering voice was unmistakable, and Gleick couldn't help sitting up a little straighter in his seat. "Report."

"Loading is still in progress, Ground Team. Can also confirm that Hellermann is in the building. Repeat: Hellermann is in the building."

"Received and understood, PSU," came the rough sounding reply. "Maintain surveillance. Let us know when the last of the chemicals are off the truck."

"Acknowledged, Ground Team One. PSU out." Gleick tapped at the camera controls, guiding the spy back towards the loading bay. Petey's voice became louder in Gleick's earpiece.

"I don't know why I'm so happy. Poppa always said I smiled so hard it made him want to take his belt to me just to see my expression change…"

Gleick sighed. It looked as if listening to this drek was going to be the price he'd have to pay to be able to boast to his colleagues over breakfast that he had worked with a legend.

Elize Hellermann strode through the storage area on the far side of the loading bay doors. Yet more of Big Jimmy's men moved around her, stacking canisters from the freezer wagon for later use, or loading other containers and mixing vessels onto hover-pallets. Her own staff handled the ferrying, especially for the items that went through a set of automatic doors to the nursery.

Whatever machinery had once been housed in the factory had been removed decades earlier. She had chosen this location within the Dust Zone – sector after sector of automated industrial units grouped around the Power Tower at the centre of MegSouth – because so many of the units had been closed down during one of the sector's periodic economic collapses. Falls like that hit every sector of Mega-City One at some time or another; businesses that took their owners a lifetime to build up could be gone overnight due to anything from an alien invasion to a dip in the sales of Mockburgers. Any increase in the numbers of unemployed from such a collapse would be barely noticeable in a city of four hundred million, with an unemployment rate of ninety per cent and holding.

Hellermann couldn't have cared less. Over the years, the number of things she cared about had dwindled sharply. At present, the number stood at one.

This.

The nursery doors opened smoothly. Hellermann walked through, feeling the downdraft of the clean air curtain – the environmental control system was one of the first things she had installed.

It was warm in the nursery. The temperature was boosted by waste heat from the equipment packed around the walls and across the floor, and the air was permeated by a constant low hum from the portable generators, brought in to ensure that no one at Big Meg Power noticed a spike in demand where there should have been no demand at all.

The factory space had been retro-fitted to her specifications with equipment of her own design, bought with money loaned to her by Big Jimmy, the diminutive – some would say stunted – grudfather of MegEast. Of course, Jimmy hadn't the faintest idea what she was doing here. All he was interested in was the money she had promised it would make him. If she had mentioned the word "treason", even a mobster like Jimmy might have balked.

Treason, she thought sourly, walking between processing units, purifiers and regulators. A stupid, small-minded word made up by stupid, small-minded people. People like those who claimed to uphold the law, and yet had reduced her to this – bowing and scraping for mobster money so she could continue her life's work in a rusting, bug-infested factory in the middle of the Dust Zone.

Technicians made their reports as she passed them. Everything was proceeding smoothly; as well it should, given the success of the first decantation.

Hellermann moved to another section of the nursery, where large, ovoid growth tanks stood in ranks across the floor. Each had a viewport set into the armour, and Hellermann peered into the nearest, through cloudy fluid and soupy, filigreed membranes. Inside, something thrashed and convulsed, powerful muscles jerking as a direct neural link downloaded terabytes of information directly into its brain.

Hellermann had selected the data for download very carefully: medical files, survival tactics, a compressed database of mankind's entire accumulated wisdom on the subject of war and ninety-five separate and distinct ways to kill a human being.

Placing a hand against the transparent plastic of the viewport, Hellermann smiled as she watched the creature twitch in its nutrient fluid.

"Soon, my child," she whispered. "Soon."

"That the last of 'em?" Arnold Crobetti asked. A man ahead of him in the human chain nodded.

"Looks that way."

Crobetti stretched. His splint shell casings the movement and kicked out, almost unbalancing him. The other mobsters in the loading bay pointed and laughed.

"That was funny, Arnold," laughed Little Petey. "You're a funny guy. That makes me happy."

"Yeah, yeah, very funny," Crobetti addressed his reply to everyone in the loading bay. An insect buzzed close to his ear, and he recoiled instinctively, waving it away with his hand. Damn bugs. "I don't remember seeing any of you mugs backing me up when I took a slug for Big Jimmy."

Getting his mech-splint back under control, he turned and made for the stacked weapons. The sooner he got back to

MegEast, the better. If any MegSouth mobsters turned up now, he didn't trust his splint to get him out of the way of any more slugs.

"PSU to Ground Team One. The chemicals are off the truck. Repeat: the chemicals are off the truck. Perps are tooling up and preparing to leave. Repeat–"

"Acknowledged. Ground Team One, we move. Team Two stay alert; Hellermann might use the back door." The gravelly voice cut across Tek-Judge Gleick's by-the-book communication etiquette. Gleick figured that was okay, though, seeing as the Judge on the other end of the comm-link wrote the book.

As he made his report, Gleick remote-guided the spy-in-the-sky out of the loading bay and into the night. Activating the infrared system, he piloted the flying camera skywards, broadening its field of view. His headset filled with a network of feeder roads, alleys and the dark hulks of abandoned, ruined buildings. The Dust Zone.

There. Half a dozen multicoloured heat signatures, moving in two ranks of three down the main drag. Moving fast.

"You hear that?" Crobetti asked no one in particular. He'd been strapping on his gun harness when he'd noticed: the sound of powerful engines. At first he thought it might be heavy traffic on the nearby skedway, but then he realised it was growing louder.

Getting closer.

"Lights."

Six sets of infrared vision filters were disengaged and the beams from six sets of powerful sodium quartz headlamps arrowed through the darkness and turned the loading bay as bright as a minor sun. In the glare, figures scrambled blindly trying to find cover, shading their eyes and bringing weapons to bear.

"Break."

The Lawmasters to left and right swung out smoothly, hugging the road's shoulder as the first volley of gunfire, fired blind from the loading bay into the dazzling headlights, swept between them. A lucky round struck the front wheel housing of the lead bike, whining off the armour and into the night. The rider's only reply was to trigger his bike cannon.

The other Lawmasters followed suit. In the sudden hail of high-explosive shells, the loading bay began to fly apart.

The freezer wagon's auto-polarising windshield had adjusted its setting the moment the Lawmasters' headlamps flared into life. Sitting behind the truck's controls, Tony Soba had a clear, though slightly tinted view of six Mega-City Judges barrelling towards him at what seemed a suicidal rate.

Tony had been one of Big Jimmy's street soldiers long enough to know what would come next if those Judges were allowed into the factory – cube-time and lots of it. Tony had done time before when he was a young man. If he went inside now, he'd be a crock by the time he got out – if he got out at all.

"I ain't going back inside!" Tony roared, and slammed the wagon in gear. The truck leapt forward and howled down the drag to meet the oncoming Judges.

"I'll deal with the truck," snapped the lead rider. The other five Judges swung their machines wider and opened their throttles, surging past the freezer wagon and toward the loading bay. Behind them, the remaining Lawmaster's bike cannon hammered streams of fire into the darkness.

The front of the freezer wagon simply dissolved. The forward grille, the bodywork, the windshield and the driver behind it; everything turned to fragments as the cannon shells tore the truck apart. The onboard computer must have gone too, locking the brakes, because the truck's wheels immediately jammed. The tyres gave out a chorus of shrieks as the wagon's momentum continued to drive them forwards, laying long strips of synthi-tread on the plascrete road.

The truck fishtailed, its rear trying to overtake its ruined cab, its long bulk swinging round to block the skedway.

Seeing thirty tonnes of driverless wagon heading directly for him, Judge Dredd simply opened the Lawmaster's throttle, kicked the rear wheel round and laid his machine down.

"Code ninety-nine red! Repeat: Code ninety-nine red! Judge down! Grud, he went under the truck!"

From the spy-in-the-sky's airborne vantage point, Gleick watched in horror as the freezer wagon began to roll, digging chunks out of the road's plascrete surface. It was only a matter of time before...

There was a hydrogen fuel cell in the truck's cab and volatile chemicals in the freezer at the back. With a heavy, flat sound the wagon spat out a sheet of flame, then detonated in a fireball that lit up half the block.

"Oh, I like this!" Little Petey was shouting. Crobetti could hear him even over the sound of the Judges' bike cannon shells punching chunks out of the rockcrete walls all around him. "This makes me really happy-happy-happy!"

Pumping his double-barrelled stump gun in a mindless, grinning frenzy, Petey fired round after round into the oncoming lights. Impossibly, despite standing in the open in the middle of the loading bay's raised platform, he hadn't been touched, either by the high-calibre munitions that were flying all around him, or by the debris blown out from the walls. Crobetti couldn't believe the man was still alive.

"For grud's sake, Petey, get down!" Crobetti shouted from where he was sheltering behind a stack of packing cases. He had nowhere else to go as the loading bay doors had slammed down like a plasteel curtain as soon as the first bullets were fired. His wounded leg was jumping like crazy, as if his mech-splint had picked up on the wave of fear and adrenaline that was pounding around his body. This was definitely not how he had imagined the night would end.

For a heartbeat, he entertained the fantasy that if he stayed where he was and crouched down really low, making himself as small as possible, the Judges wouldn't notice him when they stormed the loading bay. Then a glancing hit from a Lawmaster cannon shell tore half the packing cases to splinters.

"Ah, what the sneck," he sighed. His face was bleeding from a dozen splinter wounds as he chambered a stub-shell and struggled round, his mech-splint still twitching, to get a good shot at the oncoming Judges.

And died, quite without pain, as a cannon shell turned his skull into little more than red mist.

"Dredd here. Cancel the code red. I'm fine. Tek-Judge Gleick, consider this your official reprimand for premature use of the distress code. There might be a Judge out there who really needs assistance."

Dredd hadn't been anywhere near the Lawmaster when the truck had gone up. He'd kicked away from it to avoid being crushed between the bike and the road. While the Lawmaster had skidded away at an acute angle, finally ploughing into the perimeter fence of the neighbouring factory lot, Dredd had slid right under the truck and out the other side, letting his uniform's armoured knee and shoulder pads take the punishment. As soon as he'd shed enough speed he was up on his feet and running, Lawgiver in his fist, heading for the loading bay. His controlled fall from the bike had taken him to within a hundred metres of the ramp.

The firefight in the bay was already over. One of the Judges – probably Marks, Dredd decided – had swung his Lawmaster around and gone up the ramp sideways, pinning several mobsters against the wall, while the others had dismounted and gone in with Lawgivers blazing, a standard Justice Department containment pattern. Dredd counted ten perps dead, three wounded.

Farrell, a young Judge not long out of his rookie's white helmet, was cuffing the three wounded mobsters as they huddled against what was left of the bay wall. Seeing Dredd step up onto the platform, he turned to greet him. "Glad to see you're still with us, sir."

"Eyes on your perps, Farrell," Dredd replied. He walked past the young Judge, who hastily returned his attention to the mobsters.

Marks ran his override card across the lock. The plain-looking slug was programmed to override any electronic locking mechanism in Mega-City One, but in this case it simply emitted a sad bleep of defeat.

"No go. They've shielded the lock." He grimaced, then noticed that Dredd now stood beside him. "Hi-Ex?"

Dredd nodded and Marks moved quickly to his Lawmaster, opening stowage pods built into the rear wheel housing. He took out three slabs of plasteen, Hi-Ex charges with integral detonators. Dredd looked at the charges, made a quick mental estimate of the strength of the doors, and decided that two would probably do it.

Still, nothing wrong with a little overkill. He brought his helmet mic down. "Dredd to Ground Team Two," he growled. "We're going to blow the loading bay doors. Prepare to move on my mark. Gleick?"

"Reporting, sir."

"What can you see?"

"I'm picking up a lot of activity inside; they're either destroying evidence, getting ready to bug out or both – Judge Dredd! Behind you!"

At Gleick's warning, Dredd whirled. One of the dead mobsters was getting up again.

Later, at debriefing, he would discover that the big man with the stub gun pointing at his face was "Little" Petey Steene, wanted for numerous counts including that of strangling his own father with a synthi-leather belt at the age of ten. At this moment the man's name was less than important: by the time the mobster had chambered his first shell

Dredd had already fired two shots from his Lawgiver. The first round shattered Steene's gun and the hand that held it, and the second blew most of his head away. Little Petey died with a grin on his face, or what was left of it. The execution round had destroyed everything above his top teeth.

Dredd watched the corpse flop back down to the loading bay floor. "Watch your perps, Marks – even the dead ones." He glanced back to where Gleick's spy-in-the-sky was dropping down towards him. "Well spotted, Tek-Judge."

"Th-thank you, sir!"

"The reprimand still stands. Marks, where's that Hi-Ex? This raid has already taken longer than it should."

The shaped Hi-Ex charges blew a ragged hole in the plasteel door, roughly the shape of an inverted triangle. A white-coated tekkie must have been standing too close to the doors when they blew as Dredd had to step over his smoking corpse to get in.

"Nobody move!" he barked. Decades of street experience had given his voice a degree of authority that most citizens found themselves obeying before they realised what they were doing. "This is an illegal bio-tech operation and you are all under arrest!"

Two tekkies looked up from their terminals, stared at Dredd like frightened animals, then took off for a set of doors to one side of the main area.

"Ground Team Two, time to join the fun," Dredd snapped into his helmet mic as he brought down one of the running tekkies with a leg-shot. The second runner was reaching for the door controls when he was spun howling to the floor by a shoulder-shot from Marks, who had followed Dredd through the blast hole.

Some of the tech staff were armed. A small-calibre pistol cracked from an overhead gantry, its bullet kicking dust off the floor at Dredd's feet. In a single movement, Dredd picked off the gunman then returned his attention to his main target before the perp hit the ground. "You!"

he bellowed. "Where's Hellermann? Give her up now and you might get out of the cubes while you're still young enough to walk out!"

The tech managed to get one hand away from the wound in her leg to point towards a set of big pressure doors on the far wall of the factory. "In there," she gasped.

"I knew you'd say that," Dredd sneered. He left the woman to either tend to her wound or bleed to death, and headed for the doors. Behind him, the other Judges in his team followed Marks through the door and spread out through the factory space. Shouts of command and the occasional gunshot began to echo among the equipment.

The doors slid aside and Dredd went through, feeling the pressure curtain brush at him. Beyond, rows of growth tanks stretched away, gleaming softly in the dim light. Cables and pipes littered the floor. Dredd tapped one with his boot and felt it thrumming through the kevlar sole.

He'd seen these tanks in the briefing vid, although those had borne the Justice Department eagle crest. These bore the logo of what Dredd guessed was a Hondo-Cit chop-shop, specialists in the reverse engineering and copying of virtually any piece of high technology. All Hellermann had to do was get the specs for the growth tanks to the chop-shop engineers and they could have turned out dozens of the tanks almost overnight, ready to be smuggled back to Mega-City One.

The woman would obviously stop at nothing. Dredd glared out into the gloom, making out a set of pressure-sealed doors in the end wall. According to the last set of building plans submitted to the MegSouth zoning board, those would have led to the works canteen. If Hellermann was there, she was heading right into the arms of Judge Mexter and the rest of Team Two.

But she was clever, he knew that. And there were plenty of places to hide right here.

"Hellermann," he called, stepping carefully over the cables. "You're under arrest. Make it easy on yourself."

As if in answer, one of the tanks shifted on its base.

Dredd heard it before he saw it; a heavy impact from within the plasteel and ceramic. He took a cautious step towards the nearest of the growth vessels. The lid was pale and opaque, with a viewport set into its curved surface. Inside, something moved spasmodically in gluey liquid.

The sound of the canteen doors blowing inwards caused Dredd to turn, Lawgiver unconsciously and immediately aimed. A loose, tangle-limbed figure in a singed and tattered lab coat flew out from the doorway and rolled to a messy halt on the floor. There were shouts and orders to freeze uttered by someone with Justice Department training, then screams and several secondary explosions. A squeal of feedback made the audio pick-ups in Dredd's helmet dull for a second to protect his hearing, then the lights throughout the facility dimmed as something short-circuited with spectacular finality and a last, loud explosion. The copper tang of burning circuitry wafted from the open doorway.

Elize Hellermann soon followed, cuffed, bleeding from a cut above her close-cropped hairline and pushed ahead of Judge Mexter and his team. One of the Judges had hold of another tekkie by the ragged collar of his lab whites. Cuffing him had been unnecessary as one arm and one leg were a mess of shrapnel wounds – he must have been standing far too close to whatever it was that had exploded in the canteen.

"Doctor Hellermann was bugging out just as we came in," Mexter greeted Dredd. "The canteen's been fitted out as a sterile operating theatre. Moment she saw us, she set the gruddamned robo-docs on us." He put a gloved hand up to a thin line of blood that ran the length of his jaw. "We hit them with a Hi-Ex each and they went to pieces. A couple of her assistants, too. But that was it for the power."

Dredd nodded. "I'll see Attempted Judge Homicide gets added to her charge sheet," he replied. "It's already an impressive–"

The lid of the growth tank next to him exploded outwards.

Dredd turned his face away as shards of razor-edged plastic spun into the air. A heartbeat later the entire lid of the tank whirled upwards in a shower of fluid, as something vast leapt out and hurled itself forwards.

In an instant Dredd was being battered against another tank. His Lawgiver had been slapped from his grip before he could react, and the thing had a massive hand around Dredd's throat, crushing his windpipe, and it was slamming him repeatedly against the growth unit behind him. If he hadn't been wearing a Justice Department helmet his skull would have been shattered.

The grip on this throat was incredible, stronger than a robot. His vision had already started to grey out; Dredd could hear the other Judges yelling and shots being fired.

"Hold your fire. You'll hit Dredd!"

His vision narrowed until all he could see was the thing's face, or what it had for a face. Pure hatred with teeth, and eyes that held far more intellect than such a monster should possess.

Enough, Judge Dredd decided, was enough. He sagged in the creature's grip and let his hand drop down to the top of his boot. When it swung up again, a broad, tempered blade protruded from his fist.

Dredd slammed his boot knife into the creature's chest, but the grip around his throat didn't weaken and now the grey fog was turning black. With the last of his strength, Dredd stabbed again, driving the blade between its ribs and twisting, probing for a vital organ.

With an involuntary squeal, the creature released its hold. Dredd hurled himself back. "Now!" he gasped, through a throat that felt as though he'd been eating glass. "Open fire!"

"No!" cried Hellermann, but her protest was drowned out by the sound of four Lawgivers firing in unison.

Dredd saw the creature's pale, unfinished skin explode in a dozen places. It reeled from the impact of the execution shells, then with a roar of fury it leaped towards Judge Mexter. A sabre of polished bone had already erupted from its forearm.

"Incendiary!" Dredd dived for his Lawgiver, snatched it up even as it was acknowledging his voice command, and pumped three shots into the monster's side.

Instantly it was ablaze – a bellowing, thrashing column of greasy flame. It staggered towards Mexter, but the flesh was already twisting off its bones. Within a metre it sagged onto its knees, and finally collapsed onto the factory floor.

It didn't stop trying to get to Mexter until several minutes later, when Dredd tired of its squealing and put an execution round through its skull.

"I'm just glad we caught them before they got shipped out," Mexter said later as Hellermann was being led away. "I can think of a dozen rogue states and twice that many crime bosses who'd pay good credits for just one of these killers. Imagine if they got their hands on an army of them."

"Um, Judge Mexter, Judge Dredd. About that." One of the Ground Team's Tek-Judges, Corben, had commandeered a workstation. He stood up from his seat as Dredd and Mexter came over.

"About what, Corben?" Dredd asked, aware that his voice sounded even more gravelly than usual. "Spit it out."

Corben nodded. "I've only just skimmed the surface of Hellermann's system," he began, "but there's something you should know. These tanks are holding the second and third batches Hellermann has produced. The first was decanted a week ago with a better than seventy per cent survival rate. Seems the duds were rendered down and used to augment the nutrients for the next batch." Corben looked down at his feet with a grimace. He was standing in a puddle of the solution that was leaking from the ruined growth tank.

"What happened to the first batch?"

"They were moved to one of Big Jimmy's safe houses out by the Kennedy Hoverport while a credit transfer was arranged," Corben continued, reading the information scrolling down the workstation's monitor. "A big credit transfer. I haven't been able to piece together the name of the buyer, but I can tell you that they went over the Atlantic Wall."

"When?"

"Yesterday."

"Dredd to PSU."

Tek-Judge Gleick started at the sound of Dredd's voice, almost spilling the cup of fresh synthi-caf he had ordered from the roving robo-dispenser. Since the raid on the factory ended, he had kept the spy-in-the-sky clear of the street Judges, and of Dredd in particular. One reprimand from the legend was more than enough for one night.

"Patch me through to the Chief Judge, Code Omega." Dredd was the only street Judge with the authority to demand a direct comm-link with Chief Judge Hershey. Gleick knew that Hershey and Dredd had a history – Dredd's recommendation had carried a lot of weight when it came time to elect a new Chief Judge, a little over two years ago.

"Yes sir," Gleick's hands flew over the comm-keys, bypassing the normal channels of communication which ran from street Judge to Sector House and on up the chain of command. "Chief Judge, I have Judge Dredd on the line."

Dredd spoke as soon as the channel opened. He didn't waste time with formalities. He didn't even wait for Gleick to get offline. "We're twenty-four hours too late," he growled. "Project Warchild is already in the air."

2. SPLASH

The Lindberg was flying low over the Black Atlantic, *really* low, and that made Taub nervous. To him, it seemed as though the cargo plane was barely skimming the tops of the highest waves.

It was an illusion, he knew. The cargo jet's autopilot was keeping a good forty metres between plane and water, but the slate-black surface of the ocean was so featureless, so vast, that it filled every part of the view from the cockpit. At times it looked as though the plane was barely moving, but then Taub would see a line of grey on the far horizon, and watch as it drew closer, speeding up, and resolving itself into a wavefront of scummy grey foam before it disappeared under the cockpit. The toxic surface of the Black Atlantic broke every now and then, but reluctantly.

Mostly it was just oily swell, and that got old really fast. Taub yawned, stretched, and said: "Want another caf?"

Hopkirk shook his head without looking up. The pilot had downloaded an e-zine to his dataslate the previous afternoon, and he'd been reading it continuously since switching the Lindberg to autopilot. Taub couldn't decide if Hopkirk was just a slow reader, or if he was just keeping his nose in the slate to avoid conversation. Neither explanation appealed to him very much, but who knew about these Brit-Cit types anyway? Stuck-up, at best. A serious stick up the rear at worst.

"Suit yourself." Taub got up, steadying himself against the back of his seat as the Lindberg rose slightly to avoid a swell, and made for the dispenser unit set in the cockpit's rear wall. While his drink was gurgling into a plastic cup, Taub surveyed the choices offered by the energy bar dispenser set next to the caf-machine. Five fruit flavours, all of which he knew from bitter experience would taste like damp cardboard. "What the drokk is a dongleberry anyway?"

"Sorry, a what?"

"Dongleberry. This bar dispenser's got a new flavour – Delicious Dongleberry."

"Yummy," said Hopkirk flatly. He still hadn't looked up from his slate. "It'll taste of cardboard."

Taub nodded to himself and took the plastic cup of luke-warm synthi-caf from the dispenser. "Yeah, I know. Just making conversation. Thought it might break up the boredom."

Hopkirk glanced up from his screen. "Bored?" He smiled thinly. "Well, if you want to break the monotony you could try working out whether we're still low enough to keep under Atlantic Division's radar, and high enough to avoid a megashark if one decides to jump up and take a bite out of the tail."

Taub blinked at him. "They don't do that, do they?"

In reply, Hopkirk just waved the dataslate lazily. "Should have downloaded one, Taub. All the answers, right here."

"Ah, drokk you. You're just trying to freak me out." And it's working, thought Taub wildly. Brit-Cit snecker!

He ran his finger down the list of energy bars again, but decided against eating any more. It would have been the third one since taking off from Kennedy Hoverport and it wasn't as if he'd be expending a great deal of energy during this flight. Hopkirk had supervised the autopilot during take off, and would when they landed, too. The coffin-sized cry-otanks in the hold were entirely self-regulating. He and Hopkirk were only on board to deal with the unexpected.

Taub went back to his seat and dropped into it, plucking an empty plastic cup from the drinks holder and inserting the fresh one. The empty went into the space between his seat and the curve of the fuselage. "Ah, don't mind me. I just get nervous, is all."

"Nothing wrong in that," said Hopkirk. "Keeps you on your toes. But as far as the Justice Department is concerned, we're just a perfectly ordinary private cargo flight to Brit-Cit. And since when did Atlantic Division have the manpower to check every flight?"

Taub thought about that and nodded, feeling a little better. All the paperwork for the flight had been in place before Eddie the Belly had even contacted him. Eddie was a good payer, for a Fattie, and had given Taub plenty of work in the past – he always seemed to need a pilot who wouldn't ask questions. The flight plan, the security tabs on the cargo bay doors and the customs clearance certificates had looked so good, Taub would have sworn they were genuine.

The Lindberg-CS13 was a nondescript plane, just heading towards obsolescence; no customs officer would give it a second glance. They would touch down in Brit-Cit long enough to refuel and change crews, probably handing over the flight to a couple of Euro-Citters for the next leg of the trip. By the time it took off, the plane would be flying under a new ident-number. To all intents and purposes, the plane now flying across the world's most polluted expanse of water would have vanished while sitting on the blacktop at Brit-Cit's main air terminal.

Taub didn't know the cargo's final destination, and he didn't care. He would take the zoom train home along the Trans-Atlantic Tunnel, running three thousand miles along the bed of the same polluted ocean he was currently flying over, and pick up his payment from Eddie. Simple.

Here's to "simple". Taub raised his cup of caf, took a gulp and almost choked. "Sneck! What the drokk do they put in this stuff?"

"Dongleberries," replied Hopkirk, waving the dataslate.

An hour later, Taub was almost relieved to hear the alarm chime. He had been staring vacantly at the sickly green flashes of a storm on the southern horizon, and there was a chance he might have nodded off for a moment or two. He wondered if he should have another caf, maybe an energy bar. Having Hopkirk report back that that he had dozed off on the job would be a bad idea.

"What's up?" he asked, glancing across at Hopkirk. He was glad to see that, some time in the last hour, the Brit had put down his e-zine.

Hopkirk consulted his control board. "Proximity alert," he muttered, tapping at the screen. The chiming faded out. "Nothing serious. Whatever it is, it's on the surface and over a thousand kilometres away. It's big though. Very big indeed."

"Cityship, probably," Taub said. "They're nothing to worry about, so long as we don't get close enough for them to take a pop at us."

Hopkirk's eyebrows went up. "Do they do that?" Taub grinned at him.

"What, not in your zine?" He sat back and stretched. "Yeah, it's been known. If they brought us down, their scavengers would tear the plane apart for salvage and feed us to the megasharks. Though we won't have to worry about them reporting anything to the Justice Department."

"Quite," Hopkirk replied. And picked up his slate again.

Taub returned his bored gaze to the southern horizon. The storm appeared to have blown itself out. The swirling funnel of dirty cloud that hovered over the ocean there had cleared, and all that remained was a curtain of greasy-looking mist, pierced here and there by shafts of sunlight breaking through the parting clouds. That didn't surprise Taub at all – the vast quantities of radwaste and industrial pollution that had drained into the ocean over the centuries had produced a virulent microclimate, capable of turning from placid to catastrophic in the blink of an eye.

Taub wondered what it must be like to be caught in a storm at sea level. He imagined the muties on their city-ships closing hatches, shuttering windows and hiding in the dark, waiting for the storm to pass. He imagined the violent rolling of the individual vessels that made up the floating cities, the creak and snap of the cables, the moaning of the welded joints that held the ancient craft together.

As he thought of the rolling ocean, his eyelids began to droop.

The next time Taub woke, it was to the sound of Hopkirk swearing. Another alarm was sounding – not the chime of the proximity alarm, but a more insistent, insect buzzing.

"What is it this time?" Every joint in his body felt stiff. He must have been out for some time, and the seats weren't exactly built for restful sleep. There was a cot in the back for that.

Hopkirk was stabbing at his control board, but each time one icon blinked out another replaced it. "I'm not sure. Getting system warnings – flaps and rudder are sluggish and the engines are losing efficiency. Even the hydraulics are playing up."

That didn't sound good. Taub was instantly alert, checking his own board. "You didn't see anything unusual?"

Hopkirk shook his head. "No, just this damn mist."

"Mist?" Taub looked up, out of the cockpit windshield. "*Mist*?"

Something was happening to the plexiglass. What had been clear and transparent when he had closed his eyes had become frosted and semi-opaque. Hundreds of tiny circles, like ripples on a pond, had scoured the surface. "Oh grud. We're in an acid bank…"

Acid banks were another of the random and deadly features of the Black Atlantic's eco-system. Gases would bubble up from the ocean's floor, emanating from any one of a dozen different sources: mutant life forms, sunken toxic waste tankers, ruptured transit pipes and worse. When the gas hit the air it would vaporise, turning into a wall of corrosive vapour that would hang above the ocean surface like a dirty curtain. Acid banks were rare, but they did occur. And they were deadly.

"You dumb snecker, why the hell didn't you pull up?" Taub ran his hands swiftly over the control board, disengaging the autopilot and taking over the stick from Hopkirk. "If this stuff gets into the engines we're drokked!"

"I-I didn't see it…"

"Didn't see it?" Taub was hauling back on the control stick with all his strength, trying to bring the Lindberg's nose up before the acid chewed clear through the fuselage. "You were asleep, weren't you? Or you had your nose in that damn slate!"

"Blame me later," Hopkirk snapped. "Just climb!"

Taub didn't reply, he just kept dragging the stick back. The Lindberg was groaning, wallowing, shuddering under him. The acid bank was thick and heavy, not like air at all. It felt as though he was trying to fly the plane through soup.

Suddenly, the air cleared. The acid bank became a landscape of roiling vapour below them, dropping back out of sight. Taub eased the stick forwards, levelling the Lindberg out. "Made it!" he puffed, sweat rolling down his face. "Grud on a greenie."

Hopkirk looked white. "Is this going to screw up our flight schedule?"

Taub turned to him, slowly, giving himself time to think of something really foul to call the Brit-Citter. Finally, he fixed Hopkirk with a steely glare, opened his mouth, took a breath – and stayed with his mouth gaping wide open in horror as he saw what was happening to the port engine.

Smoke was vomiting from the sides of the pod, venting through holes and rips in the metal shell. As he stared, the smoke was joined by a belch of flame.

"Grud," he whispered. It would be the last word he ever spoke.

The engine blew up, the acid-etched fan blades giving in to the furious stress of their own rotation and whirling into fragments. The entire pod blasted apart, shattering into a ball of flame and shrapnel, tearing half the wing away. The Lindberg was instantly wrenched sideways and out of the air.

The impact killed Hopkirk instantly, tearing his pilot's throne free of the deck and slamming it with crushing force into the side of the cockpit. The plexiglass windshield, already weakened by the acid, exploded outwards. Taub felt the wind slam into him like a wall, battering him back into his own seat. The pressure was so great he couldn't even get his hands to the controls. He certainly couldn't scream even though the acid-laden air was already ripping into his skin.

His last vision was that of the gleaming Black Atlantic looming up to meet him.

The Lindberg hit the water like a missile, shearing off the remains of both wings. The shattered cockpit gaped even wider with the impact, swallowing tonnes of fluid in a second. The plane slowed in its forward motion and began to settle, dropping through the stew of toxins, rad-waste and industrial pollutants that made the Black Atlantic one of the deadliest places on earth. By the time it hit the seabed it was almost unrecognisable, but not as unrecognisable as the corroded, rapidly decomposing body of co-pilot Taub.

The nose of the plane hit bottom first, and the acid-eaten fuselage gave way as it did so, splitting clear across. Debris drifted out into the murk. Most of it sank.

But ten self-contained cryotanks, their armoured support systems affected by neither the crash nor the poisoned Atlantic, did not sink. They were built to float. So they left the Lindberg to its fate and went spiralling slowly up through the black water like glossy bubbles, one by one, heading for light and air.

3. SCAVENGER HUNT

To the untrained eye, the scavenger ship *Golgotha* was as ugly as sin. Its hull was a bulbous, blunt-nosed mess, stained black by the Atlantic's toxic waters and patched with a thousand hastily welded plates. So many winches, booms, cranes and outriggers rose above the gunwales that the ship looked more like an upturned insect than a seagoing vessel, rolling drunkenly on its back and wiggling its legs in the air. And it was noisy – the creaking of the outriggers, sullen twanging of cables in the wind and the grind of heavy chain against pulleys was almost enough to drown out the chugging of the engine.

Golgotha wasn't pretty, but it was the closest thing to a home Gethsemane Bane had ever known.

She was up on the bridge, feet braced apart against the swell, standing at the helm with her hands white-knuckle tight on the controls. A storm had passed by this spot not long ago, and while the lashing acid rain and gale force winds were gone, they had left a roiling and disturbed sea in their wake. Bane was finding it hard to keep *Golgotha* on a level heading, and the thought that the storm might have roused a megashark – or something even bigger – kept flashing uncomfortably through her mind.

"I don't like it," she muttered, partly to herself. "Shouldn't we be able to see it by now?"

Most of the crew was out on the foredeck, clustered around the prow. The plexiglass of the windshield was so smeared and streaked that she could only make them out by the brilliant yellow of their protective slickers. She resolved to treat *Golgotha* to some new windows as soon as they got back to *Sargasso*, if they made money on this trip. It was a regular expense. Plexiglass didn't last long against Black Atlantic spray.

Dray was on the bridge with her, running the sensor station. He stood peering into the scope with his one good eye, the crocodile skin of his face painted over with the colours from the readout. "It's off the starboard bow, no more than fifty metres."

Bane triggered her headset mic. "Hear that, guys?" One of the yellow blobs waved in reply, and they all moved to starboard.

"I'll go help them," Dray said. "We're too close for this to be much use now." He turned from the sensor screen and reached for his slicker, which was hanging from a peg by the door.

Bane put her hand to his shoulder. "I'll go. You hold her steady. And get ready on the outriggers."

"Aye, aye, cap'n." Dray flashed her a reptilian grin. A mutant, like everyone on the scavenger ship, Dray had skin like leather and needlepoint teeth. He had been on the *Golgotha* longer than anyone, Bane included, but he had been the first to start calling her "captain".

Bane grabbed her own slicker and shrugged into it, sealing it quickly before stepping into the wind and spray. The door whined closed behind her, and after waiting a moment to ride out another of *Golgotha*'s familiar rolling lurches, she headed along the companionway and down the stairs to the deck.

Everyone else was down there waiting for her, except for Orca. The big engineer was holed up in the drive room, as usual, tending his precious engines as though they were living things. Bane could have used his strength up at the prow, but she didn't feel it was right to disturb him. Besides, if the object was heavy, *Golgotha* might need an extra surge of power to the winches, and it would be Orca's job to provide it.

Bane had no idea what the object was. Or objects. Dray had been watching the signal it was giving out for more than eighteen hours, but he still couldn't tell her if there was one big source or lots of smaller ones close together.

One or many, it didn't matter. The object had power, components, and no one to take it home. That made it the personal property of Gethsemane Bane and the *Golgotha* crew.

As long as she could *find* the drokking thing!

She leaned over the bow rail, cupping a hand over her eyes to ward off the spray, and searched the sluggish, heaving surface for something other than polluted water and scum. Her eyes were good, but it was Angle, further along the rail, who saw it first.

"There!" he yelped, leaping up and down and pointing. "There it is!"

Angle's arms were too long, and looked as though they had been built with more than their usual number of elbows. But when he pointed at something, it stayed pointed at. Bane followed his arm and instantly saw what she'd been missing.

It was just under the surface, occasionally bobbing through and sleeting black water off its flanks. Something rounded and grey and artificial. "Good eyes, Angle! First round's on you!"

Angle grinned and punched the air. Bane could hear Dray chuckling in satisfaction, and Can-Rat was skittering from side to side in excitement. It had been a while since *Golgotha* had made a find like this. Once they got it back to *Sargasso*, it could make them a pretty cred or two.

"Dray?" She turned back to wave at the bridge, and saw Dray waving back through the grimy windshield. "It's not too big, and it floats. We'll need number four crane, but the outriggers can stay where they are. She won't tip."

"Got it," Dray replied, and instantly the medium starboard crane – number four – began to unfold itself from rest position.

"Hey, Angle." Bane moved over to where the slender mutant was still pointing and grinning. "You want to get out of buying that first round?"

"If Orca's drinking with us, yeah."

She snorted a laugh, hoping the engineer wasn't listening in. "Okay, if you can zap that thing with the magoon, I'll be buying. Deal?"

Angle let out a whoop and darted away. Damn, he moved so fast. Too fast for the deck of a ship, really, but he was young. Even younger than Bane, and she was only twenty-four. Young enough to get a real kick out of firing a magnetic harpoon at something, anyway.

She let him go and went over to join Can-Rat. "What do you think it is?"

"Coffin?" Can-Rat sniffed. "Looks like a coffin. Maybe some snecker's fancy idea of a burial at sea."

"With a tracer signal?"

Can-Rat blinked, small beady eyes bright and his muzzle wet from the sea. "Maybe he got lonely."

Angle appeared next to her, holding the magoon. The launcher was a metal tube as long as Bane was tall, with a pitted muzzle she could have put her head into. In contrast, the magnetic point of the harpoon itself looked surprisingly delicate. Like an origami teardrop.

"Maybe it's a treasure chest," said Angle, hauling the magoon up and snapping its mount over the bow rail. There was a loud metallic sound as it locked. "Fell off some rich oldster's pleasure cruiser."

"Pleasure?" Bane gave him a look. "Angle, if anyone's out here for pleasure, I don't wanna know what they keep in their treasure chests!" She paused. "What are you waiting for, kid? Zap the thing."

Angle rolled his head around on his thin neck, shrugged the kinks out of his shoulders, and then leaned down to aim the magoon. His long limbs and twitchy build gave him a combination of leverage and extraordinary delicacy of touch. When he squeezed the trigger, the magoon fizzed out of the launcher straight and true.

The point splayed in midair, faster than Bane could fol-low. One second it was a sharp point of overlaid metal plates, the next it was a wide dish slapping against the side of the object and grabbing on hard. The cable paid out behind it went taut, reeled back by the launcher's internal winch.

"Okay, Angle, hold it there." Bane slapped him on the shoulder in congratulation, and then gave Dray a signal. In response, the crane dipped low out over the water and released its grab.

"Something's wrong," Can-Rat said, very quietly, eyes fixed on the grab. "I don't like this. Something ain't right…"

Bane felt the hairs on her arms and the back of her neck bristle. Can-Rat might not have been much of a sailor – he was too short and slender for the physical demands of life on the Black Atlantic, and seawater brought out his allergies – but, either due to some telepathic mutant ability or just keen senses, he always seemed to know when something bad was about to happen. Bane kept him on board as a kind of canary – if Can-Rat got nervous, so did she.

"Don't worry," she told him. "Almost there. We'll be gone soon…"

The grab hesitated, waiting out a swell, then as *Golgotha* rolled back down it dropped, splashing heavily down onto the object. For a second Bane thought it was going to skate right off the slick surface, but Dray had been working the cranes for years. The grab scissored closed and came up in a single, soaring motion, showering the deck with grubby spray. Bane closed her eyes against it for just a moment, and when she opened them again the object was hanging a few metres above the deck. They had it.

It looked a lot like a coffin, actually. If the underside of the thing hadn't been a maze of sophisticated support pipework, she might have gotten nervous and dropped the thing right back over the side.

No, she told herself, no one was that stupid. Even a corpse could fetch a price if you sold it to the right people.

Dray was lowering the object onto the deck, and the others were moving towards it, eager to see what they'd picked up. Bane noticed that Orca had emerged from the drive room and was bouncing towards her. For such a huge man, he moved with surprising grace and lightness, as if he weighed almost nothing at all. Bane knew that wasn't true, but she also knew that his layers of protective blubber were thinly wrapped around enough muscle for three normal men. Orca's weight didn't slow him down because he had more than enough strength to carry it. A few people had found that out the hard way. As far as Bane knew one of them was still alive, but his family had to feed him through a straw.

Orca reached the object as it hit the deck and bent to study it. Bane joined him. "What do you think?" she asked, watching him running his fingers lightly over its glossy shell.

"Good quality," Orca muttered. "Mega-City workman-ship, possibly, or a Hondo-Cit copy." His fingers moved across a flat panel at one of the shorter ends. "Maybe some kind of lock?"

"I'll get a wrench and a prybar," said Angle happily. Bane shook her head.

"Wait. We'll get more for this if we don't wreck it." She turned back to Orca, who was studying a fine, barely visible seal that ran completely around the object. "What would you put in a box like this?"

"In a hermetic cask? Something perishable. Something you want to keep fresh till you need it." He paused, stroking his cascade of chins. "Food, perhaps. Med-supplies more likely."

"Paydirt!" Angle whooped. "We'll get top cred for Mega-City meds on the *Sargasso*! Right, cap?"

"Right. We keep it sealed, make it fast and head for home." Bane couldn't help but smile. If Orca was right, the chest's contents would earn them good money in the dock-side markets of the cityship. And the meds might even save some lives. Everybody wins.

Good news at last. Things had been tough for a while, with pickings so slim some trips had brought in barely enough to cover *Golgotha*'s mooring fees, and the little ship still needed fuel and spare parts, despite Orca's genius for repairs.

Abruptly, Bane glanced around. Can-Rat was back at the rail, staring out across the murky water. She trotted over to join him, and was startled to see that the furry mutant was shivering violently. "Grud, Canny, what's up?"

"I dunno." He turned to face her, his muzzle twitching with fear. "I think something's coming…"

"Captain?"

"Dray? What is it?"

"Not sure. Something funny…" She heard Dray tapping at a control. "The signal's stopped, cut out as soon as it hit the deck. But there's another one."

"Another signal?" Bane grabbed the rail and leaned over, scanning the inky water. "What, another coffin?" She was liking this less by the second. Can-Rat was spooked, more caskets were popping out of the Atlantic every second – what next?

"Hold on." Dray said, over her headset. "I've got another contact. It's weird. It only just appeared, even though the radar puts it nearby and closing fast."

"Another scavenger?" suggested Orca, next to her so suddenly that she jumped.

"Maybe." She was looking around wildly, trying to see what was coming, but the weather was closing in again. The oily spray was being joined by wisps of yellowish fog, and the swell was getting worse. A storm was coming.

"Can we get the other casket aboard before they arrive?"

"I don't know. Depends how close they are." She glanced back to the casket, still held firmly against the deck by the crane grab, and then went sprawling across the deck as Can-Rat barrelled into her from behind. She yelled in surprise and protest, but never heard her own shout. It had been drowned out by the explosion that blew a head-sized hole through the gunwale, just where she'd been standing.

The other ship was almost on top of them.

It loomed out of the rising fog, all flat panels and sharp edges. Stealth plates, she thought frantically, radar-absorbent ceramic. No telling how long the ship had been following them, guns trained, waiting for them to pick up something worthwhile.

Can-Rat had just saved her from being blown in half.

Dray was yelling in her ear, telling her to say something, let him know she was okay. *Golgotha*'s deck was up at a wild angle, so steep that she started to slide across it. Dray was hauling the ship around, trying to make a getaway before the stealth ship could fire again.

She saw the port gunwale coming up to meet her, but then Orca's massive hand closed around the hood of her slicker and hauled her back upright.

Bane scanned the deck, trying to see whether everyone was okay. Can-Rat was huddled behind the object, keeping its bulk between him and the other ship. She couldn't see Angle at all. "Where's the kid?"

"Stern," Orca shouted, raising his voice above the rising bellow of *Golgotha*'s engines. Dray was opening the throttles up, putting speed into the turn. "Said something about the guns."

Bane groaned. *Golgotha* had a pair of twin-linked spit guns mounted on a crude swivel behind the bridge. They would make a lovely noise, but the shells they fired were soft headed, designed for use against Black Atlantic wildlife, not stealth-armoured ships. If he opened up with those, the other vessel would shoot straight back at him. He was going to get himself blown to bits.

"Stay here," she yelled at Orca, gesturing at the casket. "Stay behind that thing and keep Can-Rat with you." With that she began scuttling towards the rear of the ship, keeping low to avoid drawing any more fire. The stealth vessel wasn't using up a lot of ammo. So far it had only fired the one shot.

There was an almighty noise and the light portside crane splintered in half, toppling drunkenly over the side. Two shots, Bane corrected herself, ducking under the splash. She wondered what kind of gun they had mounted in that thing. Whatever it was, it was big.

Not scavengers, then. Pirates. Tooled up and ready to make their profits the fast and bloody way.

The ship had completed its turn. Dray slammed the throttle open and it surged forwards. Bane, halfway along the portside companionway by that point, had to grab a rail and hang on as the deck reared up behind her and threatened to spill her into the stern.

Seconds later the spit guns opened up with a hellish racket.

She scrambled to a halt at the stern rail, trying vainly to cover her ears with one hand while hanging on for dear life with the other. Angle was hunkered down behind the guns, and as Bane watched he squeezed both triggers and sent another stream of shells thundering towards the pirate ship.

She saw figures on the deck scattering. Angle, to his credit, wasn't trying to damage the ship. He was aiming at softer targets. "Just keeping their heads down," he shouted, loosing off another volley. "If they're too busy ducking, maybe they can't spend so much time steering."

There was a dull sound from the pirate ship, and a puff of smoke. Part of the stern rail disappeared. Bane heard bits of it whining past her head.

"Okay, you drokkers!" Angle screamed. "You asked for it!"

The next time he opened fire, he was aiming lower. Bane almost told him not to bother, but then realised she had forgotten how accurate he had been with the magoon. Despite the wild pitching of *Golgotha*'s deck and the surging motion of the pirate ship, he put his next volley directly down the throat of the stealth vessel's big gun.

Bane didn't hear the explosion, but she saw it. A narrow slot between the stealth plates at the pirate's prow suddenly vomited smoke and fire. Seconds later, more smoke began to billow out from all the forward vents and view ports. The stealth vessel was swiftly engulfed in a greasy, flame-shot cloud.

"YES!" Angle stood up, leaning out over the guns. "Who's your daddy, eh boy? Who's your drokking daddy?!"

"Keep your head down, daddy." Bane hauled him back down. "They might send a thank you back with something smaller."

For a second Angle stayed where he was, shaking with fierce exhilaration. Then he sagged back. "Grud," he whispered. "Er, cap?"

"Mm-hm?"

"That was fun. Can we do that some more?"

The *Golgotha* powered due north until the pirate ship had been left on the far side of the stern horizon, when Dray throttled back to preserve fuel. Back on the bridge with him, Bane cranked the sensor net – another of Orca's jerry-rigged but remarkably sensitive creations – to full gain. The output screen filled with dots indicating inorganic debris on or near the ocean's surface. Solid gold to a scavenger under normal circumstances, but right now Bane was content to let it go.

There was an odd, flickering contact at the edge of the sensor net's range – the pirate vessel, its stealth shielding less efficient while it was on fire. It kept its position until it had left the scope. "Picking up the other casket?"

"Casket or caskets, yeah." Dray rubbed his chin, making a grinding sound against his scales. "Disappointed?"

"Nah. Something tells me one of these things is enough." She yawned and stretched. Night had fallen while *Golgotha* was fleeing the scene and the excitement had taken all the strength from her. "I'm going to turn in. Tell Can-Rat he's got the next watch."

"You sure you want to trust him up here on his own?"

"He'll be fine," Bane replied. "Just think of him as an extra early warning system."

Dray gave a half-amused, half-sceptical snort and went back to his instruments. Bane ducked through the aft hatch and found her way to the crew quarters. Hammocks swung lazily from the low ceiling and Bane dropped gratefully into the nearest.

Golgotha was running well, the bilges were empty and the decks were clear. Orca had taken the casket down into the forward hold, where he had locked it down firmly and covered it with tarpaulin. It would stay there until they docked with the cityship.

Not long now, Bane told herself. They had outrun the storm as well as the pirates. At this course and speed, they should be back in dock within a day and a half.

That thought was enough to comfort her, and the gentle rocking of the ship took her the rest of the way into sleep.

Down in the darkness of the forward hold, the casket lay and waited. Beneath its armoured carapace, machines tirelessly monitored the condition of its contents, logging their readings onto wafer thin data crystals. The support system continued to pump nutrient solutions around the inside of the shell; the temperature was kept constant and the final data downloads ran through their checksum routines.

And the timer, built into the lock that Orca had noticed on deck, kept counting down the seconds, just as it had been doing since the casket had been sealed.

As Gethsemane Bane fell asleep, the counter read just thirty-four hours, forty-nine minutes and a steadily decreasing handful of seconds.

A day and a half.

4. BREAKFAST TO GO

The best time for a crime swoop, Dredd had decided long ago, was dawn or even earlier. The worst excesses of the Graveyard Shift tended to fade out by four-thirty, and the day's hardcore perps wouldn't have roused themselves yet. This wasn't to say that Mega-City One in the early hours was a crime-free zone – that wasn't going to happen in Dredd's lifetime – but there was a dip in the graph before the sun came up.

Besides, a groggy citizen was a poor liar.

The doors on Les Dennis Block's eighty-seventh floor had been recently repainted; the last time Dredd had been here they were uniformly grey. Now they were uniformly green, which was as close to urban renewal as Les Dennis was likely to see in a while. Dredd strode up to number three-twenty, rapped on it hard, and waited. A few seconds later the door began to rattle: a full complement of latches, bolts and security chains were being unlocked behind the plasteen.

When the door finally opened, it only did so partway. Dredd saw a handspan of nervous, blinking citizen behind two more lengths of stout chain. "What–"

"Marcus Elizabeth Bropes? I'm here to search your apartment."

Bropes swallowed, nodded hard and eased the door back towards the frame so he could get the chains off. Dredd noticed how careful he was not to close it fully – that would get it kicked off its hinges in a heartbeat. The man had been swooped before.

Dredd pushed past Bropes and into the apartment as soon as the chains were down. Typical place: everything made from extruded plasteen, from the walls and the furniture to the half-dozen tacky souvenirs on top of the Tri-D. A table with one chair, facing the screen. Bropes had been in the middle of a bowl of Synthi-Flakes and a beaker of juice.

"You're up early, citizen."

"Uh, I have a job, Judge." Bropes was still in his night things, skinny white limbs emerging from T-shirt and shorts, red hair mussed and flattened from sleep. "I'm a pointer, down at Brendy's Pad-Mart."

"Pointer?"

Bropes nodded. "I point at things. Things in the Mart. Like pads, and stuff." He demonstrated, aiming a long finger at the beaker. "Draws people's attention to the products, makes them want to buy more."

"A laudable career, citizen. Committed any crimes recently? I'll know if you're lying."

"No Judge, no crimes. I couldn't be a pointer if I had a record."

The swoop took less than ten minutes. Bropes stood quietly to one side as Dredd went though his possessions. He didn't have that much: his clothes, souvenirs from various sightseeing tours, a collection of kneepads, all from the Pad-Mart where he worked. "Staff discount."

The apartment was clean. Dredd checked a couple of the kneepads against Justice Department records, but the sales were on file, and Bropes even had the receipts. Against all the odds, it looked as though he'd stumbled across a model citizen.

Still, he had to ask. "What's up with the middle name, Bropes?"

The man looked downcast. "The bot at the registration office had a malfunction. Pa always said he could see it sparking, but Ma wouldn't let him reregister me. Said she wanted a girl..."

"I see." Dredd got a feeling he was going to be regaled with Bropes's life story if he stayed any longer, and he

needed to be back on the street. He headed for the door.
"Thank you for your time, citizen. Enjoy your breakfast."

He was halfway out the door when it hit him. *Breakfast.*

He spun on his heel and was back at the table in two long
strides. "Mind if I try a Synthi-Flake, Bropes? Hear they're
pretty good."

Bropes was gaping. "I–"

Dredd took a single flake from the bowl, sniffed it, put it
in his mouth. And spat it back again. "Wondered what you
were spending your wages on, Bropes. Give it up."

Bropes sagged, like a puppet without its strings. He raised
his bony arm and pointed at one of the souvenirs on the Tri-
D. "Power Tower Tours," he whispered.

The flimsy plasteen tower came apart easily in Dredd's
gloved hands, and a tiny amount of white powder flowed
out into his palm as he tipped the remains. He didn't even
need to taste it. "Life not sweet enough for you, citizen?"
He crushed the replica Power Tower in one fist. "Code
twenty, section two. Possession of an illegal substance with
intent to use: two years."

"Two *years*? For *sugar*?"

"And compulsory rehab. Marcus Elizabeth Bropes, you've
pointed at your last kneepad."

How could he have missed the sugar?

Dredd tooled his Lawmaster along Mandelson Overpass,
disgusted with himself. He'd almost been out of the hab,
and there was a bowlful of sugary Synthi-Flakes sitting
right there on the table the whole time. The souvenirs
should have been the first thing he looked at, crushing
every one searching for contraband. Instead, he'd almost
made a mistake.

Almost let a guilty man go free.

Dredd pulled the Lawmaster over to the side of the overzoom and gazed out over the city. He couldn't afford to
make mistakes. No street Judge could. What was wrong
with him?

Was he getting old?

No, he wasn't ready for the Long Walk just yet. He didn't like to admit it, but the plain fact of the matter was, there was something on his mind.

Project Warchild.

Depending on who you asked, Elize Hellermann was either a scientific visionary on par with Newton and Einstein, or a borderline psychotic with no morals or scruples whatsoever. Everyone who worked with her could agree on one thing, however – her brilliance.

She was persuasive, too. Despite only being a member of Tek Division's civilian scientific staff, she had managed to convince at least one Chief Judge that a research into intelligent bioweapons was a justifiable use of resources. And once she had funding, she had spent the next fifteen years working on a modification – some might say perversion – of Justice Department's cloning procedures.

Cloning was an integral part of the Justice Department, used in the selection and shaping of suitable Judge candidates. But Hellermann wanted to take it in a new direction. She wanted to build soldiers, warriors, programmable monsters that could be dropped into the most violent, crime-ridden areas to pacify them without human loss.

The project had been codenamed Warchild.

More bioweapon than biological organism, the Warchild would be able to operate in open battle or undercover, the offensive systems beneath its skin undetectable by normal scanning. Implanted neurocircuitry would render it entirely controllable. It was stronger, faster and infinitely more lethal than the Judges Hellermann intended to replace.

The proposal split Tek Division. Some saw the promise of her plan, others were troubled by the ethics of the whole operation. While they debated, Hellermann set the project in motion without official sanction. By the time it was decided to suspend the programme pending further investigation and debate, Hellermann had proved her genius: Project Warchild

was on the verge of creating its first fully functioning
bioweapon.

When the full implications of the project were finally
revealed, Warchild was closed down in a day. The embryonic
monsters were destroyed and the staff who worked on them
forcibly reassigned. Hellermann never turned up for her new
assignment and dropped out of sight. It wasn't until a year
later her name resurfaced, when a routine crime swoop in the
MegEast docks turned up an illegal consignment of certain
chemicals. The chemicals were DNA recombinants and potent
mutagens, with molecular triggers that matched those used in
Justice Department cloning.

The subsequent investigation eventually led Dredd and his
team to a derelict sector in the Dust Zone, and to Elize Hellermann.

The woman was finally in the cubes where she could do no
harm. A consignment of prototype bioweapons had been completed, but they were out of the city, somewhere across the
Black Atlantic. As far as Dredd should have been concerned,
the case was closed.

Dredd rubbed his throat idly, still feeling the Warchild's
talons crushing his windpipe. One second after birth and the
creature had almost taken him down. It hadn't even been
properly programmed – Hellermann had triggered its early
emergence as she had escaped through the nursery, trying for
a diversion.

The creatures in the factory had already been disposed of
but there were ten more of them out there. Fully grown, fully
programmed, utterly lethal.

The case was closed. And it shouldn't have been personal.

But to Joe Dredd, Project Warchild felt like unfinished
business.

5. SARGASSO

It was Angle who saw the cityship first. He was on watch, prowling *Golgotha*'s deck and scanning the moonlit horizon for any sign of salvage or trouble. He had just started shouting when it appeared on Dray's sensor board, and the proximity alarms were what woke Gethsemane Bane. They weren't loud, but some steady, unsleeping part of her brain had been listening out for them.

Golgotha and her crew were more than twenty-four hours away from their encounter with the stealth ship, and most of that time had been spent arguing about what was in the casket and which grudforsaken hulk the pirates called home. Bane had stayed out of the chatter to a large extent. Her near-death experience had taken more out of her than she was prepared to admit, and she had spent most of the journey back helping Orca fix the gunwales. He wasn't concerned about what was in the box or where the pirates had come from: he had his engines to think about, bullet holes in the upper hull and a missing crane.

It had been a long trip and Bane was dog-tired. So when the alarms went off and Angle started yelling "Land ahoy," she was up and out of the hammock in moments, hungry for the sight of home.

Dray was up on the bridge as usual, working both the helm and the sensors. He stepped aside when Bane bounded in. "There it is," he grinned, nodding at a speck on the horizon. "At drokking last…"

"Aw, don't say you haven't enjoyed this one, Dray!" Bane hunted around for her binocs and found them on a hook under her slicker. "I was thinking of swinging around and heading back out for another week."

"Wouldn't advise it."

She winked at him and raised the binocs to her eyes. For a moment all she saw was the darkness of nighttime on the Black Atlantic, with just a slivery gleam of moonlight to pick out the horizon. She then saw a dull smear of light directly ahead, and the binocs changed their focus a fraction to bring the cityship *Sargasso* into view.

From here, *Sargasso* looked less like a vessel and more like an island, a great dark slab of metal rising from the black waters in an insane sprawl of decks and towers and support cables. It was studded with thousands upon thousands of lights: searchlights, running lights and cooking fires. A warm light shone from untold numbers of portholes, and spots of sickly green phosphorescence lit up from the churning ranks of drive screws at the stern.

Home. Gethsemane Bane had never been more glad to see it. She stayed on the bridge for the next four hours, watching it grow in her vision, never taking the binocs from her eyes until she didn't need them any more.

It was impossible to say which ships had first joined together to become *Sargasso*'s original core. There were more than five hundred vessels in the structure, everything from pleasure cruisers to fishing boats, chemical tankers to factory vessels. It was even rumoured that an old twentieth century attack sub was bolted somewhere under the waterline. Some smaller ships hadn't actually touched the water for decades; their deck space was more important than their hull volume, so they had been hauled up level with their taller companions and fixed in place.

Safety came in numbers, nowhere more so than on the poisoned waters of the Black Atlantic. Maybe it was a desire for such safety that drove the *Sargasso*'s first component vessels to sail together. Maybe it was a need to hold formation among myriad ships of differing engine power that prompted their crews to begin lashing them together. And over the years, the crews had been joined by refugees from the ABC Wars, economic migrants and mutants driven out of the Mega-Cities because of their damaged DNA. As *Sargasso*'s bulk increased, so did its population. It stopped being a ship and had become a city.

Sargasso wasn't the only cityship afloat, but it was the largest at three kilometres from multiple bows to multiple stern, with a wake that could swamp a battle cruiser and a million people calling it home.

Dray took the helm when it was time for *Golgotha* to dock. He always did. Only someone who knew every last detail about how the little vessel rode in the water would be able to manage it.

He began to alter course a few kilometres out, angling to port and *Sargasso*'s stern. The cityship's vast collection of hulls set up a web of chaotic crosscurrents and undertows that could tear a smaller vessel in half. The only safe way to approach *Sargasso* was from the stern, and even that took a master helmsman to get right.

Golgotha bucked and wallowed as it crested the outermost limit of the cityship's bow wave. Playing the helm like a musician, Dray brought the vessel in close enough to catch the wave and ride its rear slope back along *Sargasso*'s length. Then, after dropping back more than five hundred metres past the portside stern, he opened the throttles and began to catch up.

Sargasso wasn't a single, solid structure. Nothing so vast could survive on a moving sea if it couldn't flex and shift with the waves. According to its heading, *Sargasso* could gain or lose almost a hundred metres in length at any one time, and half that in width. It could open to let an especially destructive wave pass though, or narrow to let obstructions go by on either side. It had even sailed though an old Sov-Block minefield once, each ship in the structure moving apart just enough to avoid the floating thermonuclear weapons. It had almost worked. One of the mines had been sent on a new heading by the cityship's wake, and struck a trailing ship. Bane could still remember the city-wide gasp as it had hit, and the cheering a few seconds later when it failed to detonate.

That fluid structure, essential as it was for the cityship's survival, also made it the devil to dock with. Bane looked across at Dray as he worked the helm, not daring to speak. Dray was sweating, his lips working, one good eye blinking rapidly as he calculated and recalculated *Golgotha*'s course. *Sargasso* had two main docks set on either side of the pro-peller fields, but the docks were moving and the props were thundering and the water behind *Sargasso* was a thousand tonnes of leaping, hissing foam in its wake. A computer autopilot would have had them crushed between a couple of hulls on the way in, or dragged down to a close encounter with a drive screw. Gethsemane Bane, who had captained *Golgotha* all her life – or at least, the only part of it that mattered – couldn't have done it. She was in Dray's scaly hands now. They all were, and they all knew it.

Bane returned her attention to the view out of the wind-shield. In front of her, the harbour entrance was already rearing up.

The doorway was twice as tall as the *Golgotha*'s top-mast and four times as wide as its hull. There were huge doors inside made up of great slabs of formed and welded plasteen cut from the hulls of scavenged supertankers. In the event of an attack, the doors could be swung and locked closed, using power geared-up from the main engines. *Sargasso* hadn't gone to war in Bane's lifetime, but she knew there was always a danger. Not all pirate vessels were as small as the one that had taken off Orca's precious crane.

Dray was guiding the ship along the narrow safe channel between the propeller eddies, closing the last few metres of distance from home. Bane saw the shadow of the harbour scan towards her along the deck, then it was over the bridge and she could feel the sudden coolness of it on the skin of her arms.

They were inside. They were home.

A cacophony of shouts and catcalls from the maintenance crews were greeting them from twenty metres up. They hung from cradles, greasing the huge rods and gears of the door mechanisms with rendered down megashark blubber. Angle and Can-Rat, who were up at the bow rail, returned the calls with some obscenities of their own, making Bane blush and grin.

Golgotha trundled along the harbour pool, hunting for a berth. Dray had the throttles back now they were in calm water and Bane could hear the familiar noises of the dockside over the throb of the engines: more shouts and greetings, engines and drive units rumbling, sirens, and loudest of all the hubbub of the dockside market that spread across the entire forward end of the harbour.

Sargasso had a complement of twenty scavenger vessels. The portside harbour was big enough to house them all, with plenty of space for visitors.

Bane couldn't keep the smile off her face. This should have been the busy time, the time when the ship had to be unloaded and refuelled and maintained. There were deals to set up, fees to pay, spares to buy and creditors to dodge. Gethsemane Bane, as captain and master of the scavenger ship *Golgotha*, was in for a harder time in the next few hours than she would be at sea. But despite that, she was grinning like a loon.

She was back. Everything was going to be all right.

Somehow, Bane always ended up thinking of Jester when the *Golgotha* berthed.

During the first years of her life, she probably didn't think at all. Those times were just a blur of hunger and violence. She had no memory of her mother or father, assuming she had either and wasn't just expelled from the guts of a slick eel dredged up out of the *Sargasso*'s bilges. She had a vague

memory of someone telling her that was where she came
from. And hurting her.

One day, she had been big enough to hurt him back. Very
badly. Luckily, she had no real memory of that either.

The thing she could remember, far more clearly than she
would have preferred, was hunger. It was an empty belly
that had first taken her down to the harbour, driven her to
creep along the dockside and dip a fist into the tank of
bilge-filth fresh out of *Golgotha*'s pump to take that first
slimy lump of decaying mutant fish, chew it and force it
down.

She would have kept on eating the dripping waste until it
killed her too, she was that hungry. Luckily for her, she was
being watched, and before she had taken another bite she
was lifted in one giant hand and hauled, kicking and
screeching, onto *Golgotha*'s deck.

She had expected a beating. After all, that's what such
digressions had always earned her before. Instead, she got
soup.

Suspicious and terrified, she would have hurled the bowl
away and bolted off the ship and into the water, had she not
been so close to starvation. But the smell of the soup had a
direct effect on her central nervous system, forcing her to sit
and gulp it down, all the time avoiding the eyes of the big,
shark-grinned man who had brought it to her.

Then she ran. But she was back the next day, and once
again there was soup.

It got to be a habit.

Why Jester Bane, one of the most experienced scavenger
captains on the *Sargasso*, should have considered the foul-
smelling, suspicious and occasionally downright
destructive child a suitable candidate for adoption, she still
had no idea. But then again, he always did have an eye for
a valuable piece of salvage. Maybe he could see the worth
in that damaged child. That was how a good scavenger
worked: sort through the garbage, ignore most of it, but
take on board the pieces that will make a profit.

Jester Bane had never made a profit from little Gethsemane. But over the years, he did make a captain out of her.

"Remembering Jester, huh?"

Dray's question brought her back to the present with a
jolt. She looked down at the deck and saw that it was clear;
Can-Rat and Angle must have already gone down to the
crew quarters, getting their things together for shore leave.

Golgotha's crew didn't spend a lot of time together when
they were docked. Dray had family waiting for him and
Angle would go and try his luck with anything female whose
body temperature approached normal, while Can-Rat often
just seemed to wander off, then wander back a while later.
Either that or he would remain aboard and watch Orca, his
intense gaze making the big engineer nervous.

"How could you tell?"

"The way you were smiling," Dray replied. "It reminded
me of him. Without the teeth, of course."

Bane laughed quietly. "Did he ever…" Slightly embarrassed, she trailed off.

"Ever what?"

"Say why he gave her to me?"

"*Golgotha*?" Dray shrugged. "He knew you'd look after
her. Us, too."

Bane thought about that for a moment or two. Then she
shook her head and ran her fingers back through her short,
cropped hair. "Ahh, since when did I get to be the mother-
ing type? Get off the boat."

"You sure?"

"You've got a woman waiting for you, Dray. Go on!" She
shooed Dray away and backed him towards the hatch down
to the bunk-hold. "I'm going to see the Old Man, but I don't
want to see you back here till you're too exhausted to stand
up, understood?"

"Aye, aye, captain," Dray replied with a smile, and ducked
quickly through the hatch.

● ● ●

Orca, to no one's great surprise, was down in the engine room.

He had been working on *Golgotha*'s drives for hours; running tests, making small adjustments, sometimes just sitting back on his vast haunches and staring off into space. It was during these periods of trance-like thought that he would often get his best ideas: new ways of tweaking the engines, filtering the fuel, modifying yet another wrench or electro-spanner out of all recognition.

The only disadvantage to these unfocussed moments was that Can-Rat would be watching him the whole time. Orca would return to reality, full of new ideas, and get a jolt when he saw that hunched body and narrow, intense gaze aimed right at him.

Orca had been working when the others left the ship and he had continued working as night fell. And Can-Rat had been watching him the whole time. His small, jet black eyes had followed Orca incessantly around the engine room, and he had been scuttling about in swift, darting movements to get a better view of whatever the bigger man was working on.

Orca had long ago given up on being annoyed by this. Once, he had cornered Can-Rat and asked him if he wanted to learn about engines. Can-Rat had simply replied that he *was* learning.

The little mutant's mind simply didn't work the way that most peoples did, Orca had decided. Can-Rat was a bit like him in that respect, able to analyse the structure of a mechanism and thereby discern its purpose and operation, just by external study. It made Orca a great engineer, but what it made Can-Rat he wasn't prepared to say. He got the strange feeling that the furry little man wasn't just studying the engines; he was seeing the entire boat as one single, interconnected system.

And that included the crew.

However, for this night, study time was over. He had done all to the quiescent drive system that he could reasonably do. Time for other things.

He stood, wiping his hands, and backed away from the transmission unit's complex mesh of gears. The cover locked as he pulled it down, sealing the gears away. Later, he would open a lube-valve and fill the unit with oil.

Orca took the equipment he had been using back to his tool chest, stowing them carefully in their labelled drawers and niches. Then he waddled past Can-Rat and squeezed out through the engine room hatch. His curiosity, usually so easy to suppress, was getting the better of him. He sighed, and gave in to it.

Time to look at things other than engines.

Can-Rat watched Orca leave. He stayed where he was for a few moments, perched on top of Orca's workbench, then he hopped down and scampered after the engineer.

He knew Orca didn't like him much. None of the crew did, except Captain Bane, but that didn't matter. Can-Rat didn't see things the way other people seemed to. To everyone else, all the parts of the ship were separate; a vast collection of components that only worked when fitted together in a certain way. But to Can-Rat, the engines weren't distinct from the rest of *Golgotha*, any more than *Golgotha* was distinct from *Sargasso*. Even when the ship was out at sea, it was still connected, still part of the whole picture. The crew, too. On one level, they were individual people, but that level was the least interesting one to him. Without them, *Golgotha* was just dead metal. Without *Golgotha*, the crew would come apart, be homeless and hungry and miserable. Engines wouldn't work without a ship, and the ship wouldn't work without engines.

Why didn't people see that? It was so obvious.

That was why he enjoyed watching Orca at work, in as much as Can-Rat could enjoy anything. The big man often found that the engines worked better when certain parts of them were arranged in a slightly different way. Can-Rat had learned from watching Orca that there were hundreds, maybe thousands of ways that the engine parts could be arranged to work. And infinitely more ways that they could be made to stop working.

He couldn't have explained it to Orca even if he had wanted to. In the same way that he couldn't have explained how he sensed things that were about to happen before they did, because he could feel their connections shifting about. It would be like trying to describe what Synthi-Caf tasted like to a man born without a tongue.

Orca was heading along the spine of the ship, towards the forward hold. Can-Rat knew where he was going and found himself hanging back.

The casket.

It lay at the heart of a web of connections, darker and more tangled than he had ever seen. It made his head hurt just being around it. The others thought he had sensed the pirate vessel closing in on them before the sensors had picked it up, but he hadn't. It was the casket that had been bothering him.

Death lay within that thing, like a statue lies within stone, waiting to be freed by the sculptor's art.

And Orca was walking right towards it.

Can-Rat stopped where he was. The engines were part of *Golgotha*. They were part of Orca, too. If Orca ceased to function the engines would, and then the ship would. Gethsemane Bane was part of *Golgotha*. If Orca died, the engines would die, the ship would die, and Bane would... Die!

He didn't want that.

"Wait!" he called, his voice sounding reedy and thin as it bounced from the hull's metal walls. "Orca, wait up!"

Orca hauled himself along the length of the *Golgotha*, squeezing through hatches and passages and moving more easily through the ship's holds. The holds contained nothing but spare parts and provisions. The only salvaged booty lay in the forward hold.

He almost filled the narrow passage that led to the forward hold. Spinning the locking wheel in the centre of the door, he pushed the heavy metal panel inwards without even feeling its weight. Orca wore a layer of dense fat like a suit made for a giant, but he wasn't a weakling. It took powerful muscles to move his bulk, as more than one dock-side loudmouth had discovered to their cost.

He turned sideways as he stepped over the hatch sill and eased himself through. The forward hold was in darkness. Orca heard Can-Rat saying something a few bulkheads behind him, but he chose to ignore it. The little man had bothered him enough for one day.

Light from the passage cut across the hold, drawing a bright line across the deck and up the far bulkhead. Orca reached out to the bulkhead by the hatch and turned the switch he knew would be there. Above him, blue-green fluorescent tubes fluttered into life.

The casket was open.

The cables holding it down to the deck had been broken, their frayed ends glittering in the light. The lid of the shell had flipped open and was now lying on the deck next to the body of the casket. Fluid, translucent and greasy-looking, had spilled out of it in considerable quantity and now lay in steaming puddles on the deck.

Orca hesitated, unsure of whether to step back into the corridor and slam the hatch, or try to find whatever had been released from the casket. Something organic had been sealed inside, he could see that from the exposed systems. There were data leads in the casket, drug injectors, a gas-transfer system. The lock had opened by itself. A timing mechanism?

Just as he thought that, Orca saw part of the far wall *shimmer*.

One second it was just shadowy, stained bulkhead metal, the next it was fluid, mobile, casting shadows that were all wrong as it separated from the wall.

And hurled itself towards him.

Orca didn't even have time to move before it struck.

● ● ●

Back in the passageway, Can-Rat saw Orca jerk suddenly, horribly. The web of connections that linked him to the rest of the world were already unravelling around him.

Can-Rat skittered to a halt. Orca was still on his feet, but he was sagging, as if his vast weight had finally caught up with him after all these years. There was the sound of something wet and heavy hitting the floor.

"Orca?"

The engineer must have heard his voice. He turned, awkwardly, his great shoulders rolling around first until he almost lost his balance, then his foot came up and moved back, slamming back down to the deck. He ended up facing Can-Rat.

There was an expression on Orca's face that was almost infinitely sad. He opened his mouth, but all that came out was blood, because there was a wound in his body that ran from his groin up to his throat. He had his hands across it, as though trying to hold himself together, but he was too late. His massive torso had already emptied itself over the deck.

Can-Rat screamed in horror and took an involuntary step backwards. Orca raised a foot and stepped forwards too, as though trying to get away from the hold, but before he could move again a long, shining blade, white and glistening like wet bone, exploded out of his throat.

Orca went down like a loose sack, sliding off the blade to crash onto the passageway floor. Blood, sent flying by the impact of his body, went halfway up the walls and painted Can-Rat from head to toe.

He felt the warmth of it, the sudden, acrid taste of it in his mouth, and he shrieked. At the sound of his voice, what he had thought was a shadow in the hatchway shimmered and flowed and then stepped out into the light.

Its skin was blue-lit metal and rust-stained wall, and then it was pale and slick and unfinished, like something unborn. Can-Rat saw it for a split second before the terror took him and sent him scrambling for his life back along the passageway. He had seen the half-made armour growing through it in patches, the blades, the nightmare it had for a face. He saw the way it was looking at him. Then he ran.

The cold intelligence in that awful stare was something that would stay with him until he died.

6. PROPHESY

"Central Dispatch, all Judges in sector twenty-one, please respond."

Dredd finished cuffing the unconscious perp to a holding post, shook a few gobbets of blood and hair from his daystick and shoved it back into its belt loop. "Responding."

"All points request for back-up, Fresh Start Displaced Persons Habplex, off Weaver Skedway."

Dredd's Lawmaster was parked a few metres from the holding post, near the entrance to Hackin' Henry's Smokatorium. That was where the perp had been when Dredd pulled up: kicking the door and demanding to be let in. The Smokatorium staff had locked the doors from the inside, and little wonder, since the man had been wearing nothing except a small pouch of pipe tobacco. And that had been slung around his neck.

Dredd knew that tobacco addiction could do strange things to a citizen. Still, this had been an eye-opener. Even more surprising had been when the man had rounded on Dredd and tried to set him on fire with a cigarette lighter.

Dredd climbed quickly back onto the Lawmaster and gunned the engines. The big bike leaped forward with a throaty whine. "Acknowledged, Dispatch. What's the situation?"

"Attempted mass breakout, with associated damage to municipal property."

"On my way." Dredd took the Lawmaster left onto the intersked that would lead him onto Weaver. By his reckoning,

Fresh Start had been due to pop for the past two weeks. He was quite surprised it had taken this long.

There were hundreds of Habplexes all over the city, unwelcome leftovers from the Apocalypse War. Areas that had been reduced to rubble during the conflict had been bulldozed flat, levelled out and used as the foundations for sprawling, fenced-in camps. Inside the fences, temporary hab-domes provided shelter for the unfortunate citizens made homeless during the war. Often they ended up camping on ground once occupied by the blocks they had lived in previously.

The Habplexes hadn't been intended as permanent accommodation, but as the years went by and disasters like the Necropolis Event and the Second Robot War had continued to stretch the city's housing budget, plans to close the camps down had been pushed back further and further until they were basically out of sight.

Every month or so, someone from the Habplex would get lucky and be rehoused; that was usually the trigger for the remaining ten thousand inhabitants to begin ripping the place apart. The fact that they were destroying their own homes in the process always seemed to escape them.

The intersked sloped up sharply, taking the road over part of the Meg-Way. The rise afforded Dredd an early view of the camp – a wide gap in the Mega-City skyline, maybe five kilometres away, and a distant smear of yellow security lights. There was smoke, too, lit crimson from within. Fresh Starters often tried to burn their way through the perimeter fence.

Dredd tooled his Lawmaster diagonally across the sked and into the exclusive Judges' Lane. He could move faster there. As he did so, his helmet comms hissed into life again. "Central Dispatch."

"Already have that Fresh Start call, Dispatch. I'll be there in three."

"Negative, Judge Dredd," the dispatcher told him. "Message is direct from Chief Judge Hershey, your request to be appraised of developments in the Warchild case."

That, Dredd thought to himself, was fast. Hershey must have been taking a special interest. "Go ahead," he replied. "But make it quick."

"The SJS got nothing out of Hellermann."

Dredd hadn't expected to hear that. The Special Judicial Squad – the Judges who judged the Judges – were masters at interrogation in all its forms. Truth drugs, psychic techniques, dream machines; they had all the tricks and showed no mercy in using them. Dredd knew Hellermann was tough, but SJS should have cracked her like a synth-egg.

"She's had herself modified," the dispatcher reported. "Artificial glands grafted into the brainstem. They release anti-serums that neutralise truth drugs. Looks like she'd been undergoing deep hypnosis, too. She has auto-suggestive blocks set up to stop her breaking under psychological duress."

"She knew what to expect if she got caught and prepared for it," Dredd muttered, guiding his Lawmaster onto a slip-zoom. Already he could hear the dull roar of the riot, punctuated by the whiplash cracking of gunfire. Things, it seemed, were getting ugly.

"That was SJS's assessment, too," said the dispatcher. "Judge Buell has ordered that Hellermann be handed over to Psi-Division for deep psyche interrogation."

"Let the Chief Judge know I won't be holding my breath."

Ahead of him was the broad, flat expanse of waste ground on which the Habplex had been set up. Bathed in the nicotine glow of the security lights, rioting camp-dwellers moved through the area in destructive waves. At least half of the hab-domes were ablaze and most of the others were in ruins. From the look of them, many had been torn apart to provide weapons for the rioters.

A group of Fresh Starters had built a bonfire against the electromesh fence, hot enough to melt the wire and short out that section. Tearing the burning debris away from the blackened wire, they had succeeded in ripping a hole in the mesh. Dredd angled his bike towards the opening and thumbed its siren into life.

"Thank the Chief Judge and tell her I'll be in touch. Now get me Weather Control."

The journey from the harbour barge to the Old Man's chambers took Bane almost an hour, although part of that was spent in the dockside market looking for a suitable offering. Row after row of stalls were arranged around the forward edge of the harbour pool, covered against the constant rain of rusty condensation dripping from the metal roof. All the stalls had battery lamps and bioluminescent tubes strung from their frames, so that shoppers could see what they were buying in the cavernous gloom of the harbour barge. Some even had their own portable generators running noisy neon signs and matrix displays. Bane tended to steer clear of those stalls – if the owners had that much credit to burn, they certainly didn't need any of her hard-earned notes. There were plenty in the dockside market who did.

She settled on a bottle of potent brown spirits, no doubt brewed up from fruit mash and fish innards in some bottom deck bilge-still. It would probably taste ghastly, but the Old Man wouldn't mind and Bane had liked the little charms strung around the neck of the bottle on baling wire: sea creatures cut from scraps of thin metal, megasharks and octopi and long, looping serpents. They chimed against the glass and caught the light. Bane had thanked the toothless old woman behind the stall and handed over enough notes to pay for the bottle and a little more besides. An extravagance, she knew, but what was the point of making a good catch if she couldn't spread it around?

The market was packed – it usually was – and Bane had to duck and weave to get past the shoppers and back onto open dockside. From there she took the starboard ladder up five decks until she reached a hatchway in the barge hull. That led her out onto a narrow, hanging mesh bridge that swung uneasily in the wind. That bridge – quite terrifying to cross, with the cables groaning and the black water rushing past far below – had been the beginning of Bane's trek through the cityship, across eighteen decks, up and down numerous levels, through tunnels and up towers and down grimy, corroding ladders. She passed through three more markets, a wedding, two brawls, an open air drinking competition and a minor fire until she reached the chem-tanker *Hyperion*, only six hulls from *Sargasso*'s centre line.

By the time she got there she was cold, soaked from spray and very, very tired. Her limbs ached from all the climbing and carrying the bottle around hadn't helped, either. Next time, Bane promised herself, she would take the old fool a sandwich. At least she could stuff that into her coat pocket and have both hands free.

She went into *Hyperion* through the deck where hatches had been cut in the thick metal. Stairs led down through the levels until she was at a point that must have been midway between the deck and the waterline. There, a series of gangways opened out into multiple compartments, set into what had once been the tanker's vast chemical storage tanks. Now they were factories, homes, brothels, a hospital, and the chambers of the Old Man.

A chem-tanker was as big as a small town, although it was still only a tiny fragment of *Sargasso*'s total bulk.

Bane had been to see the Old Man so many times she could have made the trip blindfolded. She had to go down two more levels and through a narrow plasteen tunnel to get to his chambers and when she finally arrived she found the way blocked.

Two huge guards crouched at the chamber entrance, their heads almost touching the high ceiling. Everyone on board *Sargasso* was mutated to some degree – the Black Atlantic did that to everyone after a while – but this pair were extreme by anyone's standards. They had biceps Bane could have curled up and hidden in, and one was carrying a plasteen H-girder in one mighty hand, slapping it against the other palm like a jetball bat.

The Old Man's guards were legendary on board *Sargasso*. One of them was rumoured to be female, but Bane had no idea which.

"Hey," said the one without the girder as she stopped. Its voice was surprisingly soft and high, almost childlike, like that of a singer. "Bane. Good hunting?"

"Pretty good," she smiled. "Is he–"

"Expecting you? Yeah." The other guard stopped slapping its palm with the girder and rested its end against the deck. Bane felt the mesh sag slightly under its weight. "He's been asking for you."

"Right…" Suddenly, Bane felt unaccountably nervous. She swallowed hard, tugged her long coat a little tighter around her shoulders and stepped between the guards, the bottle a comforting weight in her fist.

It was time to meet the oldest man in the world.

The quayside under Angle's feet seemed to be pitching and rolling like the *Golgotha* in a heavy swell, which was just how he wanted it. After spending as much on grog as he had in the past couple of hours, he would have demanded his money back if he hadn't been at least partially drunk. As it was, he reckoned he was at least three quarters there, which he considered a pretty good deal.

Even though he was barely out of his teens and the youngest of *Golgotha*'s crew by far, Angle was already an experienced drinker. Luckily, the mutation that had given him his extra joints had also blessed him with a surprising capacity to metabolise alcohol, even the vicious algae-based grog they brewed on *Sargasso*. Within an hour or two he would be as sober as a Judge, which was a good thing. He was meeting Kerryanne, the barmaid from the Leaping Eel, after her shift was done.

There was a breeze coming in through the harbour doors, cool and tangy with the battery-acid smell of Black Atlantic seawater. It sent the quayside lanterns swinging on their cables and sent sprays of condensation drizzling down from the roof braces. Angle walked unsteadily between the moving cones of yellow light, feeling cold, rusty rain hit his shoulders and the top of his head as he headed for the *Golgotha*. If he was going to impress Kerryanne, he needed a shower and a change of clothes.

Behind him shone the lights of the three taverns in which he had spent his evening: the Dancing Norm, Lannigan's, and, of course, the Leaping Eel. The places had been jammed with all manner of revellers, from market traders and entertainers to cleaning crews and maintenance gangers down off the gantries. And, of course, the other scavengers. Angle had enjoyed the evening immensely, drinking the hardest of the gangers – a red-haired shift leader called Big Molly – clear off her chair, and swapping tall stories with the crews of every other ship in the harbour. But, as drunk as he was, he'd kept the secret of what lay in *Golgotha*'s hold to himself. The other scavs would find out about the casket on the day of the auction and not before.

The grog was warm in Angle's gut, the hour was late, and he was as relaxed as he had been for a while. So much so in fact, that he almost tripped over the corpse before he saw it.

It was in the middle of the quayside, in the shadows between two lanterns, and he had to stop himself stumbling into it. At first he thought it was a pile of old cargo nets, dropped carelessly in his path, but then he noticed something pale emerging from the bundle, splayed in a pool of lantern light. It was a hand.

Three of its fingers were missing.

Angle let out an involuntary yelp of shock and took a step backwards, his heart suddenly bouncing and hammering behind his ribs. There must have been an accident, he thought giddily. The crane operator, or one of the maintenance gangers, someone operating dockside machinery. Maybe the poor bastich had fallen into his own equipment.

Gingerly, he took a step forwards and rolled the body over. It flopped onto its back far too easily. Corpses tend to be heavier when their internal organs are still internal, not left lying on the quay and slithering greasily into the harbour pool…

"Oh, drokk!" Angle backed away, the alcohol-induced warmth vanishing in an instant. The expression on the corpse's face was terrible, a rictus of pure terror, and worse because it was a face Angle recognised. They'd been drinking together, not long ago; an hour, maybe less.

Ifrana Rokes, of the *Melchior*. She'd left the Dancing Norm to check on the moorings, and hadn't come back. Angle had figured that he'd been tactfully dumped and had switched his attentions to the Leaping Eel and Kerryanne instead.

And all the while poor Ifrana had been lying here. Murdered. Even in the bad light, Angle could see that this was no accident. Someone had opened the woman up in the same way as they might gut a fish.

He quickly looked up and down the quayside, his head spinning, but there was no one about. No one but him and the opened, stone dead woman at his feet. And possibly the murderer, he thought, feeling his spine turn to ice. Waiting in the shadows with a gutting knife the size of an anchor…

Angle realised that this was not a good place to be.

Golgotha was close by, bobbing listlessly in the water. Angle decided that if he had to make a stand anywhere, it would be there, where he could get the spit guns into play. He skirted around Ifrana's body, trying not to see the way her emptied torso was slowly collapsing in on itself, and climbed quickly up *Golgotha*'s gangplank.

The ship rocked slightly as he stepped aboard. Angle winced at the sudden movement and paused, holding his breath and listening intently. He heard the slow, even creaking of boat hulls in still water, the patter of condensation-rain on decks, the distant murmur of late trade in the market.

And a low moan from somewhere astern.

The noise was between him and the guns, he guessed with a mental curse. But then the moan sounded again and he realised it was Can-Rat.

"Canny? Stomm, what's going on?" Angle scrambled over to where his crewmate lay wedged between the gunwales and a winch drum. The little mutant appeared to have folded his body in half lengthways in order to fit into the gap, making himself almost invisible among the shadows.

"Angle, that you?"

"Yeah, it's me." Angle reached down, his multi-jointed arm moving easily into the awkward space. 'Let me help you up."

Can-Rat shook his head. "I'm okay," he muttered, and unfolded himself from the bolt-hole with an oddly fluid grace, marred only by a sharp intake of breath and a gasp of pain when he was halfway upright. He sagged away from Angle's grasp and leaned heavily against the stern rail. "He got Orca," he said quietly.

"What?" Angle gaped. "No way…"

Can-Rat nodded. "Down in the hold. Cut him up without trying. Then he came after me…" He tried to straighten, but the pain was obviously too much. "Grud, that hurts… I thought I'd be safe out here, but he's fast, and he can see in the dark. He hit me… Had a blade…" Can-Rat was beginning to lose consciousness. Pain and shock were dragging him down. Angle grabbed his thin shoulders.

"C'mon, you furry drokker, stay with me! What happened?"

Can-Rat swallowed, and shook himself. "Don't know. I heard screams. Maybe he got distracted."

Ifrana, Angle thought ruefully.

"I tried to get up, but I think my ribs are busted."

"Yeah, looks that way," nodded Angle. "Did you see who it was? How'd he get aboard – from the quayside or out of the water?"

"He didn't come aboard," said Can-Rat, wincing as he pressed a tentative hand to his damaged ribs. "He's been here the whole time."

The Old Man's chambers were welded deep into the inside of the chem-tanker *Hyperion*. Originally it had been a vessel in its own right, a high-speed pleasure skimmer. The Old Man himself had sailed the Atlantic in that nimble little ship, back when the seas were still blue. He had been very old, even then, and very rich.

The cabins and decks of his skimmer were now black with age and the smoke of a thousand candles. Gethsemane Bane had to walk gingerly into the main cabin to avoid knocking over the hundreds of bottles and jugs that covered the filthy wood – offerings from those who had come to the Old Man over the years to hear his weird and ancient wisdom.

People from all over *Sargasso* would make the journey down into the bowels of the *Hyperion* bearing gifts. It seemed everyone had a question that only he, in his strange trances and riddled speech, could answer – who to let a daughter marry, where to hunt for the best salvage, how to make a charm to ward off disease or turn the blade of an enemy. As long as Bane could remember, he had never done anything else.

Bane had been coming to see the Old Man since she was a child, just after Jester had first adopted her, but not for advice or readings. Despite the Old Man's reputation as the *Sargasso*'s resident shaman, Bane simply came to see him because she liked him.

He was sitting in the middle of the cabin, surrounded by his candles and bottles. His thin legs were crossed, his head bent so that the curve of his naked back showed his spine and ribs in perfect detail under the dark leather of his skin.

Bane crept towards him, very carefully, and sat down opposite. The Old Man was naked except for a pair of baggy shorts. His skin was as dark as mahogany, and his hair, cropped close to his skull, was pure white. To Bane, he looked small and heartbreakingly frail.

"Hey, eldster," she whispered, in case he was asleep. "Brought you some booze."

At the sound of her voice, the Old Man gave a reedy cry and threw back his head. "Devil child," he spat, his eyes rolling wildly. "Evil you are, evil I see! Terror you bring in your right hand, fire in your left!" He raised a skeletal arm, finger outstretched. "Get thee gone! Sinner, harridan, harlot!"

Bane was on her feet, shocked by the outburst. She felt something against her boot and heard a bottle clatter onto the deck. "Hey, what–"

"How dare you bring foulness before me!" he yelled, shaking with rage. The corners of his mouth were starting to quirk up. "Tempter, destroyer! Er, scavenger…"

"Scavenger?"

The Old Man was trying hard to keep a straight face. Eventually he gave up. "Ah, what do you expect, child?" He grinned, showing a wide sickle of very white teeth. "When all you bring me is this rancidness?"

Bane lifted the bottle and shook it at him, making the charms rattle. "You old phoney! You really had me going there!"

He shrugged. "It's my job. Hey, sit down, sit down…" He waited until Bane, now trying very hard to keep an angry look on her face, had settled back onto the deck. "I've got to keep in practise, haven't I? The punters expect so much and I'm not as young as I was."

That, Bane knew, was an understatement. The Old Man hadn't been young since before the ships that made up *Sargasso* were built. He had seen the building of the Mega-Cities, the turning of the dry land into the rad-desert known as the Cursed Earth. He had seen the Atlantic go black.

Something in his DNA had twisted, long ago, shutting down the processes of natural ageing. He had once told her that he had self-replicating telomeres, whatever they were. Then again, he had told her lots of things as she was growing up. Except his real name – no one knew that.

Bane glared at him. "Fraud."

"You and I both know," said the Old Man, "that isn't true." He presented Bane with his open hand. "Give, give…"

"Sure you want it? Rancid and all?"

He nodded vigorously. "Booze, child, is like sex and pizza. It's all good." He took the bottle from her and turned to place it among a dozen identical ones just off to his left. "You've been hunting."

"It's my job." She gave him a fond smile. "It's good to see you."

He nodded gently. It was all she needed. Embarrassed, she let her gaze drop to the deck, and changed the subject. "Look, I wanted to ask about–"

"Can-Rat," he interrupted. He often did that. Knowing what people were going to say before they said it was one of his talents. If he wasn't a natural psionic, he was something very like one.

"Mm." She looked up. "Is he one of yours?"

"Of mine?"

Bane nodded. "He sees things before they happen, I think. We were attacked out at sea, and he saw it coming." She grimaced, trying to put what she felt into words. "I was wondering if he saw things the way you do."

The Old Man fixed her with a steady gaze. "I've never met the man."

"That's never stopped you."

He shrugged. "Can-Rat sees connections. You've said before that he's odd and seems distant sometimes?"

"That's one way of putting it."

"He's like that because of the way he sees you. He's more interested in the links that bind you to everything around you, rather than you yourself. Gethsemane Bane as a wave function in the quantum network; a holistic entity, not a discrete equation."

Bane thought about this for a few moments then shook her head. "I don't have the slightest idea what you're talking about," she said. "But as long as he can keep knocking me over before bullets hit me, I guess he's okay."

"I think," the Old Man began, and then stopped. A strange expression crossed his face. "He's in danger."

"What?" Bane frowned. "What, now?"

"Yes, now!" the Old Man leapt to his feet, sending bottles flying. He hauled Bane to her feet with an astounding strength in those thin arms. "Grud, child, what did you bring aboard?"

Bane had never seen him like this before, and it frightened her. "I don't understand! Can-Rat's in danger because of what we found?" No sense trying to hide anything from the Old Man. "Because of the casket?"

The Old Man suddenly reached out and grabbed her by the forearms, holding her still. "Listen to me, Gethsemane Bane," he hissed. "No tricks now. No trances, no riddles. Whatever is in that box is death, pure and simple."

"What–"

"I don't · know!" he snarled. "There's no mind, no thought. Action, but no intent. A plan, but no purpose. Just death! And your people are in its way!"

He shoved her back. She stumbled, almost tripping over the bottles. Dozens of them scattered across the deck as she fought for balance.

"Go," the Old Man was shouting. "Go, before what you've brought here kills us all!"

7. THE SKIPPER

It was Erik, the younger and slightly brighter of the Tusk Brothers, who spotted the figure. It was gone almost before his eyes could track it, but it left an after-image in his brain: a tall, slender man, stooped, darting across the street and into the shadows of a nearby alley.

Erik might have been mistaken, but he could have sworn the man was naked.

"Hey." He used the back of his hand to slap Igor on the upper arm, drawing his attention. His brother was more drunk than he, and in a fouler mood. Hardly surprising, since it was Igor who had just been thrown bodily out of the Black Whale tavern. Erik had followed as a matter of course. The Tusk Brothers were rarely apart.

"Whassup?" Igor scowled. Erik put a finger to his lips, indicating silence. It took Igor's grog-addled mind a second or two to catch up, but when he did his big lower jaw closed with an audible snap.

Erik leaned close. "Just saw some guy, end of the street. Lurking around like maybe he doesn't want anyone to see him."

A slow smile spread over Igor's ruin of a face. "Yeah," he nodded, slowly. Igor did most things slowly, except drink. "Yeah. Right. So–"

"So," said Erik, finishing up for him, "maybe he won't shout so loud if we tap him, yeah?"

It was late; late enough for most of *Sargasso*'s honest citizens to be away in their beds. On most streets, especially in working spaces like the harbour, the only real foot traffic was security patrols by the skipper's men. The Tusk Brothers were on legitimate business, as much as they ever were – staggering home after being thrown out of a tavern wasn't illegal. But anyone darting naked into the shadows on a darkened street was obviously as eager to avoid the patrols as Erik and Igor.

The street was actually a metal companionway, slung out over two tiers of the dock district and, ten metres below, the quayside itself. The hull-side of the street was lined with stall fronts and kiosks, every one shuttered and locked for the night. Five minutes back towards the bow end was the Black Whale , its windows and open door throwing strips of warm yellow light across the mesh.

The alley was a dead end. Erik reached around to the small of his back, under his long fishskin coat, and drew the pair of narrow, double-edged daggers he kept there. Igor slipped a heavy billy club from his belt and tapped it experimentally against his palm. He grinned and nodded to himself, happy at the prospect of a little amusement.

Erik began to increase his pace, his coat – long ago acquired from an unlucky night-time pedestrian – billowing behind him. He wanted to catch the lurker before the man realised he was heading into a dead end and returned to the street. He winced as he heard Igor's heavy tread, keeping up. Igor wasn't the most subtle of men.

In fact, the brothers were not very much alike at all. Erik was small, lean and dark, while Igor was pale of skin and big in the bone. Erik was dextrous and could flip a knife more than twenty metres, hitting whatever he chose. Igor favoured a more direct approach and could shatter a man's spine in a single blow. Both had long, wicked tusks jutting up from their heavy lower jaws, but that was all they really had in common.

Apart from a mutual aptitude for relieving others of their possessions, of course.

They went around the corner together, shoulder to shoulder, blocking the alleyway. There wasn't much light to see by, just a couple of biolume strips throwing a dim, blue-green glow down the walls, but what Erik did see stopped him in his tracks.

The figure was naked, but it wasn't a man.

It had its back to the brothers; a hunched, ridged back that gleamed corpse-grey in the biolume light. There was something about the figure that looked raw, incomplete, like a statue half-made and then abandoned before all the rough edges had been chipped away. Its long, stick-thin arms were up, doing something to the service panel at the end of the alleyway.

As Erik watched, his oversized jaw dropping, the figure reached up and tore the panel free of the wall.

The screech of tearing metal as the fixing bolts ripped clear through the frame somehow launched Igor into action. Maybe the sound hurt his hangover – Erik would never find out.

Igor gave a roar and began barrelling up the alleyway, his billy club raised high and his boots crashing on the mesh.

The figure before them half-turned and made a strange, flipping motion with its hand, almost as though waving them away. The gesture seemed weird, almost effeminate, and Erik barked out a laugh of surprise. But as he did so, Igor tripped over his own feet and went sprawling to the metal floor.

Erik had seen Igor fall over drunk before but he usually got back up again. This time he stayed where he was, face down on the mesh. A shiver went through him and Erik heard him make a sound – a long, whistling groan, as though all the air was being squeezed out of his lungs. And then he was still.

When Erik looked away from his brother to see where the naked figure was, it had gone.

Something was horribly wrong here. There was simply nowhere for the figure to go unless it had climbed over the damaged panel and into the duct. But there hadn't been enough time for that. Igor had gone down almost instantly.

Erik trotted forwards, blades ready, searching the shadows but seeing no one. He reached Igor in a few paces and crouched down beside him.

Igor Tusk wasn't breathing. His face was turned to one side, his eyes wide and still. His pupils had contracted to tiny points.

There were three small needles, like tiny spikes made of plastic or bone, embedded in the skin of his face.

Erik had seen poison at work before, although nothing so fast or powerful. He shouted a curse and jumped up, and as he did so something tiny whipped past him, whining off the mesh a few metres back towards the street. Terrified, he stared up the alleyway, trying to see where the flying thing had come from.

Part of the wall moved. The rust-bubbled paintwork shifted fluidly, and just for a second Erik saw the outline the movement made: a man-shape, stooped and thin as sticks.

The figure had never gone away. It was there... with him.

Erik screamed, long and loud, and then he was running down the alley and onto the street.

It was Erik Tusk's screams that woke Dray from a very pleasant sleep.

He lay still for a moment, eyes closed, trying to identify the noise that had roused him. It had sounded like screaming, but who would be making such a deafening noise at this time of night? Maybe one of the kids was having a nightmare.

He sat up, making his wife stir and roll away from him, drawing the covers up over her head without waking. Dray smiled in the darkness and swung his legs out of bed, getting up carefully so as not to disturb her further, then padded across the room to the door.

He heard another scream just before he got there, and shouting. It seemed to be coming from below him.

Dray and his family lived in one of the dozens of habs on the upper level of the harbour barge; most of the scavenger crews resided there so they could be close to their vessels. Dray didn't like being away from *Golgotha* for long, and since he had moved into the hab he had enjoyed being able to lean over the street railing outside his door and look straight down onto *Golgotha*'s deck, twenty metres below.

It got noisy sometimes, what with the stalls and the taverns on the next street down, but he was used to that. The Black Whale had once closed for a week while roof braces were being re-welded. Dray hadn't been able to sleep a wink.

Now, however, something far worse than the usual drunken row was taking place a level below his feet.

He leaned over to see what was going on. The patrons of the Black Whale were all out on the street, surrounding a man in a coat. It was the man who was screaming, something about his brother.

About a killer.

Dray didn't like the sound of this at all. He went back into the hab and dressed quickly, making sure he had a couple of good knives in his belt. Then, with his wife still asleep under the covers, he went out, taking care to lock the door after him.

A set of metal stairs took him down to the Black Whale, but most of the patrons had gone. He'd heard them yelling and whooping into the distance as he was getting his shirt on. There were just a handful left, talking excitedly by the door.

Dray recognised a barrel-chested docker called Tome and trotted over. "What's going on?"

Tome gave him a nod of greeting. "Looks like someone's gone kill crazy. Murdered Igor Tusk."

"You're kidding!"

"I wish. Erik came in screaming the place down, then someone caught sight of the killer and they all went after him. Gruddamn lynch mob. We've sent someone off to find a skipper's man."

"Nice to see someone's still thinking." Dray puffed out a long breath. People died on *Sargasso* all the time, he knew.

The Skipper and his patrols did the best they could, but there was just too many people to keep track of, too many places to hide. Still, a murder practically on his doorstep... That wasn't a nice thing to think about, not with his wife and children asleep just a level above his head.

And the *Golgotha* below.

He rubbed his chin, nervously. "Look, Tome. I'm gonna check the ship. Kelli and the kids are still at home. You couldn't...?"

Tome grinned and slapped him powerfully on the shoulder. "I'll be right here."

Mako Quint didn't sleep much. Lucky for him he didn't need to, because the skipper of a cityship didn't get time to waste sleeping. When the telephone rang he was still at his desk, gulping at a mug of caf the size of his own head and working on his notes for the next day's council meeting.

The phone was his personal property; an antique, at least a hundred years old and held together with glue and silver tape. He lifted the handset from its cradle and spoke into the cracked plastic mouthpiece. "It's two AM!"

"Trouble at the docks, sir." It was Philo Jennig, his deputy. "Looks like three dead."

Quint closed his eyes for a second. "Where?"

"Two down on the docks, portside harbour. One near the Black Whale tavern. By the sound of it, we've got ourselves a lynch mob, too."

"Wonderful." Quint stretched, feeling the kinks in his neck and back crackle as he straightened. The harbour and the surrounding areas always had been a magnet for trouble. When people spent a long time out at sea things were bound to pop every now and then when they got home. One of his first acts as skipper was to double the number of patrols in those areas, especially at night. "Get a patrol on the tail of the lynch mob – we don't need any more deaths. I'll head down to the docks."

"The council?" Jennig asked.

"None of them will thank us for waking them at this hour," Quint replied. "Wait until we have something conclusive to tell them. I'll call you from one of the quayside boxes for an update. And, as this is a manhunt, turn on the harbour lights."

The harbour was bathed in light by the time Bane got back. She'd made good time on the journey from the Old Man's chamber. All the way she'd been trying to calm herself down, to stop her heart yammering in her chest and her stomach flopping like a landed fish. He wasn't always right, she told herself a hundred times. He'd got things wrong before. He might have been drinking some of the offering booze, or maybe he was just stringing her along. Telling her a tale, trying to scare her.

No one was in danger from the casket. Everything was going to be all right.

She almost convinced herself. But all her comfortable lies disappeared when she opened the hatch and saw the harbour lights were on.

The massive banks of halogens weren't cheap to run, and they were never turned on at night unless something bad was occurring. The last time it had happened was when Bane had been eleven and a megashark had come in through the harbour doors. It had taken two hours to drive it off.

There was no shark thrashing between the ranked vessels this time. Just skipper's men on the quayside and *Golgotha*'s deck, and thousands of people leaning over the railings on all the levels of streets above straining for a better view.

There were more of Quint's men guarding the hatch. One of them had told her that no one was being allowed in or out of the harbour, but then the other had asked which ship she was from, and when she told them they looked at each other and let her through. That was when she knew for certain something terrible had happened.

There was a mounded shape on *Golgotha*'s deck, covered with a tarpaulin.

As soon as she saw it, her stride faltered. She wanted, *needed*, to see what was lying there, but somehow her legs didn't want to move any more. She heard somebody make a choked, sobbing sound, and realised with no small surprise that it was her.

By the time she got to the gangplank all the strength was gone from her. She stopped at the foot of it, unable to take another step.

She heard footsteps and turned to see Dray and Angle coming towards her. They must have been talking to the skipper's men when she arrived, further along the Quay. Angle's face was whiter than usual. Dray's scales didn't show a colour change, but his expression was enough to confirm her worst fears. "Can-Rat?" she whispered.

Angle looked momentarily confused. "He's okay... Well, he's got a bunch of busted ribs, but otherwise he's all right."

Bane shook her head. "But the Old Man. I mean, up there..."

"It's Orca," said a quiet voice behind her.

She turned. Mako Quint was standing behind her, flanked by deputies and armed guards. Bane didn't think she'd ever seen the man this close.

"I'm sorry, Captain Bane. I truly am." He glanced at the covered body up the gangplank. "I know you were friends."

Bane's head felt as if it was going to come off her shoulders. The Old Man had seen Can-Rat in danger: why hadn't he seen this? "What happened?"

"Looks like he disturbed the killer," Quint replied. "Can-Rat too, but Orca got the worst of it."

"I need to see him."

Quint shook his head. "Trust me, girl, you really don't. Besides, it didn't end here."

Dray had stepped forwards. "Remember Ifrana Rokes, off the *Melchior*? He got her, too. And then Igor Tusk, up near the Black Whale."

"Oh my grud…" Bane stepped away, her mind spinning. "I don't get it. How could somebody kill Orca? He was–"

"He was a big man," Quint muttered, finishing the sentence for her. "I knew him. Not well, but we've worked together. Whoever killed him must be…" He shook his head. "I don't know. But this isn't over, captain. We've got a lynch-mob roaming the upper levels with Erik Tusk in charge. The harbour's locked down until my men find them, the killer or both. But that's not what I'm most interested in right now.

"I want you to tell me all about what's in your forward hold."

Quint had just finished questioning Captain Bane when one of the quayside boxes rang. When one of his deputies answered it there was a short conversation, some cursing, and then the phone was handed to him. "Quint," he barked.

"Jennig, sir. We, er, I mean…" He heard the man swallowing hard. There were other noises, too. It sounded as though someone was vomiting.

"Come on, Philo! Spit it out. Where are you?"

Perhaps "spit it out" hadn't been the best phrase he could have used. It took Jennig a few seconds to regain his composure after that. He cleared his throat. "Up on fourth, near the starboard vent ducts. Sir, you'd better get up here."

"Have you found the killer?"

"No. We found the lynch mob."

Three hours later, Mako Quint stood on *Sargasso*'s central bridge, watching the rising sun paint a sick yellow line across the horizon. He stood ramrod straight, hands clasped behind his back, his chin out, gazing through the wrap-around windows with his customary cool, steady glare. The bridge crew expected nothing less of him. He was skipper of the biggest cityship afloat and he had a job to do.

Nevertheless, he was glad that he could keep his hands locked together like that. It stopped them shaking.

He had never seen anything like this in his entire life.

Jennig had found the mob near one of the harbour's huge ventilation ducts. The ducts were big enough to drive a ground car through, sealed with armoured plasteen grilles to protect the giant fan blades inside. The killer had torn one of the grills open and smashed a fan blade to get through, which meant he had easy access to the rest of the harbour barge's giant air-system and, if he wanted, the open deck. Despite all Quint's efforts, there was a multiple murderer loose on the *Sargasso*.

Before he had escaped, however, he had turned on the lynch mob.

At first, Quint thought the bodies must have been caught in the fan and then thrown back out by the airflow, but there was no blood inside the grille. It was everywhere else, though, spattered against walls and metal. The killer had gone through the mob like a mincing machine.

Later analysis of the bodies would reveal that, far from dying in a frenzied attack, the mob had fallen prey to an assault of almost unimaginable precision. Each corpse had sustained only a single wound, although those wounds were horrific beyond belief. Torsos had been sliced open, heads severed, throats and arteries cut. Erik Tusk had died when a blade had taken off the top of his head, from the eyebrows upwards. Another man had been sliced in half at the waist.

A couple of the Black Whale's patrons had tried to escape, but were put down with the poisoned needles that had claimed Igor Tusk. And with that, the killer was gone. People living close by reported hearing a disturbance that only lasted about half a minute.

In the hours that remained before dawn, four-man patrols of skipper's men had begun to move through the cityship, reporting back constantly to the central bridge. Meanwhile, Quint had interviewed Can-Rat, whose ribs had been tightly bandaged, then Angle and Dray, and spoke to Gethsemane Bane for a second time. What they told him had confirmed his worst fears.

There had been more than one casket.

The "man down" call came shortly after his second interview with Captain Banc. A patrol had come under attack as they moved through a hydroponics farm on board the bulk carrier *Castiglione*. Their attacker had shot one man and maimed a second, reportedly with a blade that was part of his arm, then made off in the direction of the *Mirabelle*, the *Castiglione*'s immediate neighbour. *Mirabelle* was another ancient tanker, but its hold space had been fitted with hab-units made from stacked and racked cargo containers. Almost twenty thousand people lived there. Fearing a bloodbath, Quint directed his men on the neighbouring ships to converge on the *Mirabelle*. The moment he gave the order, he found himself wondering how many of his people he had just sent to their deaths.

The dawn's yellow line had become a purple bruise across the sky. An hour ago the city council had been woken and called to an emergency session. The session was still in progress, but Quint wasn't chairing it for the moment. He had something more important to do.

There was a very good comms set on the bridge and Quint's radio officer had already set it to the emergency frequency used by scavenger ships at sea. That frequency was on at all times, by *Sargasso* law. Every scavenger still out there would hear him.

The coiled wire stretched as Quint raised the microphone to his mouth and thumbed the "talk" button.

"*Sargasso* to all scavengers," he began. "This is a warning. Repeat: this is a warning. An unmarked watertight casket was salvaged and returned to the *Sargasso* in the last two days. Its contents are lethal. Repeat: lethal. We have at least twenty dead.

"If you have picked up a similar artefact, dump it immediately. Under no circumstances should it be brought aboard the city; anyone who does so will be shot on sight. Details of salvage coordinates to follow."

Quint paused. The sun's bloated bronze disk was rising

above the horizon. The black ocean seemed to burn. He took a breath and began again.

"Repeat: *Sargasso* to all scavengers, this is a warning…"

8. DROPZONE

The floors of the Grand Hall of Justice were synthetic marble, polished to a near-mirror finish, and Dredd's footsteps echoed as he approached the office doors. On any other surface in the city the soles of his boots would have made no sound at all, but the builders of the Grand Hall had been very particular about such things. Dredd could have worn boots made of spiderweb and his footsteps would still have echoed loudly as he walked up the corridor. There were electronics involved.

The acoustics of the place had been specifically calculated to inspire awe. And to let the Chief Judge know who was walking up to her doors, of course.

The doors in question, Dredd was pleased to note, had been reinforced again since he had last been here. Extra layers of bonded plasteen armour had been added to the outer panels, making the doors capable of withstanding assault by anything up to and including battlefield lasers.

Dredd approved of that. He took the safety of the Chief Judge very seriously indeed.

The doors opened as he approached them, smooth and whisper quiet. Dredd went right through across the wide floor and stopped in front of the Chief Judge's desk, rigidly at attention.

"At ease, Dredd," said Hershey quietly. She waved to an empty chair set to one side of the desk. "Take a seat."

"Thank you, Chief Judge. I prefer to stand." Out on the streets, Dredd didn't give two drokks about anyone's ideas of protocol or petty etiquette. But here at the home of the

Law, it was always going to be different for him. Here he could be nothing but the model of propriety.

Besides, one of the other chairs was occupied by someone Dredd preferred not to sit with, however persuasive Judge Hershey was.

Judge Buell was the head of the SJS – the Special Judicial Squad. He was slender and sharp-featured, with the look of the now extinct hawk to him. The personality, too, Dredd knew from bitter experience. Predatory, he was. Carnivorous. And more than willing to use the Law as a tool to further his own ends. Quite frankly, Dredd would have rather taken his rest next to an active Warchild. At least you knew where the attack would come from.

Across from Buell were Judges Duffy and McTighe. Duffy was head of the Atlantic Division; his remit was everything from the Mega-City Docks out as far as the territorial limit, two thousand kilometres offshore. McTighe was the Tek Division Chief. He and Dredd had crossed swords before, normally about McTighe's constant desire to redesign every piece of Justice Department hardware he could get his hands on. Personally, Dredd liked his daystick the shape it was.

"Duffy, McTighe," he nodded to the two men, and without turning back: "Buell."

Hershey raised an eyebrow at him. "Hmm. Anyway, now that the pleasantries are over and done with… I assume you've guessed what this is about?"

"The Warchild," Dredd replied. "Either you've located the first shipment, or Hellermann's cracked."

"The latter's proving difficult," Hershey muttered, sitting back in her chair. "You'll notice Psi-Chief Shenker hasn't joined us; Psi-Division's still working on Hellerman, but not having much luck. Her psyche's got more dead ends than a Mazny estate."

Buell sniffed. "Give her to me. She'll crack, given enough time."

"Time, Judge Buell, isn't on our side." Hershey touched a control on her desk, and a circular section in the centre of her desk fell away. The silvery disc of a Tri-D projector popped up to take its place. "Judge Duffy?"

Duffy leaned forwards, and set a small data slug into the projector's base. A globe of hazy light sprang up, filling the air above the desk. Justice Department eagle logos scrolled around its equator. "This is an electronic intercept, picked up by one of our listening posts along the territorial margin." In response to his words, the Tri-D globe unfolded into a map, showing the coast and most of the Black Atlantic. The margin lit up as a jagged line of bright dots. "It's audio only, I'm afraid, and not of the best quality."

"Let's hear it," Dredd snapped.

The map showed crosshairs and zoomed in to a point marked "Transmission Source." Dredd noticed its position was at least four thousand kilometres into the Black Atlantic, and then the air was filled with the raw scratching of static. And a man's voice, rich and commanding, with a hint of Euro-City in his accent.

"*Sargasso* to all scavengers," the man began. "This is a warning…"

The message ended. No one spoke. The map disappeared and the image returned as a spinning globe.

"Any thoughts?" asked Hershey after a few seconds.

Dredd folded his arms. "Sounds like they found a Warchild."

Hershey nodded. "Not much doubt about that. Dredd, what do you know about cityships?"

"Not a lot. Think I flew over one, once – a hundred or so surface vessels chained together into a kind of raft. It shot at us."

"No surprise there," sneered Buell. "Probably trying to knock you down for salvage. It's how those… " he paused, hunting for the right word, "*people* live."

Hershey shot him a glare, then turned her attention back to Dredd. "*Sargasso* is the biggest cityship afloat with over five hundred vessels. Last estimate put the population at almost a million."

"A million?" whispered Duffy. "Dear grud. If one of those things has gotten loose in there, the casualties–"

"Are nothing we need concern ourselves over," Buell interrupted. "Chief Judge, the cityships are out of Mega-City jurisdiction. And full of mutants, I might add."

"What do you suggest, Buell?" Dredd snapped, still without looking at the man. "Sit back with a long lens and count how many it eats?"

"Something like that."

"Gentlemen!" Hershey was on her feet. "Bickering is not going to help us here!"

"I concur," said Buell mildly. "Perhaps Judge Dredd would prefer to offer his own take on the matter."

"I would, " Dredd answered immediately. "The Warchild is the product of criminal activity. It's evidence and it belongs in Justice Department hands."

"Thank you, Dredd. My thoughts exactly." She cast a dark glance in Buell's direction. "Not to mention certain ethical considerations. And there is one more factor to be taken into account: Hellermann claims she can control it."

"Really," Dredd grated. "Psi-Div finally get something out of her?"

Hershey shook her head. "Unfortunately not. The woman's as smug as they come. Believe me, I'd like nothing better than to see her snap. But whatever Psi Division came up with, it was bad enough to make her offer a deal."

"A deal? Chief Judge–"

"I know, Dredd! I know!" Hershey raised her hand. "Your feelings on these matters are on record. But we've verified with Tek Division that each Warchild has a control code, a word that will shut it down. Hellermann says she'll know which word when she sees the Warchild."

Dredd didn't like the way this was going. "And what does she want in return?" he asked.

"An end to the interrogations and transfer to a low security cube," Hershey replied. "I share your misgivings, Dredd. But as you say, the Warchild is our business and it belongs here. Not running wild on a ship full of civilians."

"Or possibly falling into the hands of our enemies," said McTighe, quietly.

"If Hellermann is able to do what she claims, I judge it to be a reasonable trade," Hershey continued. "Dredd, I want you to assemble a team. Get Hellermann close enough to the Warchild and let her shut it down. The Sargassans may not be pleased to see you, but I can't see them complaining if you can get rid of their problem."

"And if the word doesn't work?"

Hershey gave a small shrug. "Then I guess it'll eat her."

Dredd squared his shoulders. "A win-win situation. I like it."

"You'll need to come in fast and high," McTighe told him, as they walked through the Tek Division prototype lab. Dredd had followed McTighe there after the briefing had broken up. Buell had skulked off somewhere on his own and Duffy had gone to prepare margin clearances for the mission, plus any extra intelligence he could find on the cityships. He had warned Dredd that there might not be much – the titanic vessels tended to keep themselves fanatically to themselves.

McTighe was confirming that fact right now. "If they see a plane coming in low they'll shoot it down. Probably think it's an attack, plus they'd want the salvage. So we'll take you up to a safe altitude and drop you from there."

Dredd thought about parachuting on to the moving deck of a ship full of angry mutants and decided there was no harm in exploring other options. "Grav-belts won't do the job?"

"Not from the altitude you'll need," McTighe told him, as they walked past benches covered in components and various items of hardware. "You'd reach terminal velocity before they got low enough to activate. Never slow down in time."

Better to land on the deck than plough straight through it, Dredd had to agree. "So what are you thinking?"

McTighe had stopped near a rack of grey, rubbery-looking bodysuits. "The PFE Shrike. High-altitude, pressurised flight envelopes; radar invisible, with integral life-support." He reached into a nearby locker and pulled out a slim, stream-lined casing fitted with heavy straps and covered in the same slate-coloured material as the suits.

"There are lift-generating surfaces built into the suits, under the arms. Equipment storage in the backpacks, along with nano-composite parafoils. You'll free-fall most of the way, then activate the foils and come in so fast they'll never be able to draw a bead on you."

Lift-generating surfaces, thought Dredd. Wings, in other words. They were going to jump out of an aircraft halfway out of the atmosphere and sail down into a combat zone wearing something a bat burglar would laugh himself sick at.

"Great," he muttered. "Reckon I'll need to assemble a team who can flap hard."

It took two hours to get the team in place. Dredd knew three street Judges with para-drop training, not including himself, but one was on secondment to Brit-Cit and couldn't be brought over in time. That left Larson and Adams, neither of whom Dredd had worked with before. Still, they had jumped out of aircraft at high altitudes and survived, which made them as qualified for the mission as anyone.

McTighe had insisted that a Tek-Judge be part of the team too and Dredd had to concur. Some scientific know-how could be invaluable when there was unknown technology involved, and Hershey had reminded Dredd that the Warchild wasn't the only X-factor he would be facing. The entire cityship was, at present, a virtual unknown.

The man McTighe had supplied would not have been Dredd's first choice. Tek-Judge Peyton seemed to be some-one far more at home in front of a lab bench than out on the field, and he was less than happy about the para-drop. In his favour, however, was the fact that he had worked on the original Warchild Project.

Somehow, Buell had managed to get one of his people involved. When Dredd had arrived at Kennedy Launch Strip, SJS-Judge Vix had been waiting there for him.

Dredd had met Vix once, and not in the best of circumstances. He regarded the woman as acid in a uniform, a worthy student of Judge Buell and all his teachings. Buell's excuse for Vix's presence was that she was qualified in airborne operations and para-drops. She was also, Dredd knew, spying for the SJS. Dredd would make sure he didn't keep his back to her for any length of time.

Which, of course, left Elize Hellermann. She had arrived at the strip last in a pat-wagon. The look she gave Dredd when she saw him could have burned holes in plasteen.

So Dredd's team, at take off, consisted of himself, two Judges he didn't know, one he didn't trust, one who was scared witless and a mad scientist who would probably feed them to her pet monster at the earliest opportunity.

The day was just getting better and better.

They sat, three facing three, in the cramped body of the strat-dart as it arrowed across the Atlantic. The dart performed best in high, thin air, and the pilots had taken it up to forty kilometres as soon as they had left the launch strip. It had been a long climb, during which the occupants of the drop bay could do nothing except sit on the hard benches, review their mission data and think about what was to come.

There was little in the way of conversation. Dredd wasn't surprised, given the make-up of the team, and found it something to be thankful for. There was work to be done and he could do without the idle chatter.

The dart had been flying level for almost two hours when Dredd got a signal from the cockpit. He unstrapped, stood as upright as he could in the low-ceilinged bay, and went forward.

The pilot had activated a monitor screen between himself and his copilot. The screen must have been for Dredd's benefit since both fliers were wearing head-up display helmets. Everything they needed to see would be right in front of them.

There were no windows in the cockpit.

The pilot gestured at the screen. Concentric circles were scanning outwards from a bright point, partway across a stylised map of the Atlantic. "We've got your target."

"Can they see us?"

"Not yet. We're picking up passive scans from a spy-sat, so we're as good as invisible."

"That's about to change," Dredd replied. "Take us below the cloud layer and stand by to broadcast."

"Commencing descent to drop altitude." Dredd watched the pilot ease the control collective forwards and felt the angle of the deck beneath his boots begin to change. On the screen, the map disappeared and was replaced by an external view. Dredd saw an endless landscape, white and billowing, rising like a tide. It swallowed the view and the screen went blank.

"We'll be through the cloud layer in a few seconds," the pilot told him. He flipped down part of his control board, revealing the comms panel, and pressed several buttons. "Okay, Judge Dredd. Give the word and I'll slave this into your personal comms channel."

"We don't know what kind of equipment the cityship might be using," the copilot told him, "so we'll be sending across a wide frequency spectrum. I'll record as you speak and put it on a continuous loop until touchdown."

"Sounds good. Patch me in."

The monitor screen turned from white to black. One second it was blank and in the next the view had turned to that of a vast, oily sheet, glittering with tiny ripples of sunlight.

"Calling whoever is in authority onboard the cityship *Sargasso*," Dredd began. "I am Judge Dredd. I represent the law in Mega-City One. A piece of our technology has been taken aboard your city and I am leading a team that will remove it. Your assistance is not required, but your cooperation and that of your citizens would expedite our mission.

"My team will arrive by air. This is not an attack. Repeat: this is not an attack. But be advised, we shall defend ourselves if fired upon. This message will now repeat. Dredd out."

The copilot pressed a key on the comms board. "We'll keep broadcasting until we hear you're down safely," he said.

"We're now at drop altitude," the pilot cut in. "Five minutes to marker. You ought to get back and buckle up."

Dredd turned awkwardly in the confined space and squeezed back through the hatch and into the drop bay. He was already wearing most of McTighe's Shrike suit: the radar-baffling grey fabric was a tight fit over his uniform and didn't allow for any great freedom of movement while walking. The lift surfaces under his arms flapped uncomfortably and he could barely turn his head. But already Dredd could see how it would turn a man into a missile in the air.

The rest of the suit was waiting for him in the bay. Adams helped him into the backpack which strapped on securely with reinforced webbing across his chest. The top of the pack – which contained not only the parafoil but also the bulkier sections of his uniform – looked oddly truncated, until he put on the flight helmet and locked it down. The helmet was designed to fit over a Judge's helm and turned his entire torso into a nearly rigid and highly aerodynamic capsule.

The others were already suited up. As soon as the dart had reached drop altitude the lights in the bay had changed from white to amber, giving them the signal to suit up and lock down. Dredd saw the inside of the flight helmet light up with icons and guide indicators, a full HUD that would tell him everything he needed to know on the way down.

He turned to Peyton. "How are you doing?"

"I'm, ah, okay, sir." Peyton was a faceless teardrop with arms and legs just like the rest of them, but his body language was all nerves. "My suit's slaved to Larson's flight controls, so I guess I'll be okay."

Larson slapped him on the shoulder. "Don't worry, tekkie. I won't put you down too hard!"

"See that you don't, Larson," growled Dredd. "If Hellermann doesn't come up trumps, Tek-Judge Peyton could be our last line of defence."

"So it's true." That was Hellermann. Her Shrike was covering up prison greys, and slaved to Vix's. More for reasons of security than to give her an easy ride. "You were part of my operation."

Peyton's suit bobbed. Probably nodding in the helmet. "I was lead analyst on the resequencing team."

"No wonder it failed."

"Button it, Hellermann." Dredd moved down the line to stand at the bay doors. "There's only one word any of us want to hear from you."

The lights in the bay went red and an armoured pressure door slid across the cockpit hatch.

"We're nearing the drop zone. Helmets on; make your final checks. Larson, make sure Peyton's harness is good to go."

They came out of the strat-dart in a long line, Dredd jumping first.

For a few seconds the slipstream tore at him. He tumbled, his view a spinning mess of black water and white sky, and then the Shrike took control. The lift surfaces between his arms and torso were filled with a complex array of hollow, flexible spines. The suit's onboard computer worked these effortlessly, filling some with air and emptying others, modifying the flight characteristics of Dredd's body until he was sailing through the air straight and true.

The strat-dart was a triangle of black shadow, already peeling out of Dredd's view and back into the clouds.

Dredd kept his body straight, his arms back and level with his torso splayed at forty-five degrees to give the lift surfaces their best angle of attack. He was moving forwards as fast and far as he was falling downwards.

Ahead of him, the cityship was a ragged island of metal, trailing a hundred kilometre wake.

"There's the target," Dredd reported. "Drop team, sound off."

"Adams here."

"Larson, all okay."

"Vix."

"Grud," gasped Peyton. "Grud! This is fantastic!"

"Don't get too fond of the experience, Peyton. We'll be down in sixty. Hellermann?"

There was a pause; then: "I hear you."

The cityship was growing like a stain. Dredd could see that every square metre of its upper surface was covered in buildings, everything from the original superstructure of *Sargasso*'s component vessels to skyscrapers made from upended chemical tanks and great stacks of cargo containers. Everything was linked to everything else. Great spans of gantry and support cable and haphazardly swinging bridges glittered in the sunlight, looking from this altitude like the work of a deranged and hyperactive spider. There wasn't a flat spot anywhere.

"Drokk," muttered Larson. "We'll be in trouble if we can't find a landing strip."

Alarms began to go off in Dredd's helmet HUD. "Foil altitude!" he barked. "Drop team, deploy parafoils!" As he spoke, he keyed a control in the palm of his flight glove.

He felt the backpack shudder as it unfolded, and then he felt a massive impact against his chest and shoulders – the parafoil had deployed. Instantly his flight-wings went limp and disengaged from his torso, leaving his arms free. He reached up and grabbed the foil's control handles, swinging himself around towards the port side of the cityship.

It was rushing up to meet him, filling his field of view, becoming more insanely complex with every metre he

dropped towards it. There was detail everywhere: the
stepped superstructures of luxury liners and the blocky conning towers of supertankers and anti-pol ships. Bridges and
walkways were slung between individual vessels, while
elsewhere the hulls of several ships appeared to have been
welded tightly together. And, on every level, untold numbers of dots that grew and resolved themselves into figures.

Dredd watched as one of the dots looked up and stabbed
a pointing finger skywards. There must have been shouts of
surprise or alarm as other dots followed the first figure's
lead, looking up and pointing. Some ran for the nearest
doorway or hatch. News was spreading.

"There!" called Vix. "That Sov-ship in the middle, near
the conning tower!"

Dredd scanned the cityship for the distinctive lines of a
Sov-Blok vessel. He quickly saw that Vix was right; almost
at the centre of the *Sargasso* was a gigantic mass of grey
metal that looked like a Putin-class assault carrier. While
most of the deck was taken up with hastily-constructed residential areas there was a large, uncluttered space just
ahead of the superstructure. From what Dredd remembered
about the Putin-class, that's where the primary weapons
mounts would have been.

"Drop team, follow my lead. We're setting down." Dredd
tugged at the control handles, spilling air from one edge of
the parafoil and angling towards the open space. Whatever
passed for city defence on board the cityship would almost
certainly have realised where they were headed and, if they
were anything like City-Def back in Mega-City One, they
would be itching for some target practice. The presence of
the Warchild would only make them more trigger-happy
than usual.

"Get down and ready as fast as you can," he told the others. "If we're going to be sitting ducks, I'd sooner have my
feet on the ground."

● ● ●

Seconds later, the deck came up and hit the soles of Dredd's boots – hard.

Instantly he slapped the foil-release on his chest webbing. There was the dull thump of explosive latches and the parafoil whipped up and away from him, skating across the deck. Around him, the rest of the team came down with varying degrees of success: Adams, Larson and Vix made good landings, but Hellermann seemed to crumple as her boots hit, and she went down heavily onto one knee. Peyton made a textbook landing but missed the release pad – the wind against his parafoil had him over – and for a few seconds he went slithering across the deck. Larson had to trigger his release by remote control.

Dredd hauled off his flight helmet and dropped it, undoing his webbing with his other hand. The backpack slid off his shoulders and he pulled it round and slapped a panel on the side. The pack popped open along a pressure seal and dropped a Lawgiver into his palm.

The rest of his uniform could wait. He checked the weapon over, made sure it was set to deliver standard execution rounds. By the time he had done that the rest of the team were assembling around him. Vix was helping Hellermann along – it looked as though the woman had damaged her knee on descent.

Peyton was last to join them, dragging his helmet off as he did so. "No welcoming party yet," he puffed, obviously unused to the effort. "Maybe Dredd's message worked."

"Judge Dredd – diplomatic attaché to a ship full of mutant scum," Hellermann sneered. "That has a nice ring to it."

"So does 'life without parole,'" Dredd growled. "I'd bear that in mind." He looked up at the long window of the *Putin*'s conning tower and saw faces pressed against it. They were unashamedly looking back at him.

"Defensive formation," he ordered. "Cover the angles and watch the shadows. Move slowly. We don't want to spook the locals."

Dredd could see movement all around: figures darting from cover to cover, heads peering over rails and out of windows. Weapons were no doubt being passed around. He needed to connect his sudden arrival with the message he had broadcast earlier.

He dropped his helmet mike and turned on the internal amplifier. "I am Judge Dredd!" he roared.

"And I'm Mako Quint." The voice was as commanding as his own, and very nearly as loud. Dredd turned to find its source and saw that a hatch had opened halfway up the conning tower. A man stood on a platform there, flanked by armed mutants, although he was a head taller than any of them.

At the same time, more mutants popped up from their hiding places. A lot of them. Dredd found himself, not for the first time in his life, standing in the crosshairs of several hundred weapons.

"This is my city, Judge Dredd," snarled Mako Quint. "And you are not welcome here."

9. POWER TO THE PEOPLE

Luckily for the mutants, none of them tried to take Dredd's Lawgiver away.

The drop team had been led into the *Putin*'s conning tower by a squad of armed men and women who appeared to be under Mako Quint's direct command. Some were obviously mutated, although many seemed human. Dredd guessed that everyone on the cityship must have been mutated to some degree but he also knew that DNA tended to start kinking on prolonged exposure to Black Atlantic water.

Quint had met them at the base of the conning tower, looked them over, and then turned away and walked inside without a word. He was a big man, physically larger than Dredd, and he carried his bulk easily. Under his clothes – dark shirt and trousers, fishskin jacket, heavy utility boots – he was all muscle. Dredd noted that if he and Quint came to blows, the other man would definitely have the advantage in strength. And Dredd couldn't rely on being too much faster, either.

Life on the Atlantic not only made people into mutants, it also made them tough. It would be a mistake, Dredd knew, to underestimate any of them.

Once inside the tower, they were taken by elevator to what had been the fire control deck. According to what Dredd knew about this class of warship, the *Putin*'s deck would have been ringed with weapons boards, sensor stations and comms equipment when it was operational. All that was long gone and in its place were blank walls painted

a grim brown, biolume strips around the ceiling, and three
rows of bench seats against the far wall. The seats were set
at different levels with highest at the back. To Dredd, who
had spent a lot of time in the Cursed Earth, it was a familiar enough arrangement.

"Mutants," he growled, mainly to himself, "sure do love
a council."

Quint had gone in ahead of them and his guards had stationed themselves around the rear wall of the chamber. The
benches were already occupied – Dredd counted thirteen
mutants there, none of whom could have been mistaken for
human, even in the worst light.

Out in the rad-deserts and wastelands that surrounded
Mega-City One, every second town or settlement Dredd had
ridden through had some kind of council, quorum or
elected body making life difficult. He didn't know why and
didn't much care. They just seemed to like it. Maybe it
made them feel important, worthwhile.

Human.

Dredd looked across at Quint. "I got the impression you
were in charge here."

"Skipper Quint," said a mutant on the lowest bench, "is
responsible for maintaining the rule of law on board the
Sargasso." The mutant's voice was rich and fluid;
strangely so, given that he seemed to consist of a head
and very little else. The fleshy tentacle making up the rest
of his body was curled up and strapped into a padded
chair that was studded with interface jacks; presumably it
could be bolted into a robot prosthesis to give the man
mobility.

Dredd hadn't taken his eyes off Quint. "Then we have at
least that in common."

"However," the mutant continued, "matters that concern
the safety of the entire cityship come before us. My name is
Jubal Haab, and we are–"

"The ruling council," Dredd cut in. "Or some variation on
the theme." He stepped forward.

"Listen to me, councillor. You're wasting time. You know who I am and why I'm here – if you hadn't got my message we'd be shooting our way in to see you right about now."

"You wouldn't be getting far," rumbled Quint.

The limbless mutant gave Quint a dark look, then turned his attention back to Dredd. "I've no doubt you would have tried, lawman. And it would have been Quint's duty to stop you. We selected him for the post of skipper, just as we were elected to the council by the people of *Sargasso*. And we are very good indeed at choosing the right man for the job."

"Oh, terrific," snapped Vix. "A democracy. We could be here for a week."

At the SJS-Judge's words, the temperature in the room seemed to drop by several degrees. Dredd kept his gaze firmly on the wormlike mutant, but in his peripheral vision he could see Larson and Adams tensing up, shifting their body positions to allow for a quick draw from their temporary holsters.

He could also see that, while the guards still weren't aiming directly at him, their guns weren't exactly pointed anywhere else, either. This was bad. If push came to shove, the drop team were badly outnumbered, and they hadn't had a chance to take their Shrike suits off. Dredd didn't relish the idea of trying to shoot his way out of this place with ten kilos of McTighe's radar-eating rubber spoiling his aim.

"Perfect," he heard Peyton mutter. "I survive the drop and then get fragged because she doesn't like their politics."

Dredd pointed a gloved finger at Haab. "You can vote all you like," he grated. "Fact is, you've got a killing machine making synthi-mince of your population. All you have to work out is what's less welcome – us, or it."

"It's thanks to people like you that it's here in the first place!" hissed out the councillor to Haab's left. This one had three eyes staring out of a blank sac of a head and his reedy, outraged voice whistled from an opening at the base of his throat.

"Grafton's right," said a woman whose arms were as boneless and ceaselessly mobile as a squid's. "I say put them over the side and we'll kill this evil toy of theirs ourselves!"

At that, everyone on the bench was yelling. Thirteen councillors, thirteen opinions, thirteen voices raised above that of its neighbour in an attempt to get its message across. Instant chaos. Fights broke out. Pieces of paper flew up into the air. Jubal Haab was howling for silence and Dredd saw that Quint was standing with his eyes closed, his head shaking slowly from side to side.

"Wonderful sight," said Dredd quietly. "Democracy in action."

"This *toy*," snapped Hellermann, stepping past Dredd and right up to the first bench, "is the most sophisticated biological weapons platform ever produced!"

The hubbub gradually died down. Within a few seconds, every one of the mutant councillors were looking at Hellermann, the sharp-featured, crop-headed woman with the bulky grey bodysuit and the voice that could cut through hull plating.

Hellermann folded her arms and glared up at the council with utter disdain. "What do you think this is, some B-Vid monster? Wandering about with its arms outstretched, picking off the odd screaming victim until the hero catches it off guard and pushes it off a cliff?"

She shook her head as if amazed by their stupidity. "The Warchild project took fifteen years and over two billion credits of research to develop. It's designed to operate independently for an indefinite period under the harshest battlefield conditions. It has internal weaponry, stealth skin and bullet proof armour. It can be programmed with any number of specific mission profiles, or left to its default settings – and believe me, even under default settings this thing is your worst nightmare!"

Hellermann stepped back, knowing she had the whole council's attention and obviously loving it. "Trust me; no matter how many people you send after this thing there's only one way you'll know if they find it. They won't come back.

"There's only one person on this cityship who can stop it. Me."

There was a long pause. Then Jubal Haab twisted in his support harness. "Is this true?" he demanded, staring directly at Dredd.

"That's what she says," Dredd replied. "She's the closest thing it's got to a mother."

Again, the council members began to talk at once. Haab called for silence and this time the noise ceased almost immediately.

"We should consider this carefully," Haab said. "In private."

Two council members – the one with the neck-mouth and a woman who had vestigial hands sprouting from either side of her neck – picked up Haab's seat and carried it out of the room. "Make yourselves comfortable," Haab told Dredd as he was carried towards the door. "Uninvited you may be, but you are our guests."

"I can't believe they thought we brought it here on purpose!"

Gethsemane Bane stopped pacing as Angle spoke. It was the first time in a long while that anyone in the cell had said anything, and sitting in silence had been driving her slowly insane. She often paced about on *Golgotha*'s decks, when the seas had been empty and the way home long and slow.

Of course, there wasn't as much room here.

There were five decks under the conning tower in the brig. The *Putin*'s superstructure housed the council chamber, Quint's office and the central bridge; all the machinery of law and order on *Sargasso*, in fact. So it was quite appropriate that anyone who transgressed those laws should be kept on the same vessel.

"They don't," Dray replied. He was sitting on the cell's one, narrow bunk, his eye closed and his back against the wall. "They're just drokked off with us."

"We'll still be punished, though." Can-Rat was next to him, curled up around the pain of his bandaged ribs. "Maybe they're trying to figure out what to do with us."

Angle, who had found a corner of the cell as soon as he had been thrown into it and had stayed there the whole time, punched the wall in frustration. "Should be a short debate," he spat. "I mean, what would you do to the dumb sneckers that brought a box-wrapped killing machine home to Mama?"

Can-Rat realised what Angle was talking about. "They wouldn't. Would they?"

"Exile?" Angle said, then shrugged. "Sneck. I would."

Bane closed her eyes. Exile was something she'd not been letting herself think about.

Even for a scavenger whose life was measured by long periods on the open sea, the idea of exile was a nightmare. Those sentenced to it would be cast adrift in a small vessel, sometimes with a little food and water, sometimes without. The lucky ones would find themselves prey to Black Atlantic wildlife; megasharks, most usually, but there were bigger and nastier things under those inky waters. The less fortunate wouldn't be eaten at all. They would die slowly from hunger and thirst and the slow, insidiously corrosive effects of the ocean itself.

If you were strong and they gave you some water, you might last a fortnight.

Exile was the worst punishment available to the cityships – worse than execution, by far. When you were exiled, you had time to regret what you'd done.

"They wouldn't exile you," Bane whispered. "They wouldn't do that. *Golgotha*'s mine, I'm responsible. I won't let them punish you." She started pacing again, head down so they couldn't see the fear in her eyes.

"How, cap'n?" Angle was glaring up at her. "Sorry and all, but it doesn't look like you've got a whole lot of leverage from here!"

Dray opened his eye and gave him a look. "Calm down, kid."

"The sneck I will!" Angle leapt to his feet. Dray was up to, in an instant.

"I told you to calm the sneck down!"

"That's enough!" Philo Jennig had appeared at the cell door. As the crew fell silent, he gave a nod to the skipper's man who had been posted outside.

The guard unlocked the door and slid the bars aside.

"Jennig." Bane stepped quickly towards the deputy. The guard began to raise his rifle but Jennig shook his head.

Bane took a deep breath. The way things were going for her right now, she reckoned she had one chance at this, and one only. "Listen," she said, "I've told Quint and now I'm telling you. My people had nothing to do with this. If anyone should be punished, it's me."

Jennig cocked his head to one side. "You sure you know what you're saying?"

"Yeah. Tell them I'll accept exile." Behind her, Dray gasped, but she ignored him. "Drokk, I'll jump over the side myself if that's what it takes. Anything they want, as long as my crew go free."

A grin spread over Jennig's face. "Captain Bane, I believe you just said the magic words."

For the drop team, comfortable meant being rid of the Shrike suits.

By the time the councillors began to file back in, Dredd was in full uniform again. His shoulder and knee pads were strapped on, his Lawgiver and daystick were at his belt, and his badge of office was chained onto his uniform.

He was ready for work.

After the councillors had settled themselves, Mako Quint strode back into the chamber. This time, someone was with him; a tall, slender woman with short dark hair. She wore heavy trousers with pockets sewn onto every spare centimetre of fabric, a vest and heavy boots. She wasn't armed.

Her skin, under the glow of the biolumes, had a strange sheen.

"We have discussed the situation," began Jubal Haab, speaking as soon as his padded seat had been set onto the bench. "And your claim that you can solve it."

"And how many of your people have been slaughtered while you've been 'discussing?'" Vix spat.

Dredd raised a hand. "That's enough, Vix."

Haab fixed Dredd with a liquid stare. "You can take your weapon," he said. "Hunt it down, make it safe and take it back to your Mega-City. You will be escorted to the location of its last kill. From there, Gethsemane Bane will guide you." With a jerk of the head Haab indicated the new arrival. "She captained the ship that brought your monster here."

Dredd gave the woman a sideways look. "Bad luck."

"No drek," he heard her whisper.

"You will receive no more help from us," Haab continued. "Find the rogue weapon and you are welcome to it. Die and we shall find another way to deal with it."

"Sounds fair," Dredd replied. "Let's get to it."

10. THE HUNTER

They began at the vent. There was something at the site of that bloodbath Dredd needed to see.

The bodies had been taken away but the stains had not. No one had wanted to stay near the vent long enough to clean the deck – simply moving the corpses had been done with unseemly haste. Bane found herself treading carefully between the grisly evidence of what had occurred a few hours before: broad, ragged-edged puddles where men's lives had poured out onto the deck, wide triangles that spoke of arterial spray and tracks where hands and feet had skidded in blood.

There were round spots, too, where droplets had flicked through the air. In their thousands.

Most of the blood had dried in the warm wind from the vent, gone from bright crimson to a dark, rusty brown, but some of the puddles were too deep. Distressingly, those were often the ones that contained fragments of what Bane could only allow herself to think of as "material."

Others had walked here without as much care. Bloody footprints crisscrossed the deck.

Just being here was making Bane feel shivery and ill. Before this, she had only been told of what the Warchild was capable of – she hadn't even been allowed to see Orca's body. But now, although the corpses themselves were gone, the tale of their final moments was told in painful detail.

And the Warchild, as these intruders from dry land called it, could be anywhere. It could be watching her right now.

Bane drew her coat tight around her thin shoulders and stuffed her hands deep into the pockets. She allowed herself a quick, surreptitious glance at the intruders to see if they were as frightened as she was.

Apart from the woman that called herself Hellermann, the rest of them wore glossy armoured helmets that covered most of their faces. What little she could see showed different reactions: Dredd, the leader, seemed completely unaffected by the carnage, as did the female Judge with the skull on her helmet. Larson and Adams had gone a little pale, and the small chubby one, Peyton, looked positively sick.

Dredd had noticed that too. "Pull yourself together, Peyton," he growled. "Gonna get worse than this."

Vix, the skull-headed one, was crouched next to the vent. Bane watched her, trying to work out what she was doing; the way she was tipping her head this way and that seemed odd, until she spoke. "How many do you make it, Dredd?"

"Fifteen."

"That's what I got." Vix stood up. She must have been down there to get a different angle on the bloodstains, Bane realised. And from this mess they were able to tell how many had died?

Despite herself, she was impressed.

"Doesn't tally," said Peyton. "I asked that Jennig guy, the one with the head? He told me there had been fourteen bodies pulled out of here." He put his hand to his mouth and coughed weakly. "Well, he said it had come to fourteen when they put them back together."

"So we're missing one." Dredd rubbed his chin, thoughtfully. "Maybe he got away."

"I doubt it," Hellerman cut in. "It's not built that way."

Vix walked over to Hellermann and put herself right in the scientist's face. "Enlighten us, *doctor*," she sneered.

There was a long silence as the two women stared each other down. Vix, behind her grisly-looking helmet, had the advantage. Eventually Hellermann shrugged. "It doesn't leave witnesses," she said.

Vix snorted and walked away. As she went past Dredd, Bane heard him say: "Feel better?"

"Much."

I'm doomed, Bane thought wildly. These people were supposed to find Orca's killer, track it down through the kilometres of steel maze that made up the cityship's interior, and make it safe. Instead, they seemed more interested in scoring points off each other.

Anyway, Hellermann was wrong. "Can-Rat's alive," she said.

Suddenly, everyone was looking at her. "Say again," Dredd told her.

"Can-Rat. He's one of my crew. He was there when the, er, Warchild killed Orca, and it hit him, but then it got distracted and ran away."

"Which means?" Dredd was looking at Hellermann. The woman seemed momentarily confused.

"Another situation must have overridden its default program. It thought it was in more immediate danger from another source."

"Did you build it that way?" asked Larson.

Hellermann shook her head. "Not exactly."

"Great," muttered Adams. "It's malfunctioning."

"Which makes it even more dangerous." Dredd turned to Bane. "Okay, captain. This is where you come in."

Bane's eyebrows went up. "Me?"

"You're supposed to guide us, right?" He leaned close and pointed his gloved finger at her nose. "So get guiding. Or we'll throw you back to the council and make our own way."

He turned and stalked away, back to the vent. Behind him, Bane sagged.

An invisible killing machine in front of her and a troupe of bickering, trigger-happy fascists behind? Gethsemane Bane was beginning to think that exile would have been the easy option.

• • •

Unlike the Warchild, neither Bane nor the intruders had the strength to simply stop the fan and climb past the shattered blade. Dredd favoured putting a bullet through the motor but Peyton saved him the ammunition by tracking down the main power supply and shorting out the connections.

The fan whined slowly to a halt, rattling on its damaged bearings as the missing blade threw it off-balance. Dredd caught it once it was slow enough and hauled it to a stop. Thankfully, he didn't make Bane go through first.

He made her go second. "All clear," she heard from inside the duct. "Send the mutant through."

She climbed in gingerly, aware that the missing fan blade had left razor-sharp shards of metal sticking out from the hub. The rest of it, she saw once she was through, lay in dozens of scattered fragments all over the duct floor. Some of them had embedded themselves in the walls.

The rest of the team followed her in. The duct was big enough to stand up in and constructed from heavy gauge steel. It still rang like a gong as soon as anyone took a step, and echoed horribly. "Say goodbye to a stealthy approach," said Larson ruefully.

"You won't be creeping up on it anyway, mister," Hellermann said from just inside the grille. Bane had noticed that the Judges were always careful never to let her get behind everyone else. As though they thought she might make a break for it. "It's got hearing that would shame a bat."

"You're proud of it," said Bane, in spite of herself. Hellerman gave her a withering glare.

"At least I have something to be proud of, *mutant*."

"Screw you." Bane turned her back on the woman and walked ahead a few metres. "Are you guys coming, or are you just going to stand there arguing about who's got the biggest helmet?"

"Hey. Hey!" Vix was striding up behind her. Bane felt a gloved hand come down on her shoulder. "Don't get mouthy with us, girl. We're the ones who're going to save this cesspool of a city!"

"Oh yeah?" Maybe Vix was used to browbeating rookies or juves off the street, but Gethsemane Bane, for all her lack of years, was a captain of a Black Atlantic scavenger, and she got tired of her attitude very quickly. She threw the hand off and spun on her heel.

"Okay, skull-head," she snarled. "Riddle me this – two corners away down this vent shaft are three exits. They slope down at a real sharp angle, and they all look the same. One of them leads to the service ladder, the others don't. Which one are you going down?"

The outburst seemed to bring Vix up short. "Ah, the middle one?"

Bane made a buzzing noise in her throat. "Is the wrong answer! You're in the water, skull-head. And that's gonna burn that uniform off your ass pretty drokking quick."

She noticed that Dredd was suddenly next to them, not saying anything, just standing there with his arms folded. She hadn't even heard his approach.

Up close, he was big. Quint was bigger, but even the skipper didn't have the aura of raw command this man had. So far, she realised, he'd just chosen not to use it.

"Finished?" he said.

Bane nodded. Vix lowered her gaze and stepped back.

"Good." His voice level and even. "Defensive formation, Hellermann and Peyton in the centre. Bane, you and I are on point. Larson and Adams, watch our backs. Anyone tries getting into a pissing contest again and you'll have me to answer to when we get back to the Meg." He pointed to Bane. "Except for you. You'll answer to me right here. Now let's move!"

To get to all the areas of the harbour barge, the vent had been built in a series of sloping corners and wide loops. The team had been moving through the duct for about five minutes when Bane rounded a corner and saw something that stopped her dead in her tracks.

In the centre of the duct was a seething puddle of fur. Rats; dozens of them, as big as her forearm. They were feeding.

She could hear the steady crunching of teeth on bone.

Dredd had pulled his gun – a bulky, blunt-nosed automatic with a rotary indicator above the trigger. Bane had just enough time to get her hands over her ears before he pulled the trigger.

The gun thumped heavily in his fist and one of the rats flew apart. Bane felt the noise of the shot slam into her eardrums, even past her clasped hands. The rest of the rats were already gone, a scuttling, screeching mass whirling away down the duct.

Dredd walked up to the object they had been feasting on. "Looks like number fifteen didn't get away after all."

For a moment Bane couldn't grasp what she was seeing. Dredd was talking as though it was a body, but it couldn't be, could it? It was far too small and the wrong shape. Then her brain made sense of the image and her stomach flipped.

It wasn't an entire body. Everything below a ragged line diagonally across the torso, taking off one arm, was missing. What was left had been chewed to ruin by the rats.

"Peyton!" Dredd barked. "Hold onto your lunch and take a look at this."

Warily, the shorter Judge joined Dredd. "Grud," he whispered, just once. Then he knelt down by the carcass.

"Bite marks," he said, pointing at the torso. Bane, hanging back, didn't want to see in detail. "Big ones, not the rats. He's been chewed through here, here and here. This is a straight cut."

"So what are you saying?" asked Adams, obviously horrified. "It's eating people now?"

Dredd crouched by the corpse and reached down to the torn neck. He tugged something free and brought it up to the light.

It was a slender needle, as long as a finger, and carved from pale bone.

"Toxin dart," Dredd muttered. "Shot this one and brought him along as a packed lunch."

Peyton nodded. "It needed to feed. But it waited until it was safe then ate what it could and left the rest."

"Which tells you what?"

"It's planning a lot of... activity" Peyton bit his lip.

Vix nudged the corpse with her boot. "At least we know we're going the right way."

"From here," Bane said, "there's only one way we can go. It's when we get on deck we have to start thinking."

She led them through the duct, luckily without further incident. By the time they got out of the harbour barge, night had fallen and a storm wind was whipping at the deck.

Bane came up first, climbing the service ladder she'd quizzed Vix about. Dredd was next to her in a second, scanning the deck with a flashlight clipped to his gun. Within a few moments the whole team was up, moving smoothly into a spread pattern, everyone covering everyone else's back.

The Judges' guns had integral viewfinders at the rear, above the grip. Bane caught a flash of Dredd's as he swung the weapon about and saw an instant of brilliant blues and greens. Thermal imaging. "Will it show up on that?"

"Probably not. Everyone else will, though."

Bane had to plant her feet apart against the wind. It was rising to a gale, whipping her coat about. "We're not all against you, Judge! The word will have gone out by now – news travels fast here."

"Forgive me if I'm still not expecting open arms. Which way?"

She pointed. "You can't get to the ship ahead directly from this one. No bridge." She turned her head to the side as spray blew at her. "We'll have to go starboard, to the *Castiglione*. From there to the *Mirabelle*, that's starboard too. But that's the last anyone saw of it. I don't understand why we didn't start there."

"You don't need to. After the *Mirabelle*, where then?"

Bane shrugged. "You tell me where you want to go, Judge, and I'll get you there. But tracking this thing is your job."

"That's right. It is. Which is why I needed to start back at the vent."

There were eight bridges from the harbour barge to the *Castiglione*, but most were too slender and unstable to use in the storm. Bane led the team downwards, using the mesh stairways that zigzagged down the side of the barge, until she reached the Bridge of Calm. Some weird pattern in the air-currents around the cityship caused a dead spot there. No matter how hard the wind blew, the Bridge of Calm was always rock steady.

As such, it was a common romantic spot for courting couples. But there were no lovers on the bridge tonight, just nervous skipper's men. Bane led the team quickly across and into the *Castiglione*.

A giant hydroponics farm took up most of the *Castiglione*'s internal space and they were able to move through that vessel quickly. But the *Mirabelle*, into which the Warchild had disappeared, was a different matter.

"It's a residential ship," Bane explained, as they moved through the short tunnel installed between the inner and outer hulls. "The habs are mostly cargo containers, shipped down there and welded together. I used to live there a long time ago."

"Where do you live now?" asked Larson.

"On the *Golgotha*. Well, I used to. Right now, I don't know."

"It depends on the outcome of our mission," Dredd told her. "If we succeed, you get your ship back. If we don't, it doesn't matter."

"I hadn't thought of it like that," said Bane. Her voice sounded very small.

The tunnel opened onto the lower deck of the *Mirabelle*. Bane stepped out of the hatchway and into open, smoky air. Behind her, she heard one of the Judges – Peyton, she was sure – give a low whistle.

She had to admit the *Mirabelle* was impressive in a certain way.

The chamber they now stood in was forty metres high, from the mesh deck to the roof braces. It stretched away in every direction for a much larger distance, but it was impossible to see how far – thousands of cooking fires had turned the air into a thick, pungent smog.

Stacked from floor to ceiling were the habs: ten metre cargo containers, bolted one on top of the other and side by side, in some places ten or more high. Open mesh walkways ringed every level of every stack, connected by an insane spider web of ladders and stairs. Washing lines were strung between the walkways, dripping processions of laundry hanging from them like limp flags. The walkways were strewn with potted plants, bicycles, children's toys, and garbage of every description – the accumulated detritus of human existence, poured into a big metal box and left to rot.

Great halogen lamps strung from the ceiling cast a sickly glow at street level, but most of the light came from windows. Rough cut squares glowed in every hab, far too many to count. Most of them also showed the silhouettes of watching figures.

Five thousand people lived in this compartment, and *Mirabelle* had four compartments. Even so, there was no one about on the streets or up on the walkways. Bane had never seen the vessel so empty.

She turned to the Judges. "Okay," she began, "now listen to me. This is a low cost residential area. I'm sure you have them in your city too. If you do, you'll know that there are places you go, and places you only go in pairs, right? Same here. I'll lead you through the safest way, but we go quickly, we go quietly, and we don't make any trouble."

"No argument," said Dredd. "If the Warchild came through here, it didn't stop. We'd know about it by now."

They began to move into the stacks. Bane knew that the biggest spaces between the habs would be the safest, as more light filtered down to the deck on the widest streets. She led them quickly around several corners, skirting an area she knew contained six dead ends and four taverns, and another where the lights were constantly being knocked out by juves on the top hab roofs.

Bane was heading for the Main Drag, a wide street that carved almost clear through the centre of the hold. She took the team along a row of small shop-fronts to get there, but when she turned the next corner it was blocked.

Someone had piled scrap metal into the space between two habs. There was tonnes of it, mainly rusted H-girders, but the gaps were filled with a lot of broken sheet steel and plasteen. Metre-long spikes of grimy metal stuck out from the girders at every angle. Climbing over the blockage would be impossible without getting impaled, or crushed as the whole unstable lot of it collapsed.

Bane didn't find either choice attractive. "They're barricading themselves in," she told Dredd. "They're terrified of the Warchild."

"No surprise there," the Judge replied. "Find us another way, fast."

She lead them back the way they had come, then took a different turning. Around the next corner she found the same result.

On the third roadblock she gave in. "No way through, not without getting ourselves torn up. We'll have to back onto the upper deck, see where we can get from there."

"And if the Warchild is in the middle of that lot?" asked Vix.

"As Dredd pointed out, I think we'd know about it by now." She walked past the group and back towards the tunnel. "Come on."

"Wait," called Vix. "Dredd, there may be another way. A couple of Hi-Exes should bring one of these barricades down, then we could go where we pleased."

Bane looked back and saw Dredd pondering the nearest roadblock. "Civilian casualties?"

"Probably minimal."

Then the air shifted.

Gethsemane Bane had been born with certain mutations and had developed others during her life on the Atlantic. Her tough skin, with its blue-steel sheen, had been with her since childhood. Another was a certain sensitivity to air vibrations and weather patterns.

It made her an exceptional sailor. Right now, it also told her that something terrible was about to happen.

She leapt at Dredd, yelling. She was fast, too, always had been. Certainly faster and stronger than he and his Judges had considered. He had barely turned towards the sound of her shout when she barrelled into him.

He went off-balance, but instantly corrected, only being driven back a metre or so. Vix went further because as Bane hit Dredd she'd also kicked back at the same time, catching the skull-head Judge below the ribs. All the breath went out of Vix in one go and she crashed backwards into a hab.

There was a massive, ringing pain across Bane's skull. Dredd had backhanded her away, slamming her across the deck and before she'd even hit the mesh his gun was centred on her heart.

Behind him, the first girder shrieked into the deck where he had been standing.

Another one came down next to it, huge and crudely sharpened. It punched into the mesh with a deafening howl of torn metal, tilted sideways, and was smashed flat by the next five girders that came down after it.

Bane was sitting on the deck, her head whirling from Dredd's blow. He'd hit her very hard indeed, she realised, and before she knew it the floor was tilting up behind her and hitting her in the back of the head.

Metal was still falling from the sky. Instead of girders, it looked like about two tonnes of nuts and bolts in a chain net.

Coming down right on top of her.

Far away, on another ship entirely, the Old Man woke from his slumber.

He had been asleep for a long time, since just after Gethsemane Bane had left. Reaching out through the multiple hulls and decks of *Sargasso* to find Can-Rat had been difficult enough. Worse still had been the waves of pain and fear that had come back up the connection to hit him.

He'd managed to hide the worst of their effects from Bane, but after she'd gone it was all he could do to make it back to his bed and collapse on it. He was sure that several bottles of offering spirit had been broken on that stumbling journey, a loss he would mourn later.

He blinked in the darkness. Hours must have passed. His guards had turned the lights out.

There was something ticking away at the back of his mind. Something that hadn't been there when he had gone to sleep.

A presence...

He reached out. A new mind had arrived on *Sargasso*, several new minds. Only one was of any interest to the Old Man, however.

"Dredd? Judge Dredd?"

It wasn't possible. The Old Man sat up, shaking off the last of his fatigue. He reached out again and found a mind made of steel.

The Old Man was no telepath. He had never read a thought in his life. But minds made ripples in the stranger surfaces of his world, like stones thrown into sump oil. Dredd's mind was like cold metal; utterly unyielding, totally hard. Unbreakable. To a psyker who sought out minds directly, the lawman would have been a blank as he was immune to such effects. But the Old Man's powers were far more subtle. He saw the oil, not the stone.

The Old Man felt a wide, predatory grin spread across his face. "Judge Dredd," he chortled. "This is a turn-up for the books, and no mistake."

He reached down and fumbled in the dark until his fingers brushed a bottle. Metal charms chimed against his knuckles as he lifted the bottle and twisted the lid off. It was the bottle Bane had brought him. He lifted it in salute.

"To Judge Joe Dredd," he laughed quietly. "Who I never thought I'd see again."

11. THE FALL OF THE GODS

"We shouldn't be out here," grumbled Sanny Fane. "They should give us guns if we're going to be out here."

Sanny was griping because he'd lost three rounds of rock-scissors-paper and thus was going down the access stairs first. Voley, who'd only lost two, was at the rear, and she could see Sanny's head turning left and right like a scanner dish, trying to see everywhere at once.

Personally, Voley thought that the stairway was probably the safest place to be because it was right out in the centre of the *Royale Bisley*'s main deck. Suspended from the ceiling girders, it took workers all the way from distribution on the upper hull to the maintenance level fifty metres below in one huge, narrow flight of open mesh steps.

No place for anyone suffering from vertigo, but it gave the only uninterrupted view of the *Bisley's* interior.

Lox was going down second. He was three metres tall and there wasn't a single part of his body, head included, that Voley couldn't have circled with two hands. His ear-defenders had to be modified specially. "Guns wouldn't help," he said, ducking under a support brace. "Thirty guys from the Black Whale went after it with harpoon rifles and it took them all down."

"I heard that," nodded Sanny. "Reckon the thing's the size of a hab."

Lox leaned right down to him. "Long Sally from B-shift? Her sister goes with one of the skipper's men, and he said that they found the Tusk Brothers snapped clean in two!"

"Yeah," grinned Della Satori. "But anyone on the ship could snap you in two, Lox." She shook her head and turned back to give Voley a wink. "Grud, you guys are so full of it."

"Drokk you, Della," snapped Sanny. "If we're full of it, why did Quint call Mega-City One for a platoon of Judges, eh?"

"Guys?" Voley didn't talk much, so when she did the others tended to stop and listen. Sanny, in fact, stopped so suddenly that Lox almost tripped over him.

"Look, maybe this thing's as big as a hab, or maybe it's one futsie with a blade. But let's walk this shift together, okay?"

"That'll take four times as long," said Lox, gently.

Voley's long tail twitched. "Not if we go four times as fast."

Back in the day, *Royale Bisley* had been an anti-pollution ship. A century ago it had trawled the waters of the United States coastline, one of a vast fleet attempting to stem the tide of industrial waste seeping into the Atlantic. They had failed, of course. No fleet would have been large enough to deal with that amount of liquid garbage.

Now the vessel served a far more effective purpose. The huge pumps mounted in its blunt prow still dragged in thousands of litres of seawater a second, but certain other elements had been reversed in their function. Instead of housing the pollution and releasing clean water back into the sea, *Royale Bisley* and its sister vessels now did exactly the opposite. Together, the four ships provided clean drinking water for the entire city-ship.

The system was largely automated, but it was also vital. Lack of water could wipe out *Sargasso* in a week. So every thirty minutes, the maintenance shift walked the length and breadth of the plant, checking the readouts on every filter, pump and boiler. And when that was done, they started all over again.

Whether there was a monster loose in the city or not.

Standard shift pattern was to start at the bow and work back. There were four pumps in *Bisley's* nose, and four sets of initial filters – gleaming steel cylinders as big as scavenger ships set on their ends. Each pump sent water back through three separate filters, only merging the flow when the water was clear enough to go into the big central boiler. And that was only halfway through the system.

There was a lot to check.

D-shift usually took a pump each, but not today. They ran through the system in a tight group, ear-defenders clamped on hard to protect their hearing, soaked with sweat almost instantly. The filtration plant was ancient, and as a result, it was big and hot and deafeningly loud. The shift had become adept at communicating in sign language.

It was Voley who first noticed something was wrong. She had been on D-shift for almost six years and she knew the pressure tolerances on the filter cylinders like she knew her own heartbeat. As soon as she looked at the reading on C-3, she knew something was amiss.

Voley skittered to a halt and went back to the cylinder readout. There was a big, easy-to-read display, and a smaller, more detailed version next to it. Voley had to climb a short ladder to get to that as she was very small at only a metre high.

The rest of the shift had stopped as soon as they realised she wasn't with them. They clustered around the base of the ladder. Lox didn't have to climb anything, of course. "Grud," he yelled, over the hammering din of the pumps. "Ten per cent down!"

Voley leaned back on the ladder, craning her neck to see the top of the cylinder. It stretched up above her, gleaming damply in the *Bisley's* dim internal lighting. She couldn't see anything amiss and was about to climb back down and call a supervisor when a fat drop of water hit her between the eyes.

It hit quite hard, slapping her back a little. She blinked, feeling the water running down her face, then scampered quickly up the ladder.

Heights didn't worry Voley, which was a good thing, since she didn't see anything of interest until she was at least twenty metres above the maintenance deck. At that height, the cylinder had already begun to curve inwards at the side, forming a blunt dome. It was here, where the metal skin of the filter could no longer be seen from the deck, where Voley found a hole.

She had been expecting corrosion, or maybe a split seam. Both had happened in the past. This, however, could only have been an act of deliberate sabotage. Something massively sharp had been simply punched through the metal, clear through both the outer and inner skins, plus the solid insulation between. Warm and frothy water from the filtration spinner was spitting fitfully through the opening.

Voley suddenly realised she was awfully exposed up there on the cylinder. She began to climb downwards, carefully, making sure she didn't lose her grip on the wet rungs. She might not have been worried about heights, but slamming into the deck from twenty metres wouldn't have done her any good at all.

When she got within a metre of the bottom she hopped off, ready to tell the others what she had seen. Driven by such tiny lungs, her voice wasn't loud and she was hoping they'd be able to hear her, as she wasn't sure what kind of signs she could use to tell them that someone had punched a spike through the cylinder cap.

There was no one at the base of the filter.

Voley stood where she was for a few seconds, trying to listen over the roar of the system, looking about for any evidence of her friends. After a time she called out, but there was no answer. Perhaps they hadn't heard her. Or maybe they had gone to some other readout, expecting her to be longer up the ladder.

If the shift was operating under normal circumstances, Lox would finish with filter C-3 and start tracing the pipes back to the boiler. The plan today had been to go back towards the prow after the C-line, and start on the D-filters in turn. Voley decided to go to cylinder D-1, closest to the bow pump. The others would be there, waiting for her.

She began trotting down the line of filters, peering around each one before she ran across the gap. She got all the way back to D-1 without seeing a soul.

By this time, Voley's heart was bouncing in her chest, and not from the heat. She resolved to head back to the boiler, and if they weren't there she would go back up the stairway and get help.

There was no one at the boiler, either.

Voley sprinted for the bottom of the ladder just behind the boiler and its bulky power units. She was most of the way along the port side when she ran through something slippery. Her boots went out from under her and she fell.

The boiler often leaked. Voley got up, cursing her own clumsiness, and then saw that her hands had blood on them. She must have come down harder than she thought.

There was blood on the floor, too. She walked back to where she had fallen and realised that she had slipped in a wide, crimson pool, collecting near the boiler's massive base.

The blood on her hands was not her own.

There was movement above her. She looked up, and saw something sticking out over the edge of the boiler. It was a long, thin arm, emerging from the sleeve of a maintenance worker's coveralls. There was most of a hand at the end of it.

Below the arm, blood was pouring down the side of the boiler, smoking from the heat within.

Voley gave an involuntary cry of pure horror. And as she did so, a face appeared at the edge of the boiler, near Lox's ruined hand, and peered down at her.

That was when Voley began screaming. It was a very long time before she stopped.

"Remind me of the penalty for assaulting a Judge," groaned Vix, wiping her mouth. The Bane woman had hit her in the guts so hard she'd thrown up.

"Code two, section one," Dredd replied. "Ten years. And you shouldn't need reminding, Judge Vix. Your ignorance of the Law will go on record to Judge Buell."

"Oh, give it a rest," Bane groaned wearily. "We're outside the territorial margin." Her face was badly bruised from where Dredd had backhanded her, and she was nursing any number of other contusions. They all were.

Dredd had seen the second half of the booby trap – the bundle of bolts pushed off the top of the hab stack – and had blasted it with Hi-Ex before it was halfway to the deck. That had separated the solid, lethal bundle into about four thousand separate components, but it hadn't altered their downward velocity. A hard rain had fallen on *Mirabelle*, and they had all been caught in the storm.

Bane was sitting with her back to the wall, near the access tunnel, and Judge Peyton was spraying the side of her face with something from a small surgical kit. Dredd stood over her. "You could have yelled."

"You could have been squished by a girder."

Peyton stopped spraying and Bane stood up a little shakily. The spray would have taken most of the pain away, but she wouldn't be able to see out of that eye for a while.

"Maybe. But you wouldn't have broken the Law."

Bane waved him away and walked back through the tunnel. The team had retreated there after the attack, safe from any more falling debris. Dredd let her go.

"We oughta get in there and bust the whole block," Larson was snarling. His uniform was cut in several places from the bolts and the skin beneath was lividly bruised. "They tried to wipe us out."

"They were trying to protect themselves," Bane told him. "They thought the Warchild was trying to break through. They have children in those habs, you know. Old people. What else could they do?"

"They should be letting us deal with it," said Larson. "Not dropping half a scrap heap on our heads."

Dredd was about to tell the pair of them to can the chatter when he heard footsteps pounding along the walkway from *Castiglione*. He pulled Bane to one side. Impetuous or not, the woman was valuable here. "Got company!"

Seconds later a skipper's man skidded to a halt just inside the tunnel and came face to face with the muzzles of five Lawgivers. Yelping in shock, he froze.

Dredd stepped forwards, the muzzle of his Lawgiver centred unerringly on the man's forehead. "What's the hurry, citizen?"

The man swallowed hard. "Judge Dredd?"

"What do you think?"

"Sir, I have a message for you from Deputy Jennig. He says there's been another attack."

It had taken Bane less than fifteen minutes to get Dredd and his team to the site of the attack. According to the shift supervisors on the upper deck of the *Royale Bisley*, D-shift had been observed no longer than ten minutes before the alarm was raised.

The Warchild was no more then twenty-five minutes away. Maybe less.

Dredd's first action had been to spread his team out, leaving Hellermann with the skipper's men while he searched the area. It didn't take him long to realise that the Warchild was no longer in the immediate vicinity, at which point he had sent Peyton up to check the bodies. Then he had taken Bane to see the survivor.

The woman was an obvious mutant, little more than a metre tall and with a long, naked tail poking out from under her orange work coat. Dredd had let Bane do the talking, but even her kinship with the mutant proved useless. The mouse-like woman was terrified beyond the capacity for rational thought. A doctor brought by the skipper's men had been forced to sedate her just to stop her shrieking.

Eventually Dredd gave up and pulled Bane aside. "We're wasting time. She's no use to us."

Bane nodded agreement. "Maybe later. Right now she needs to rest."

"Not my concern." Dredd stalked away. They were close to the Warchild; he could feel it. But there was a piece missing from the puzzle. He needed more information. For a moment he thought about retrieving Hellermann and grilling her, but the woman was too good a liar. He wanted to be sure about what he was hearing.

He went to the boiler, a massive cube of welded metal in the centre of the deck. The noise of the pumps was greater here and he was glad he could talk to the other Judges via helmet comms. "Peyton?"

The Tek-Judge was halfway down the ladder when Dredd arrived. "Here, sir." He jumped down the last few rungs. "Three bodies," he reported. "Two received fatal wounds from an edged weapon, one from toxin darts. Looks like the Warchild killed them on the deck then dragged them up out of sight." He lifted his helmet briefly to wipe his face with his hand. "Sorry, sir. I'll request more time in the Sector House gym when we get back."

"See that you do. Anything else?"

"No sign of, ah, ingestion. It must have eaten its fill back in the vent."

Dredd nodded. "What's its next move, Judge Peyton? Speculate."

Peyton appeared surprised. He must have known what Dredd usually thought of speculative thinking while on a case. Still, these were hardly usual times.

"You must understand, sir, I was only on the sequencing team. All the downloads, the important neural stuff, that was Dr Hellermann's field. She designed its brain." Peyton took a deep breath. "But from what I know, I don't think it's following the default program."

"Explain."

Peyton gave a little nod as though he were getting things straight in his mind before he said them. "Okay," he began. "The Warchild is built to follow certain mission profiles; I'm not sure how many, but I think it's about fifteen. Stuff like all-out combat, single-target assassination, terror tactics, that kind of thing. Those programs are all hardwired into its brain before it comes out of the tank. If it doesn't get a mission program, it will follow a default program and then go dormant until it gets one. That's what Dr Hellermann was talking about in the council chamber." He spread his hands. "Sir, you should really be asking her about this."

"I would if I trusted her further than I could throw a Lawmaster," Dredd growled. "What's your best guess?"

"I think the Warchild units were programmed before they left Mega-City One. I think whoever bought them wanted them to perform in a certain way in a hurry, and the Warchild here is following that program. Otherwise it would have gone to ground."

"So it thinks it's in a war zone." Dredd rubbed his chin thoughtfully. "That's why we've got survivors – creep's mission is more important than not leaving witnesses."

"Judge Dredd!"

That was Adams, over the comm. "What have you got, Adams?"

"A lead, sir!"

Adams's lead was a scrap of human tissue that Peyton identified as part of a finger. It was lying near one of a row of service panels, where it had snagged on a sharp edge of metal. The service panels were all intact, not ripped open like the vent or the panel in the harbour barge, but when

Dredd began tugging at those nearest the finger fragment one of them came away without effort.

Peyton inspected the other side of it while Dredd leaned carefully into the space behind the panel, Lawgiver ready and throwing out a steady cone of light from its clip-on flash. "Well?"

"The locks have been severed," said Peyton. "It pulled one corner open, used an integral blade to cut the locks then straightened the panel out and put it back. Stomm, do you know what that means?"

"Creep's getting smart," Dredd muttered. "Get the civvies. We're going hunting."

The team followed the same formation as in the vent: Dredd and Bane in front, Adams and Larson bringing up the rear. Vix kept an eye on Hellermann who, along with Peyton, was in the centre of the group for protection.

The machinery behind the service panel had been ripped away and a hole was torn in the wall behind it. The Warchild had escaped into the space between the inner and outer hulls of the *Royale Bisley*.

It was a strange place; an echoing plasteen corridor only a couple of metres wide but dozens high. Girders crossed it at every level, strewn with pipe work and cables, and walkways had been set into the hull material at irregular intervals. The entire space stank of rust – oil and ancient metal.

There were places where the Black Atlantic had obviously eaten clear through the outer hull, and the plasteen had been patched on the outside with welded metal.

The constant racket of the filtration plant was muted here, but there was another noise that Dredd had trouble identifying for a moment. It was a rushing, thrumming sound, rising and falling and creating weird echoes that boomed and rattled between the hulls. Dredd had to listen for several seconds before he realised that the noise was that of the sea, moving past him just a few millimetres of plasteen away.

He tapped Bane on the shoulder. "You've got some pretty fancy mutant senses there, captain."

"Er, thanks. I think."

"Just keep 'em sharp. This is a great place for an ambush."

They moved on, heading towards the bow. "It'll open up, not far from here," Bane told him. "The power chambers are on either side of the boiler and the hull space connects directly to them. There should be a hatch."

Dredd nodded. "Let me know if you see it."

As he spoke, something scuttled past his head.

He snapped a hand out and brought it back with the scuttling thing clamped between finger and thumb. It was a pale, fleshy spider, with a body that seemed to consist entirely of one spherical eye. Dredd turned it over, his lip wrinkling in disgust.

The spider reminded him of something but he couldn't tell what. "Anyone else seen anything like this?"

There was a chorus of negatives. "Just some kind of mutant bug," said Larson. "Place is probably crawling with 'em."

Dredd showed the thing to Bane. "These common around here?"

She shook her head. "I've not seen one before," she said levelly. "But like Judge Larson says, we mutants live in such filthy conditions it's a wonder we're not knee deep in them."

The spider's eye was rotating wildly, looking at everything. Dredd squeezed his thumb and forefinger together until the creature burst wetly and died. He was wasting time. "We need that hatch, Bane."

"It's just up here." She ran forwards and stopped next to a doorway on the inner wall. Dredd hadn't seen it, even with the clip-on flashlight. The mutant's night vision must have been phenomenally good.

Dredd's wasn't bad. Better since he'd been given his new eyes.

Bane was smart enough not to try opening the door. Dredd got on one side of it and Vix took up position on the other. Dredd counted down from three on his fingers and then put his boot to the door. It crashed inwards, pieces of lock skating away across the deck.

He dived inside and came up with his Lawgiver aimed and steady. Vix was right behind him.

The room was empty. Blue-green biolume light shone off dozens of pipes and ducts, lining the walls from top to bottom in a maze of tubes. There were more pipes on the ceiling, too – it was like standing inside a giant junction box.

There was another hatch ahead of him, but that one was already open.

Dredd stalked forwards, his boots silent, his gaze flicking from the view straight in front of him to that through the viewfinder of his Lawgiver. He heard Bane and Hellermann come in behind the Judges.

There was movement at the hatchway. Another spider appeared around the frame, regarding him steadily with its great, liquid eye. It looked at him for a few seconds then darted away.

"Dredd," hissed Bane. "Wait."

"Spit it out, captain."

"It feels wrong here. I think–"

Something next to Dredd's left shoulder exploded with a deafening roar.

The blast threw him into Vix, knocking her off her feet. Dredd just managed to keep his balance, whipping the Lawgiver up around to find the source of the explosion. As he did, his gaze caught the edge of his shoulder pad. The armoured foam had been peppered with shrapnel and there were three pale, bonelike needles sticking out of it.

"It's a trap!" he roared. Ahead of him, pallid, fleshy pustules were oozing from between the pipes, swelling visibly as he watched.

"Behind us," called Larson. "They're everywhere!"

Dredd picked a pustule at the far end of the next chamber and put an execution round through it. It popped messily, vomiting white pus down the wall. "Standard rounds," he yelled, blasting another two. "Take them out before they arm. And watch for needles!"

The chamber became a flashing, booming nightmare of gunfire and bursting pustules. Dredd took out the nearest, with Vix using her SJS marksmanship training to rid the far chamber of dozens more. A couple had grown too quickly and exploded before she had the chance to shoot them. Poisoned needles whistled through the air, one bouncing off Vix's helmet.

Behind Dredd, the gunfire was joined by the sound of another explosion. He heard Adams give a choked cry, Peyton yelling that he was hit. "Judge down!" Larson screamed. "Judge down!"

"Fall back!" bellowed Dredd, hauling Vix up and throwing her bodily back towards the hatch. "Get the wounded outside, now!" Within seconds, all the Judges were out of the chamber. Dredd paused at the opening, grabbed the hatch with his free hand and brought his Lawgiver up. "Incendiary," he grated.

He had the hatch closed before the incendiary shell hit the furthest wall. There was a familiar thumping impact as it hit, and then the chamber walls were hammering as the inferno set off the remaining pustules. In a few moments, the hull space was silent.

Except for the sounds of Judge Adams trying to breathe.

The man was on his back on the walkway, every muscle rigid. Peyton was kneeling next to him, helmet discarded, bleeding from a dozen wounds of his own but completely ignoring them as he busily hunted through his surgical kit for a syringe. Captain Bane had both hands crossed over Adams's straining chest, pushing rhythmically, trying to keep his heart beating.

Dredd watched Peyton slam a pressure syringe to the fallen Judge's neck, take it away to adjust the dose, and then administer it again. It had no effect. A few seconds later, Adams gave an agonised, rattling groan, and died.

Bane sat back, her soot-streaked face running with tears. Peyton gave a snarl of fury and took her place, thumping Adams's chest five times, dropping his ear to the man's sternum to listen, then back up and thumping again.

"Let it go," Dredd said quietly. "He's gone."

At those words, Peyton sagged back against the hull. "There was too much toxin," he whispered. "He only took one needle, but there was too much…"

Abruptly, Vix leapt to her feet. "Drokk!" she yelled. "Where's Hellermann?"

While Dredd had been watching Judge Adams die, Elize Hellermann had escaped.

As soon as Hellermann had seen the spider, she knew that she was close to the Warchild's base of operations.

The bug that Dredd had so carelessly crushed was actually a miracle of biotechnology. Grown from spores hidden within the Warchild's body, it matured in hours into a tiny mobile surveillance unit, equipped with an organic radio link between itself and its onetime host. Mineral deposits in the legs formed an antenna array, capable of sending back pictures from the eye over a distance of almost a hundred metres.

The booby trap bombs were spore-grown, too. Once the Warchild had started eating its victims, she realised that it was planning to mature some of its on board weapons store.

She was close now. If the Warchild had been watching them, it couldn't have been too far away.

Hellermann had slipped away as Dredd ordered his retreat. She had seen Adams go down – a needle in his neck – and guessed that they would spend time trying to revive him. Fruitless, of course – the Warchild's toxins were based on those of the most lethal Black Atlantic shellfish. The man's nervous system had been pulp within moments. But it had given her a chance to escape.

She ran as fast as she dared down the space between the hulls. Ever since Justice Department had taken her project from her, she had frequented far worse places than this. A little grime meant nothing to her if it got her back within range of her creation.

Hellermann found the service panel where they had come in and squeezed back out onto the maintenance deck of the *Bisley*. The whole journey into the hull space had been a set-up, including planting the tissue fragment to lure the Judges inside. Thinking about that, Hellermann couldn't suppress a grim smile of satisfaction.

Constant self-improvement and evolution had been part of the Warchild's design from the beginning. It was, however, far exceeding her expectations.

Her offspring was doing better than she could possibly have hoped.

Hellermann paused a few metres from the service panel. The Warchild would have to stay within a hundred metres of the spiders to receive their signals. There wasn't anywhere within that distance it could hide, unless...

Royale Bisley was only about eighty metres across.

Hellermann belted across the deck, under the huge pipe that led from the boiler to the desalination filter, and towards the opposite side of the ship. There was a power chamber there, too, just like the one Dredd had just incinerated.

She wondered how long it would be before the fire shorted out some vital wiring and shut down the whole filtration plant.

Hellermann reached the power chamber in a few moments and searched until she found the hatch. It looked locked from the outside; even the display panel next to it said that it was. But she had taught her creation better than that. She looked quickly around to make sure she had not been followed and then pushed her way in.

The Warchild was waiting for her. There must have been spiders watching her approach.

She saw it for less than a second before it shimmered to near-invisibility, its mimetic skin perfectly matching the wall behind it. But that second was all Hellermann needed. "Götterdämmerung!" she snapped.

The Warchild froze. As she watched, it bleached back into visibility.

Hellermann let out a long, relieved breath. She hadn't been entirely sure the code word would still work.

She had been lying to Dredd all along, of course. Although each Warchild did have its own abort code, there was another code that would shut any one of them down. Dredd himself could have used it. That, however, would not have left Elize Hellermann out of Justice Department's clutches, on neutral territory and with the Warchild completely in her control.

Once she had demonstrated to the mutant council that she herself had rid them of their problem, she couldn't see any reason why they wouldn't grant her asylum.

The Warchild remained in front of her, swaying slightly. It skin had faded back to a blank, pale grey, dry and leathery now it had been out of the tank for so long. The creature still looked rough and unfinished, but that was an illusion. It had matured perfectly.

Blades had emerged from each of its forearms, long and lethally sharp. They had hinged forwards, ahead of the slender, three-fingered hands.

"Well," Hellermann whispered. "Here we are. Together at last."

The Warchild stayed frozen, arms limp at its sides. Drool glittered below its toothy, lipless mouth. Only its eyes moved, following her as she moved.

Hellermann smiled at it, warmly. "You need a name," she told it. "After all, you're all grown-up now. Calling you child is… insulting."

She took a step back to admire her work. "I shall call you Freedom," she said. A movement on the ceiling caught her eye. There was a spider above the Warchild, watching her with its one limpid eye.

As she watched, another joined it. And another. They stood, upside down, in perfect formation.

"Wait," she whispered. "They shouldn't be able to do that. Not on their own..."

There were spiders all over the ceiling now. "But if they aren't acting on their own, that means you must be–"

The Warchild snapped forward, faster than she could think.

12. QUIS CUSTODIET IPSOS COSTODIES

On the cityship *Sargasso*, very little was ever used for its original purpose. It was something you got used to after a while; the fact that everything was made out of something else, or rebuilt to do a different job, or stapled to the deck and used as a family home. When a city's economy was based on fishing and scavenging, in roughly equal measure, recycling became a fact of life.

The same was true of Mako Quint's office. Correction: the skipper's office. Quint had to remind himself of that on a regular basis. Although he had been re-elected as skipper four times, and had held the post for seven years, he could be stripped of that title at any moment. Then he would have to pack his things and move back to his old hab in the *Middleton*, while someone else got to sit at the desk and read reports.

He had been in the office for so long, it was easy to forget that he didn't own it.

Perhaps the captain of the assault carrier had felt the same way, in the days when the ship was a potent and independent vessel. There was no way he could have known, back when the Atlantic was still partly blue, that one day his ship would form the governmental centre of a mobile city-state with almost a million inhabitants, and that his quarters would house the man whose word, in that state, was law.

Right now, Mako Quint didn't feel much like the law. He felt less in control of events with every report that dropped onto his desk.

Shift-workers killed on the *Royale Bisley*. Hab-dwellers on the *Mirabelle* setting traps for the Warchild and almost flattening Dredd's entire team. The Old Man had gone missing.

And now this.

In addition to being deselected by the council, the position of skipper would also pass on if Quint was dead, or too severely injured to carry on. With everything he was hearing about the progress of Judge Dredd and his team, that possibility seemed more and more likely.

The telephone jangled abruptly, jarring him out of his morbid thoughts. Time to be the skipper again. He lifted the receiver.

"Quint."

"Jennig here, skipper. You wanted me?"

That hadn't taken long. Quint had put the word out that he needed to speak to his deputy just ten minutes previously. He'd told one messenger, who had then told every skipper's man he could find. Each of the men he told then did the same thing, and before long Jennig knew he had to report in.

It was an efficient system, and vital since there was no centralised communications system on the *Sargasso*. Unless you included gossip.

"That business in the *Royale Bisley*," he said into the mouthpiece. "Heard it got messy."

"Wasn't pretty, skipper, no."

"Philo... Look, I hate to ask this, but did you get everything cleared away? I mean, no, er, body parts missing?"

"Grud, skipper, what do mean?"

Quint sighed. "Sorry to ask. But I'm getting reports about the water coming out of the *Bisley*. People are saying it tastes bad. Just wanted to make sure there wasn't a body in the boiler."

Jennig made a disgusted sound. "Charming thought. I'll get right on it, have a crew check the tanks. If we can't see anything obvious we might have to shut *Bisley* down and steam out the whole system."

"Thanks, Philo. Let me know what you find."

Quint replaced the handset and sat back. Four separate reports had come in about foul water being pumped out of the *Royale Bisley*. On a closed system like a cityship, that kind of situation could get out of hand, very badly and very quickly.

The last thing Mako Quint needed right now was a water riot.

They found most of Elize Hellermann outside the power chamber. The rest of her, the steaming mass that had spilled from her opened belly after the Warchild's attack, was still inside the hatchway. Hellermann had managed to crawl out of the chamber without it.

The expression frozen on her face was one of confusion rather than pain.

Bane gave a whimpered curse and stumbled away at the sight. Dredd let her go. She'd seen more horror on this trip than any civilian out of wartime, and none of the other bodies had been nearly so fresh. Heat from Hellermann's ruined corpse was still in the air, along with the coppery, faecal stench of death. Dredd saw Bane hit the chamber wall with her back and slide down it, her head in her hands, and – mutant or not – couldn't bring himself to despise her for it.

"Vix, Larson – you're with me. Peyton, see if you can work out what went wrong. Looks like Hellermann's word didn't work. I want to know why."

As Peyton trotted back to the power chamber, Dredd began to run a sweep of the surrounding area, with Vix and Larson watching his back. He knew in his bones that the Warchild had escaped them again; it never stayed around once it had made a kill. But procedure, not to mention plain common sense, dictated that he had to be sure.

He also wanted to get Larson and Vix back on track. Larson was taking Adams's death hard, and Vix was beating herself up for not keeping an eye on Hellermann. In normal circumstance Dredd wouldn't have hesitated in hauling Vix over the coals for it, but they were already a Judge down. He needed everyone frosty and aiming true.

The sweep took five minutes. Dredd had planned to order Vix and Larson back to the chamber and continue alone for a while, get a better feel for the place. But Vix cut in before he could speak.

"Judge Larson, we've already lost one scientist today. Go back to the chamber and assist Judge Peyton."

Larson frowned. "Ah, I'm not sure–"

"You're questioning my orders, Judge?" snapped Vix. "Consider how that would look on your SJS dossier."

Larson cocked his head slightly towards Dredd, looking for confirmation. Dredd knew that Vix was up to something – SJS Judges always were – but he wanted to know what. He gave Larson the nod and the other Judge walked quickly away.

When he was gone, Vix sidled closer to Dredd. "This is a disaster."

Her voice was quiet, despite the noise from the filtration plant. She was using its hammering to mask her words, even while speaking over a private comms channel. Typical SJS procedure.

"Like to tell me something I don't know, Judge Vix?"

"Dredd, I'm serious. We're really in the drek now, worse than you can imagine." She glanced over her shoulder. "Your mutant looks like she's lost the plot. With Adams down we're a gun short, and now Hellermann's toast. No way we can bring the Warchild to heel without her."

"Hate to break this to you, Vix, but Hellermann struck out. We'd have been no better off if she'd stayed." He fixed the SJS Judge with a steely glare. "You can take that back to Buell right now."

"My report to Judge Buell will be…" She trailed off. Dredd could see that, oddly, she was unsure of herself. Perhaps losing Hellermann had hit her harder than he'd thought.

"Judge Buell and I don't agree on everything," she said finally.

"Not what I heard."

"For grud's sake, Dredd! If you're watching anyone it should be Peyton!" She spun away from him and stood with her arms folded tightly. She's said too much, Dredd thought. And she knows it.

He didn't have the time or inclination to do this the slow way. "Judge Vix! If you've got information pertaining to this case, I suggest you give it up. Withholding evidence will get you ten to fifteen!"

She gave him a wry smile. "If I was afraid of cube time I'd never have joined the SJS." Still, she made that quick, almost unconscious look left and right before she spoke again.

"I didn't say this, Dredd. But the SJS are investigating McTighe's people. We've got good evidence that Tek Division didn't dispose of all the Warchild units like they were ordered to."

Dredd shook his head. "Impossible. McTighe's a tinkerer of the worst order, but he's not insane."

"No, but some of his people might be. Remember, when Project Warchild was broken up, Hellermann's staff were sent all over. Some of them ended up back in Tek-Div." Vix tilted her helmet back towards the power chamber. "Like Peyton. Not too hard to believe one or two might still be devoted to the dream."

Dream? More like a nightmare. The idea that Tek Division could be corrupted from within, that some of Hellermann's acolytes were still active and trying to bring the Warchild project to fruition was a disturbing one.

"My job was to keep Hellermann alive until she got a chance to use the word," Vix continued. "And to come back with it. So we could control the Warchild units if there were any still in the Meg."

"Hellermann said there was one word per Warchild. She had to see it to know which one."

Vix threw her arms up. "Oh, sure! If she got to read the barcode on the back of its neck!" She strode up to the nearest piece of machinery and kicked it, hard. "We've got the Psi Division reports. That's the only way she could work out which Warchild was which, and you know how fast they move. What was she going to do, offer it a hair-cut?

"There had to be one word for all of them. She got us to bring her out here on the pretext of a unique word, but there had to be a master key. Drokk!"

Vix sighed. "My guess is she was going to bring the Warchild down, then escape into *Sargasso*. Maybe even claim asylum."

"But it got away from her." Dredd turned and began to walk back to the power chamber. Vix followed him.

"Keep this to yourself," he told her. "Maybe Peyton's bad, and maybe he isn't. But right now, he's the best chance we've got."

When they reached the power chamber, Bane was drap-ing a piece of tarpaulin over Hellermann's body. She'd already used a smaller piece to cover what lay in the chamber.

Peyton was waiting for them, his helmet off and dan-gling from his belt. "I found this," he said simply, and held out his hand.

One of the spider-like creatures lay there, half its legs smashed. It twitched and pulsed feebly. "There was another one, but I've already dissected that."

"People are dying here, Peyton," Vix hissed. "And you waste your time cutting up bugs?"

"Bugs," he replied, "is right in more ways than one. Look." He had a scalpel in his other hand, and he used this to lift and prod one of the spider's shattered limbs.

Dredd saw metal gleam among the ruins. "Wires?"

Peyton nodded. "Connected to a kind of organic trans-mitter behind the eye. The Warchild's remote sensors."

"Surveillance devices?" Vix leaned in closer. Trust the SJS to be fascinated by anything to do with spying. "What's the range?"

"A hundred metres, I'd guess."

Dredd lifted the spider out of Peyton's gloved palm and dangled it by one leg. "So if we see one of these things giving us the eye, that means the Warchild won't be far away." He dropped the creature and trod on it, felt it burst messily under his sole. "Good work, Peyton. Anything else?"

"Just speculation."

Vix folded her arms. "Spit it out."

"The Warchild's getting smarter. You said it yourself, Judge Dredd. It's covering its tracks, setting traps for us. Acting more like an enemy agent than a predatory animal."

"You think it got smart enough to ignore Hellermann's word?" Dredd saw the answer in Peyton's eyes.

"Grud," he snarled, turning away. "It's gone rogue."

As soon as Philo Jennig had finished his call to Quint, he had gathered a patrol of skipper's men and headed for the *Royale Bisley*.

He knew how serious a problem with the water supply could be, just as well as anyone. *Sargasso* relied on the four filtration ships like he relied on the four chambers of his heart. Out here, on the open ocean, there was simply no other source of water. A man can live for a fortnight without food, but without water he'd be dead inside two days.

If he tried to drink Black Atlantic seawater, make that two minutes.

Jennig had seen a cityship burning, once. It was on fire from bow to stern, so hot that the air above it caught alight and the pollution in the sea below solidified, turning to ragged strips of plastic that floated there to this day. The city had been small, with only a hundred thousand people aboard. But every single one of them had died.

The fires had started during a water riot. The city had only one filtration ship, and that had failed when a slick-eel had been dragged into one of the pumps. The way Jennig heard it, no one checked the grilles over the inlets.

Bits of the eel had gone into the boiler, contaminating the water supply. The cityship had run out of drinkable water before anyone could reach it and the population had torn it apart.

Sargasso was ten times as big. A riot could spread ten times as fast.

Jennig had been on the *Camberley* when he had made the call, using the telephone on its bridge. Once he had his patrol, he had taken them across *Camberley*'s deck and into the *Pride of Macao*, a residential vessel three ships starboard of the *Mirabelle*. It was during the journey through the *Macao*'s hab-stacks that he saw the first sick people.

Someone had recognised him as he led the patrol through the vessel's main street and begged him to help his children. Jennig, who had kids of his own, found it hard to refuse; besides, the man's hab wasn't far out of his way.

The man told him that the children had fallen ill very quickly, in less than an hour. Jennig peered into the hab doorway, saw the state of the sick kids, and backed out fast, promising to call a doctor as soon as he reached a phone point.

By the time Jennig was out of the *Macao*, he had seen nearly forty people with the same affliction. As soon as he was off the ship he found a phone point, connected his personal handset and called Quint.

"Philo, that was fast. You at the *Bisley* already?"

"Not yet. Skipper? I think we've got another problem." And, making sure that none of the skipper's men in his patrol could hear him, he told Quint what he had seen.

There was a plague on the *Pride of Macao*.

13. THE CORE DRIVE

When the telephone rang next, the voice on the other end of the line was not that of Philo Jennig. "Quint, this is Dredd."

The skipper's eyebrows went up into his hairline. "Dredd? How did you–"

"Trust me, Quint. It's not difficult."

Quint cursed silently. The phone points were for the exclusive use of the skipper and his men, not these gun-happy intruders from the Mega-City. He would have to increase security around them, or maybe invest in some kind of line encryption.

If Dredd could patch in to his office, anyone could. He'd never get a moment's peace. "The council's already given you all the help you're getting, Dredd. What do you want?"

"Two things. First off, I need your people to collect the bodies of Judge Adams and Dr Elize Hellermann. They're in the *Royale Bisley* starboard hull-space and portside power chamber respectively."

"Grud," Quint groaned, putting a hand to his head. "You lost Hellermann?"

"Let's say she lost herself. Secondly, I want you to put the word out for me. There's a new kind of bug loose on your city."

Quint almost spoke, then snapped his mouth closed. Did Dredd know about the disease? And if he did, just how far and how fast had the news spread?

He decided to play it cool and try to find out more. "What do you mean?"

"It looks like a white spider," Dredd replied. Quint let out a silent sigh of relief. "As big as your hand – okay, my hand. Body's just a big eye. They're the Warchild's pets, and if your men see any of these things around it means the creep's close by."

"Okay, Dredd, I'll spread the word. Anyone sees big bugs, we'll let you know."

He put the phone down. Let Dredd chase his pet monster. Right now, Mako Quint had other things on his mind.

Down among the hab-stacks of the *Pride of Macao*, the plague was racing out of control.

Bane had recovered a lot of her composure by the time Dredd had returned with the skull-headed Judge. She hadn't wanted to lose control in front of everyone like that, but the sight of Hellermann's carcass, sliced open so bloodily, had been one horror too much.

Orca had died like that. She wondered if he'd tried to crawl away, too.

The remaining team was heading up out of the filtration plant, using the long maintenance stairway. The respite from the plant's noise was welcome, but it's heat increased as they climbed higher and the stairway seemed terrifyingly narrow and flimsy. If she looked down, she could see the deck through the open mesh, tens of metres below her boots. She did that once, and after that made sure she didn't look down again.

It was a relief to get out of the wet, yammering heat of the plant and onto a solid deck. Bane led them through the distribution section, where bottles were filled with water pumped up from the final filters, and shipped out in their thousands to this quarter of the cityship. Once past that, they were in the open air again.

The storm seemed to have eased down since they were last on the cityship's upper surface. They were also shielded by some of the bigger structures – the *Bisley* was closer to the centre of *Sargasso*, and more habs and towers had been built around it. Bane took them into a street between two vast racks of storage drums. The drums had once held oil and noxious chemicals but now they were bolted together amidst great sheets of gantry and kilometres of support cable. Ladders were welded to every stack and windows sawn out of each circular end. The drums were big enough for one person to sleep in if they weren't too tall and slept curled up.

"Cheapest kind of housing," she told Dredd.

He seemed unsurprised. "Stackers," he said. "Got the same thing back in the Meg."

"Why are we here, Bane?" Vix asked, her voice as sneering and acidic as ever. "Maybe you need a place for the night, but personally I wasn't intending to stay that long."

Bane gave her the sour eye. "Keep your skull on. This is just the best place to get to anywhere else. Like an intersection."

"And what do we do now?"

"Well," Bane said carefully, cocking her head to the side. "Either we can run around all over the cityship like idiots, or we can wait."

They waited.

The Judges used the time to check and reload their Lawgivers, running checks on the voice-select systems and making sure the magazines were full, with spares in easy reach. Bane just paced.

She guessed that they probably wouldn't have to stand around in the drum stacks for very long. Once the word went out on *Sargasso* it tended to spread at an exponential rate. Every Sargassan was part of the communication chain – everyone would simply pass a message along to anyone they met, and even with most people hiding in their habs, terrified of being disembowelled by a rampaging killer, there would still be enough links in the chain to get the word from one end of *Sargasso* to the other in minutes.

She wondered if it was like that back in Dredd's city. No, she thought, looking at the reinforced knuckles on his gloves and the size of the gun he was reloading. It probably wasn't.

As it turned out, she was right about not waiting for long. Within a few minutes, a skipper's man came to find them.

The man was Loper, one of the more extreme mutants in Quint's employ. His short torso was balanced on a pair of supernaturally long legs, bent backwards at the knee and partially armoured to support their own weight. He looked like a human grasshopper. He was also the fastest man in the cityship, which made him invaluable as a message runner.

Bane knew that as long as *Sargasso* remained without a proper system of integrated communications, Loper would never be out of work.

The man bounded across the deck towards them, actually stepping over a couple of low-lying habs on his way to the drum stacks. "Judge Dredd," he called out, skidding to a halt and folding himself down to a more human level. When he did, his knees came up to the back of his head.

"Skipper Quint sends his regards," he quoted. "And he says that spiders have been reported in the *Kraken*."

Dredd threw a glance at Bane. "Know it?"

"*Kraken*'s one of the core drives, back at the stern. Dredd, there's only one way into a core drive. If we can trap it there…"

"Maybe it's thinking the same thing," said Peyton warily.

"Either way, that's where we're headed." Dredd gave Loper a nod of acknowledgement. "Give the skipper our thanks, and tell him to pull everyone back from the *Kraken*. We'll make a stand there."

"Hop along, now," Vix smirked. Loper raised an eyebrow at her.

"If there's any justice at all," he told her quietly, "you'll end this day knowing what your own guts look like." With that he stretched way up over their heads and stepped away. In a few strides he was out of sight.

Bane gave Vix a look. "You really do have a way with people, skull-head."

Vix shrugged. "If you find any 'people' on board this wreck, do let me know."

Bane put her face very close to the glossy front of Vix's helmet, smiled politely, and blinked at her. All three sets of eyelids. The Judge flinched involuntarily.

"Sure I will, " Bane said cheerily. "If you're still alive."

Bane ran next to Dredd as they belted across the deck towards the stern. "There are six core drives," she was telling him. "They're just floating engines: chem-tankers emptied out and fitted with the propulsion systems from old nuke subs. They give *Sargasso* most of its power."

"Motive or electrical?"

"Both. Left here." She pointed to the turning they needed to take, between two outlet funnels. "Most of the other ships run their engines on fossil fuels, and we can distil that straight out of seawater."

"Wondered how you kept running."

There was something she needed to make him understand, something she'd only thought of as they had begun running. "Listen, Dredd. Just because the drives are nuclear, doesn't mean they're clean. There's this stuff we call darkwater – mixture of coolant, lube oil, old fuel and concentrated Black Atlantic. The core drives get full of it, and it's not nice."

The lawman might have been big, but he certainly wasn't stupid. He caught on to what she was saying before she said it. "Flammable?"

"Sometimes yes, sometimes no. Look, I'm not saying don't use your guns. Just keep the incendiaries to a minimum, okay?"

Bane hadn't been exaggerating when she'd said *Kraken* was nothing more than a floating engine. The days when it could have been anything else had ended decades ago, when *Sargasso*'s work crews had sliced off the entire upper deck and stripped the inside of the hull bare. They had left the propulsion screws, but nothing more. Even the engines themselves had gone, lifted out on cranes and broken down for spare parts. In their place was a Sov-built nuclear power plant, the great armoured globe of the fusion core taking up the entire forward end of the ship.

The work crews had left the *Kraken* a vast, blunt-nosed slab of a vessel, covered in enormous welds. It didn't even have a superstructure any more, save the massive braces that connected it to the rest of the cityship. The core drives were the only vessels in *Sargasso* that weren't covered in buildings, partly because of their function, but mostly due to the lingering, if irrational, fear of radioactive contamination.

The only raised structure on *Kraken*'s upper surface was a small blockhouse, two-thirds of the way towards the stern. When Bane and the Judges reached it, a wide half-circle of skipper's men were waiting for them, weapons centred on the blockhouse hatch. Spotlights from the nearest vessels had been trained on the *Kraken*, and in their harsh glare Bane noticed the shattered remnants of several eye-spiders.

"Skipper's men," called Dredd as he strode into the centre of the deck. "Stand down. We'll take it from here."

None of them budged, although at the sound of Dredd's voice a few lowered their weapons on reflex. One of the men gave Dredd a snappy salute. "Sorry, sir, but Skipper Quint's orders are to keep that hatchway covered, even after you've gone in. If it tries to go past you, it'll run into us."

Dredd seemed to mull this over for a second. "Agreed," he said. "But in that case, move your people back a few more metres. This thing's quicker than you can imagine."

With the warnings given, there was no reason for Bane not to open the hatch and go inside. Except that she didn't want to. Suddenly, on this wide open deck with the spotlights and the weapons all aimed at the small of her back, and the Warchild almost certainly waiting for her below and sharpening its knives, Gethsemane Bane found she had some difficulty getting her legs to move. From the neck up she was fine: determined, alert, anxious to find the creature and see it destroyed for what it had done to Orca and Judge Adams and all the others. But the rest of her body was a different matter. Her guts had turned to ice water and her boots were welded to the deck.

"Drokk it!" she growled angrily to herself. "I'm gonna take up fishing."

The hatch swung open as Dredd pushed it inwards. He had the flashlight clipped to his gun again, but there was no need for it as the interior of the blockhouse was as well lit as anywhere on *Sargasso*. The crews who provided maintenance for nuclear reactors liked a lot of light to work by, and the *Kraken* had power to spare.

Dredd ducked inside. Bane followed, trying to look everywhere at once. The blockhouse had no floor and the steps down into *Kraken*'s belly started right at the hatch. Dredd was already moving down, Lawgiver held near his shoulder with the muzzle vertical, ready to drop down and fire in an instant. Watching him, Bane was struck by the fact that Dredd moved like a cat. He was encumbered by his shoulder armour, a helmet that couldn't have done anything for his field of vision, kneepads, bulky boots and gloves, but he went down the stairs in perfect silence. Not a single part of his uniform even brushed a wall.

Bane, who barely came up to Dredd's chin if she stood on her toes, could only wish for such grace.

The stairs went down for three flights before they reached a walkway. When Bane got to the bottom she moved past Dredd as carefully as she could, in order to spread out and let the others down. The stairs finished in the centre of the vessel, on a circular platform of open mesh. Bane looked down through the gridwork under her boots. Ten metres below her was a metal grille, just covering a long pool of evil-smelling black fluid.

She pointed. "Darkwater," she mouthed. Dredd gave a brief nod.

The interior of the *Kraken* was mainly one single, huge chamber. To the stern a bulkhead sealed off the drive shafts, and far away towards the bow was another lead-lined bulkhead that protected the work crews from the fusion core. Or possibly the other way around. The remaining space was filled with massive pieces of networked pipes and gantries. Bane saw rows of control boards with walkways between them, huge cylinders of coolant, and pipework everywhere.

A thousand places for the Warchild to hide, especially if it had chameleon skin.

The *Kraken* made surprisingly little noise, given that it was partially responsible for pushing the impossible bulk of *Sargasso* across the Black Atlantic. Instead of the deafening hammer of the *Bisley's* filtration plant, this was more of a constant, almost subsonic drone. If Bane put her teeth together, she could feel them vibrating.

The whole team was on the platform now. Walkways connected the disc fore and aft to bridges stretching clear across the width of the hull, and they in turn led to more platforms with railings ranged around the chamber's outer edge. Occasionally, ladders ran down to the lowest deck. Bane hoped she'd be able to stay on the walkways. The idea of being level with a sumpful of darkwater didn't appeal to her in the slightest.

Dredd was gesturing at the bow. He probably wanted to start a sweep there and flush the Warchild out towards the stairs. All the better, Bane thought to herself. If they drove it out of the blockhouse it would run into multiple weapons fire from the skipper's men.

She was just wondering how, if they didn't find the creature, they could get up the stairs and out without being shot themselves, when she saw the Warchild.

She froze, trying desperately not to scream. The others hadn't seen it.

Instantly she realised why. It was still camouflaged, its skin perfectly mimicking the clean grey walls of the *Kraken*'s interior. It was only because her eyes were different from theirs that she could see it at all, and then it was only an outline.

It was crouched on one of the bridges, near the control boards. Its posture was loose, relaxed; hunched on the mesh with one hand on the railing, the other arm dangling. She couldn't see any details – no eyes, or teeth, or whatever it used to open people up so efficiently – but its head was slightly to one side.

The Warchild was watching them. And Dredd was walking right towards it.

Bane knew that it could hear her. By now, it was probably smart enough to understand what she said, and if she just screamed and pointed it would be on them, or away, before they could do anything about it.

"I spy," she whispered, "with my little mutant eye, something beginning with Hellermann…"

To his credit, Dredd didn't alter his pace or make any physical sign he'd heard her. "Where?" he hissed.

"Two bridges forward, near the centre." Bane forced herself to look somewhere else entirely. "Watching us, real close."

"You're sure?" Vix said. "I don't see it."

"Advantage of being a filthy mutant, skull-head."

"Stow it," Dredd replied. "We've only got one chance at this. Hi-ex. On my mark, cover the bridge."

There was the soft, metallic sound of four Lawgivers having their ammo loads manually reconfigured. Bane knew the guns could understand voices, but if the creature could too…

The Warchild was on its feet. Dredd brought his Lawgiver up and said: "Mark."

The bridge flew apart in a cloud of fire and whirling metal.

The racket of the Lawgivers going off was hellish. Bane was crouching, hands over her ears, feeling hot shell casings hit her in the back. For a moment she thought the Warchild was gone, that it must have been shredded in the multiple blasts, but then the closest bridge to her shuddered under a sudden weight.

The Warchild had jumped out of the explosion and landed on the bridge, only metres away.

Bane saw it for a fraction of a second before it leapt again, too brief an instant to react to but enough to form a picture in her mind that would stay there forever. The Warchild, standing, its camouflage bleaching out into bone-white skin, lipless mouth frozen into a razor-sharp snarl. One of its arms had grown a long blade, extending a metre forward of its hand. The other was a shattered twist of flesh and broken armour.

Before she could even draw breath it had jumped again. It came down on the walkway between her and Dredd.

And it *moved*. Later, Bane would realise that the Warchild wasn't impossibly fast, even though it was quicker than she could ever hope to be. But it moved so fluidly, almost ballet-like in motion, as though unfettered by mass or gravity. Every separate part of it seemed to be doing something different at once, even the smashed arm, as though it had already adapted to the loss. It was like a master swordsman and an expert dancer rolled into one.

The remaining arm-blade sang out in a wide arc, taking Larson's head off without trying. At the same moment Dredd's Lawgiver had been kicked from his hand and another foot had slammed into the small of his back. The blade whipped around on the backswing to find Vix's belly, but Bane had moved too, launching herself up and back, powering into the woman at waist level. The blade corrected in mid-flight and carved a track across Vix's ribcage.

The broken arm belted Bane across the face, exactly where Dredd had struck her. Pain erupted through her skull and she tumbled back onto the mesh. Vaguely, she heard Peyton yelling that he couldn't get a clear shot.

The Warchild snapped round, its sword-arm poised to skewer her, and took Dredd's fist right in the teeth.

Its head rocked back under a blow that would have sheared the vertebrae of any human. Bane heard the impact and kicked blindly out at the Warchild's legs, and must have actually connected by pure luck. Unbalanced, the creature found itself being hammered by the reinforced knuckles of Mega-City One's finest fist.

Behind it, Judge Larson's body dropped to its knees. The fountain of blood from its severed neck hadn't even had a chance to slow. His heart didn't realise it was dead yet.

The Warchild darted away and Dredd's next blow hissed past. The blade came up, but the creature must have been affected by the punches, because it left Dredd enough time to leap forward and grab the bioweapon's remaining arm.

Bane scrabbled away from them, beyond all terror now, seeing the bone-white sword whipping left and right in Dredd's grip. The lawman's other hand was wrapped around its throat, trying to crush the life out of it.

Bane watched incredulously. Dredd was actually gaining the upper hand. The Warchild, for all its insect grace and speed and impossible strength, couldn't break his grip.

The sword twisted down and up, scooping out a half-metre of railing. Bane saw the piece of metal bar spin away, and in a moment of awful clarity realised what the creature was going to do. "Dredd!" she howled. "It's trying to take you down!"

It was already too late. The Warchild had bent back and to the right with inhuman flexibility, its torso curving almost completely around on itself. Before Dredd could react the creature's right leg folded, sending the pair of them tumbling through the gap in the railing.

Dredd couldn't let go of the Warchild's arm or throat. He went over without a sound.

There was a second of silence and then the ghastly cracking of two bodies, one human and one not nearly so, colliding with the metal grille over the sump.

Her head pounding, Bane rolled over and looked down through the mesh. Dredd couldn't have survived a fall like that. She wondered if the Warchild had.

Her vision was blurry from pain. She blinked rapidly, her extra eyelids sweeping away tears and blood, and when her eyes cleared she saw that neither Dredd nor the Warchild was lying dead on the grille.

The metal had given way when they had struck it. They were in the sump.

14. SHIVERS

Mako Quint's office was full of people, more full than it had been for years. From his position behind the desk, all the skipper could see was faces. Some of them were angry. All of them were frightened.

The faces belonged to local councillors, minor officials who ran the affairs of small areas of *Sargasso* – sometimes four or five ships, sometimes just one. Usually they kept themselves to themselves, but in times of need they would report back to Quint, or even the ruling council.

There were twenty of them packed into the office, which represented about a quarter of the entire city.

"I've never seen anything spread so fast," Lorton Umax was telling him. Umax was councillor for a small group of vessels that included the *Pride of Macao*, and he'd been down in the underdeck habs not long before. The rest of the councillors were trying to give him a lot of personal space.

"I'm not sure what the vector is," Umax went on. "In a place like the *Macao* it could be anything. Skin contact, droplet... Grud, it could even be airborne."

A woman next to him – Quint recognised her as councillor for the *Elektra Maru* – practically jumped. "Airborne? Skipper, we need to shut down their ventilation. What if plague germs come out and blow across the deck?" She glared at Umax. "Everything windward and astern of the *Macao* could take them in!"

"If you shut down the ventilation, the *Macao* will be dead in a day!"

"Better that than the whole city!"

"Calm down, Borla." Quint raised his hands in an attempt to soothe the woman of her fears. "No one's shutting down any vents. And I've never met a bug yet that could survive Black Atlantic air."

"It's not just that," said Umax. "Some of the skipper's men won't come down on patrol. They say they're being diverted away from normal duties, something to do with this Warbeast."

"War*child*."

"Whatever. We've got a crime increase down there, a big one. If it carries on like this we'll have a riot and people really *will* die."

Quint had taken more than enough of this. He got up, his hands flat on the desk, using his massive height to lean over them. "Councillors, I hear your concerns. And I understand that the situation on board the *Macao* is serious." He raised his hand again to stem a rising babble of voices. "Please! I'll double patrols in the *Macao* to keep order and help where they can. I've got Philo Jennig calling me every ten minutes, regardless, and I've stepped up the delivery of reports. I'll know what happens, when it happens."

"But skipper–"

Quint raised a finger at Borla, halting her in mid-sentence. "This disease is not fatal, but it is infectious. We need time for the doctors to determine the best treatment for those who are ill, and they need space in which to work. So I've sent skipper's men to the *Venturer*. They're moving the occupants away and setting it up as a hospital.

"We've been through this before," he continued. "We came through it then, and we will today. But I need your help. Stay calm, keep your people calm, try to carry on as normally as possible."

He straightened, raising himself to his full height. "Oh, and councillors? One more thing. If I hear anyone, and I mean *anyone*, use the word 'plague' outside this office, they'll find themselves changing blankets in the *Macao* in damn short order. Clear?"

As they filed out, Quint sank back into his chair. He moved a file on his desk, one that had been covering up the last two reports to come in. He couldn't let any of the councillors see what he had just read.

The first report had told him of the plague's first fatality. An old woman, in her nineties, had slipped into a coma and died not half an hour before. The eldsters were always the first to go, Quint reflected. Then the children would begin to die. When adults started to succumb, the first victims would be the parents of the dead children and the relatives of the eldsters.

The second report was worse. Far worse. Four victims had just been confirmed on the *Horizon Hope*, two ships to port.

The disease was already off the *Pride of Macao*.

The Warchild was gone.

Dredd had kept his grip on the bioweapon all the way down. As he felt himself toppling off the walkway he'd made a snap decision, not trusting the fall alone to kill it. He could have freed a hand in time to grab the walkway and hang on, but he'd gambled that he could do more damage to the Warchild by making sure it hit the deck just before he did.

He hadn't gambled on the sump grille giving way under him.

The darkwater Bane had told him about was hot and foul, thick as phlegm on the surface but watery beneath. When the Warchild hit, the impact had been so great Dredd had almost lost consciousness; and for a second, when the blackness swooped up to envelop him, he thought that he had. But it only took a second to realise he'd gone through the grille and into the sump. The darkwater had blinded him.

The thick surface layer hid something else about the sump. It had a current.

There must have been a pump forcing the stuff back towards the stern, probably to be filtered and recycled. As soon as they had gone under, the Warchild was torn from his grasp, ripped away by the undertow. His hands abruptly free, Dredd had managed to grab something and hold on, his legs trailing in the vicious current. With his other hand he reached up to the front of his helmet and slid his respirator down over his nose and mouth.

The respirator wouldn't let him breathe under water, or under darkwater, for that matter. It was purely an air filter. But in the absence of air it formed a perfect seal over his nose and mouth, keeping the toxic stuff from getting into his lungs. Dredd could hold his breath for a long time and the respirator would give him a vital few minutes.

He couldn't tell where he was in the sump.

He wasn't even sure which way was up. The hot liquid was rushing past him so fast that it was robbing him of all sense of gravity. He wasn't sure if the object he had grabbed was a dangling part of a grille, and thus near the sump's surface, or whether it was something sticking out of the side. He was sure he hadn't gone down as far as the bottom of the sump, but no matter how he moved his free arm he couldn't feel the surface. And, bionic eyes or not, he couldn't see a thing in the darkwater.

It was getting hard to think. He'd not been able to take a full breath before he'd gone under the surface. How long had he been down here? The stench of the darkwater was getting through the respirator, a sickening chemical reek.

The situation was getting desperate. He reached down to his belt to see if there was something there he could use. Perhaps if he dropped a grenade into the current it would destroy whatever pump was trying to tear him away. But did he have any grenades? He was no longer sure, and the darkwater was starting to burn his skin.

Something grabbed at his collar.

He twisted away and tried to reach down for his boot knife. The Warchild must have beaten the current and come back for him. But before he could get his hand down as far as his ankle he was wrenched free of the handhold.

And pulled up through the gluey black surface of the dark-water.

He shook his head violently, feeling the slimy liquid drooling off his face and away from his eyes. When he opened them he saw Gethsemane Bane in the sump with him, her hair plastered to her scalp, skin black with dark-water residue. She had a hold of his collar in one hand and part of the broken grille in the other.

Dredd grabbed the grille and held on, then used his other hand to push his respirator back up and out of the way. He dragged in a breath.

His thoughts cleared. "Nice work," he told Bane. "You can see under that drek?"

"A bit." She blinked, three sets of eyelids clearing the muck from her eyes. "Where is it?"

"Gone. Current took it."

"Think it's dead?"

Dredd's lip twisted. "Not a chance." He got a good grip on the grille and hauled himself up, then reached down to pull Bane out of the stuff too.

"Thanks." She fell back onto the deck and stayed sitting there for a moment. "Larson's dead."

"I saw. Vix too."

She shook her head. "Skull-head's still alive. Cut up, but I think she'll live. Peyton's spraying stuff on her."

By the time Dredd had climbed back up the ladder and retrieved his Lawgiver from the walkway, Peyton had finished spraying and started bandaging. Vix was slumped against the walkway railing, her helmet on the mesh next to her. There was a deep cut in her torso, starting from her left armpit and stretching diagonally down to just under her sternum. Blood had soaked her uniform and Dredd caught a glimpse of white bone in the wound before Peyton covered it with a compression bandage.

She was, however, alive. Her eyes opened as she heard him approach and rolled towards him. "Sorry," she croaked.

"Save your strength," he told her. "You'll need it to get back up those stairs."

She gave a tiny, pained nod. Her face was paper white and her sandy hair was glued into rough spikes by sweat and grime. Dredd realised he'd never seen her without the helmet. She was a lot younger than he'd thought.

He couldn't resist one dig. "Looks like you owe Bane twice."

A weak smile spread over Vix's face and she chuckled, wincing. "Looks like I do."

Dredd moved past her to where Judge Larson had fallen. His body was sprawled over the mesh, the metal around it dripping crimson. His helmet lay a few metres away with his head still in it.

"Another street Judge down," Dredd grated.

"He died doing his job," Bane said quietly. "Doesn't that mean something?"

"Not enough." He walked back to the circular platform, and pointed down to the sump. "There's a current down there – some kind of pumping system. Know where it leads?"

"Not really. Sternwards, something to do with the coolant. There might be a vent out to open sea, but I'm guessing." She moved closer. "Dredd, we have to go back. Vix is badly hurt and there's no way we can search for the Warchild down in the sump, even if it is still there. It might be at the bottom of the Atlantic by now."

"You said you could see down there."

"See, yes. Survive, no." She spread her hands. "Dredd, we've got to fall back. At least talk to someone who knows the layout of the sump system, and get Vix to a medic."

Dredd didn't like it, but she was right. Hellermann's creation had slipped out of his grasp again, in more ways than one. Still, it was injured now. Dredd didn't know how fast it would heal, but even if it was able to self-repair at high speed, nothing could just regrow an arm.

That gave him an advantage. For a while. He just needed to know where it would end up.

Bane went up the stairs first, shouting a brief conversation with the skipper's men still on deck. When she'd convinced them that she wasn't actually the Warchild in disguise she helped Peyton carry Vix out.

Dredd didn't like having to leave Larson's body on the walkway, but that was part of the job. A fallen Judge was always treated with respect, but not at the cost of the case in hand. And Dredd had a monster to catch.

Monster. In a way that was the right word because the Warchild did things that were monstrous. But to call it that was to underestimate it. Dredd had tracked killers before, more than he could count. Seldom had he been on the trail of one so resourceful, so adaptable and dedicated.

Hellermann had wanted an army of these things doing Judges' work. If Vix was right, certain elements of Tek Division still wanted the same thing.

Dredd decided that he would be watching Judge Peyton very carefully from now on.

Bane thought the best place to go and regroup was the central bridge. The skipper would be there, and he would know whatever there was to know about the *Kraken's* outlets.

They began to make their way back across the decks. Bane took them on a different route this time, further towards the stern. It wasn't the quickest way, but it was easier, since the height of the above deck structures lessened towards the cityship's edges. With her torso strapped up tightly by Peyton's compression bandages, Vix could walk, but not climb.

The SJS-Judge had asked Dredd to leave her and go on ahead, but he refused. "I don't want this team broken up any further. You're still capable of watching our backs, Vix."

They were about halfway there, moving down a long ramp between two rows of storage drums, when Bane stopped them. "Dredd, do you hear something?"

He listened hard. There was the sound of the sea, the rushing slap of waves against multiple hulls, but he'd become so used to that he almost didn't hear it any more. Behind him, at the stern, the core drives and other engines were still churning the ocean into froth. But there was something else, borne towards him on the dawn breeze from somewhere ahead. A familiar murmuring, shot through with higher cries and shouts of rage and fear.

Things breaking.

"Drokk! Citizen riot!"

"Here?" Peyton moved out from under Vix's arm – he'd been supporting her every now and then – and moved up level with Dredd. "Grud, I hear it too. What's going on?"

"Only one way to find out." He turned to the others. "Get to the bridge. I'll meet you there when I've suppressed this."

"Suppressed? Dredd, you're insane!" Bane was looking at him incredulously. "What about the Warchild?"

"Could be a direct result, especially if it's gotten into a hab deck." He put a hand up, stopping her protests. "No arguments. Get to the bridge and find out about the *Kraken* anyway. I could be wrong." With that, he turned and sprinted down the ramp.

The sound was coming from two or three ships ahead. Dredd was becoming used to the layout of *Sargasso* now, in as much as the place had a layout. Most of it hadn't been planned so much as evolved, as though structures had been dropped randomly from a great height and then bolted to the deck where they hit.

He skirted around a pyramid of containers and headed across a rigid walkway to the next hull. The sound of the riot was much louder, now. Unmistakable. Pity he couldn't rely on Weather Control to quell it with a few well-aimed downpours, like he had at the Displaced Persons Habplex. No Lawmaster, either.

Ahead of him, a cordon of skipper's men had formed around the blocky superstructure of a bulk hauler. People were packing the balconies of the structure, crowding at the portholes, yelling and raging. Chunks of debris were being ripped away from the vessel and hurled down at the skipper's men on the deck.

Dredd could see groups of Sargassans sitting on the deck, apparently under guard. He ran up to the nearest skipper's man. "What's happening here?"

The man glanced around and almost recoiled in shock. "Judge Dredd!"

"Right first time."

"Ah, minor disturbance, sir. Nothing to be concerned about." As he spoke, a porthole in the hauler's upper structure shattered, vomiting shards of glass. Someone inside had put a prybar through it. Seconds later a bottle fizzed out of the broken port, trailing flame and shattering into a wide puddle of fire when it struck the deck. There was cheering from the balconies.

This was getting out of hand. "Minor disturbance? Sounds like somebody wants out."

The skipper's man turned to glare at Dredd. "Sir! This doesn't concern you. Go about your business!"

Two more bottles whirled trails of fire through the air. One bounced harmlessly across the deck, but the other hit a railing on the way down and exploded, showering the deck with flames. Several of the skipper's men fell back, howling, batting at their clothes where the burning liquid had struck them. A few droplets came down on Dredd's shoulder eagle.

He watched them fizzle out. "It concerns me now," he grated, and raised the Lawgiver. "Ricochet."

He aimed high and put the bullet through the broken porthole. The wasplike keening of the ricochet slug was drowned by a sudden chorus of screams as the bullet bounced wildly around the confined space. With its hard, rubberised tip, the ricochet slug was less likely to kill than an execution round, as it didn't spread out upon impact. It just barrelled on through and went on to hit someone else. But it was capable of taking a large number of perps out of action, very quickly indeed.

Dredd followed the bullet in, putting his boot into the hatchway so hard that the man crouching behind it was knocked senseless. Dredd could hear skipper's men yelling at him from outside, but he ignored them. Like any riot, this needed putting down fast and hard.

He dropped his helmet mike, setting the amplifier to maximum volume. "Attention citizens!" he roared, his voice hammering around the inside of the superstructure like thunder. "This ship is under arrest!"

He was in a short corridor at the port side of the structure, leading to a hatch forward and set of stairs aft. Dredd made for the stairs, going up two at a time. The skipper's men could handle anyone trying to get through the hatch.

The stairs opened out into a wide room, possibly the ship's bridge. Bottles of raw, reeking fuel were lined up against one wall. Two men had been filling them from a small plastic drum, using a funnel. As Dredd burst in they looked up and one reached for the knife at his belt.

Dredd put a stun shot into the first man, letting the residual power of the energy burst take the second down too. They rolled to the deck, twitching feebly. Dredd would have put an execution round through them in a second, but he hadn't wanted to set the fuel alight. The wrong bullet in the wrong place here could turn the structure into an inferno.

There was one more stairway. The bottles had been thrown from the level above. Dredd took these stairs more carefully but he needn't have worried. When he got to the top he saw that the ricochet slug had done his work for him.

One man was sprawled on the deck, a prybar in one hand and his left eye a bloody mess. The slug had gone in there and out of the back of his head. A woman was slumped in the corner with a shoulder wound and one more man was cowering against the far wall. Dredd wondered why, seeing no wounds on him, but then realised that the slug had gone through the bottle he had been holding. The man was soaked in raw fuel.

Dredd walked towards him. "Code thirteen, section two. Rioting: five years. Code seven, section two. Setting fires with intent to damage property: thirty years. I don't know what you people have instead of iso-cubes, citizen, but you're going to be spending a long time in them."

The man sank to his knees. "Dredd, please–"

"No appeals, creep. I've heard it all."

"I'm not making an appeal." The man wiped fuel from his face with one hand. "I'll go to the brig if that's what it takes. But please, tell them to let our people out."

Dredd frowned. "From where?"

"From this ship!" He pointed downwards. "We live here – the *Pride of Macao*. Some people aboard are sick, and the skipper's men have sealed us in. They're trying to shut down the ventilation system!"

The man's name was Viddington. After making sure his female accomplice wasn't going to bleed out, Dredd followed Viddington down through the superstructure and into the *Pride of Macao*.

It looked a lot like the inside of the *Mirabelle*, with stacks of cargo container habs filling a large internal space. The *Macao* was smaller, but it still housed a lot of people.

A lot of them were sick. From what Dredd could see, many were dying.

He was shown children, listless and semi-conscious, wracked with shivers, their dead white skin covered in tiny red sores. It wasn't just children, either; there were eldsters in the habs with the same symptoms, and younger adults, too. The whole ship seemed to be silent except for the ragged breathing and sobbing of the afflicted.

"There haven't been skipper's men down here in days," Viddington told him. "Some of the sick have been taken away, but they won't tell us where. People started saying they were being thrown over the side."

"Is that why you rioted?"

Viddington hung his head. "It didn't start out like that. We wanted to send a delegation to the skipper, to voice our concerns and get help for our people. But the deputies wouldn't let us out. They said *Pride of Macao* was under quarantine and we weren't allowed to leave." His voice turned abruptly hard. "Then we found someone trying to shut down the vents."

Dredd remembered the groups of Sargassans under guard on the deck. Could they have been responsible? But if the citizens of one ship were turning against those of another...

Sargasso could be on the verge of tearing itself apart.

"I'm going back on deck, Viddington. Hand yourself over to the skipper's men for sentencing under your laws. Maybe they'll be more lenient with you than me."

"I doubt that," Viddington sighed. "But will you help us?"

"I'm on my way to see Skipper Quint right now," Dredd told him. "He's got some explaining to do."

The Old Man was on the move.

Years had passed since he had last set foot out of his chambers. It had been a way of life he had come to enjoy, the lack of change. He liked the feeling of permanence and the knowledge that tomorrow, if it brought anything at all, would bring just what today had done. He had seen far too much change in his life, and very little of it had been for the better.

Besides, it helped him block out the screams.

Over the past few hours he had come to realise that changes happened anyway, whether a man cocooned himself away in a decommissioned pleasure skimmer or not. He also knew that it wasn't escape he had been trying to find. It was atonement.

All these years – wandering through the Cursed Earth, finding his way to the *Sargasso*, setting up home in the skimmer he had owned before the deaths – it had been one long pilgrimage. He had dispensed his drunken wisdom, blearily telling simple sea folk about the things he saw in his head, and their thanks had been a kind of forgiveness.

But not enough. People had died because of him. A lot of people. He had paid for it, but he could never stop paying.

It was hard to find peace with dead people constantly screaming in your head.

But now Judge Dredd was aboard the *Sargasso*. The circle was completing itself and maybe that would afford the Old Man an opportunity to find the peace he craved.

The Warchild was still in the cityship. He knew that it had been damaged, although he had no idea how. All he felt were the changes in the patterns it made, the subtle ripples and vibrations in the background medium of thought and life. The Warchild moved through the medium like a shark's fin through black water; utterly without mind but filled with driving intent. It was a weapon – a simple weapon, like a bullet or an arrow. It had been fired and forgotten. While those who had launched it looked away, the weapon would find its target.

Now the weapon had sustained damage and the ripples it made were ragged and chaotic. Somewhere, the Warchild was hiding, setting all its energies to making itself the way it was before.

If the Old Man knew anything at all, it was that Judge Dredd must have had something to do with the Warchild's wounding.

He had never thought to see the lawman again, not after all this time. Now that seemed unavoidable. His own patterns, those of Dredd, those of the Warchild and Bane and so many others, they were all merging, rippling across each other like still water in rain.

It was quite possible, the Old Man knew, that Dredd could still fail in his task. The Warchild could kill them all. If the full might of the Law wasn't enough to stop it, maybe something else was.

Him.

15. ABRAXIS

When Dredd got to the central bridge, Mako Quint was waiting for him. And he was spitting mad.

"Dredd," he bellowed. "What in grud's name did you think you were doing?"

"Putting down a riot," Dredd replied. "Stopping your men from being incinerated. Quint, what's going on down there?"

Quint turned away, obviously trying to keep a lid on his anger. Dredd noticed the rest of the bridge operatives studiously keeping their heads down. Bane and Vix were sitting over at the far wall.

"More than you know," Quint grated.

"Care to fill me in?"

"This isn't your concern, Dredd."

Dredd snorted. "Second time I've been told that today. From what I can see, I'd say it was everyone's concern. Your city's diseased, Quint."

"I know that." The skipper hadn't moved. He was still gazing out of the long front windows, over the city. The towers and gantries of *Sargasso* were beginning to gleam in the rising dawn. "There's an outbreak on the *Pride of Macao*. You know, you were there. We are doing everything we can to contain it."

"Somebody thinks you're not doing enough. Your men have arrested some citizens for trying to shut down *Macao*'s vent system."

Bane leapt to her feet. "What?"

"Is that why they went on the rampage?" asked Quint. Dredd shook his head.

"They rioted because some of them tried to see you and your men wouldn't let them off the ship. Because their sick relatives are being taken away to grud knows where. And yeah, because someone – and they think it was you – was trying to close off their air supply."

"Is that what they told you?" Quint looked over his shoulder at Dredd. "The sick have been taken to the *Venturer* – it used to be a pleasure liner and it still has plenty of facilities. We've converted it into a hospital for now."

"There are still sick on the *Macao*."

"I know," said Quint, very quietly. "The *Venturer*'s full."

Bane gave a shocked gasp and stepped back, covering her mouth.

"As for the ventilation incident," Quint went on, "some hot-heads from the *Elektra Maru* tried to do that. *Elektra*'s sternwards of the *Macao* and they've already voiced concerns about germs being blown back into their ship."

"Are their concerns genuine?" asked Vix. Her voice was still weak, but she seemed alert.

Bane shook her head. "I shouldn't think so. Black Atlantic air is pretty lethal to germs because of all the toxins in the water."

"Try telling that to a ship full of frightened citizens," muttered Dredd. He knew all too well how irrational fears, let loose among a close-packed community, could spiral out of control.

The plain fact of the matter was that in any given population, most people simply weren't very bright. It was one of the prime reasons that the Mega-Cities had given up on the idea of democracy decades ago; important decisions should be made by people smart enough to make them, Dredd had always believed. Leaving things to the citizens was a charter for catastrophe. They simply weren't bright enough to make the right choices.

It was also a truism that the more people there were in any given area, the stupider they seemed to get. On a city-ship, with a million people packed onto cargo containers and set drifting off across a poisonous ocean, they could be very stupid indeed.

And stupid people could be dangerous.

"Dredd!" Vix called. She was getting up, leaning heavily on the back of her seat. "There's something else. Peyton's gone."

Bane gnawed her lip. "Once he heard about the disease, he said that there was something he needed to do. He left about ten minutes ago."

As soon as Judge Bryan Peyton heard about the disease outbreak, a nasty suspicion had entered his mind. He hoped he was wrong; after all, cityships had suffered plagues in the past. *Sargasso* itself had been the site of an outbreak of Spike Fever just nine years before.

But it was something that he had to check out and it couldn't wait. Dredd might have taken some time at the citizen riot, so Peyton had taken his own initiative and ventured out into the cityship alone.

He was, he thought as he sprinted across the deck, going to suffer one of two possible outcomes from his action. One: the Warchild would find him and kill him. Or, two: Judge Dredd would find him and kill him.

Peyton regarded both outcomes as equally likely. After all, in the vids the chubby guy always went off on his own and got eaten by the monster. As for disobeying Dredd's direct orders and leaving the team, well...

He'd sooner face the Warchild.

But it felt good to be away from Judge Vix, if nothing else. The woman was as nasty and spiteful as any Judge he'd met. That must have been a prerequisite for SJS personnel, but she really took it to extremes. Peyton wondered if the injury she had suffered was likely to mellow her at all while she was forced to stand down and recuperate. On reflection, he doubted it.

He got three-quarters of the way to the *Royale Bisley* before he had to stop. His lungs felt as though they were being sandblasted from the inside, and there was a stitch above his left hip that felt like someone had put the boot in. Tek Division Judges rarely went out on field missions and Peyton had fully expected to spend his entire career in a lab. While the Justice Department provided full fitness training for all its personnel, no matter how sedentary, Peyton had always been able to find other things to do.

"Not any more," he gasped out loud, holding his side and bending forwards to ease the pain. In the unlikely event that he should survive this mission, he swore he'd be in the gym every shift-end, and would only eat synthi-salad for lunch. If he never set foot outside the lab again, he'd be the buffest Tek-Judge there.

He reached the *Bisley* at a slow trot. There was heavy security around its superstructure and had been ever since the Warchild had attacked D-shift. Peyton waved to the skipper's men guarding the place and they let him in without a word.

Once inside, he went straight along to see the shift fore-man, a reptilian-looking mutant called Teague. He'd interviewed Teague when the dead shift-workers had first been found, and although the man hadn't been able to tell him much, he'd been pleasant and helpful.

Teague's office was at the *Bisley*'s stern, past the bottling and distribution plant. But when he got there, the place was empty. A worker directed him down to the filtration plant.

"Great," Peyton muttered darkly. "Down the drokking stairway again..."

He met Teague down by the boiler. The mess from the Warchild's attack had been cleaned up and maintenance crews were once again moving between the filters and pipes, checking the readings. They were walking in pairs now, he noticed.

A sudden vision of Judge Larson's head spinning away from his shoulders filled his mind. He shook it away and decided not to tell the shift workers that it didn't matter if they were in pairs or not.

"Foreman Teague?" He had to shout the man's name as he walked up to the boiler. The filtration plant was as loud as ever.

Teague heard the shout and turned. "Ah, Tek-Judge Peyton. Back again?"

"Just briefly, foreman. I need you to tell me something. Since the, ah, incident, have there been any breaches in the system? Something that maybe caused a loss of pressure?"

Teague's scaly face creased in surprise. "Why yes. Once poor Voley Sparxx had recovered somewhat, she told me that she'd been investigating a pressure drop in cylinder C-3." Teague's voice was rich and booming and Peyton had no difficulty hearing it. "That's what she was doing when she was separated from the rest of her shift."

"Did you check it out?"

"We did. There's a split in the cylinder, up at the end cap. Not big, but enough to drop ten per cent of filtration pressure. We're hoping that's what is causing the bad taste in the water."

"Bad taste in the..." Peyton's heart flip-flopped behind his ribs. "Tell me you haven't sealed it yet."

"We're about to. We have a man working on it right now."

Peyton turned and ran, haring towards the cylinders. "Stop him!" he yelled. "For grud's sake, stop him!"

Peyton was in time. He was up the cylinder ladder, staring down at the hole Voley Sparxx had seen, when the call came in from Judge Dredd.

"Peyton, you obviously like the idea of a permanent posting to the Undercity."

"Sir, I'm sorry about leaving the team. But what I'm doing is extremely relevant to our investigation."

"Explain."

"Give me a few minutes, Judge Dredd. I'll give you all the explanation you need."

What Peyton needed was light. He took the flashlight from his belt pouch and instead of clipping it to his Lawgiver, he snapped it into a concealed port in the right side of his helmet. He wanted both hands free for this.

The beam from the flashlight speared down into the hole. Peyton could see where the two skins of the cylinder had been punched through, and then the hole deliberately widened. Inside the cylinder the water was dark and churning, frothy with heat and the constant rotation of the filter heads.

There was something in the water that should not have been there. Hoping his arms were roughly as long as the Warchild's, Peyton leaned in and thrust his hand into the scalding water.

"It was attached to the inside of the cylinder," he told Dredd later. "The Warchild ripped a hole in the top of the filter and just stuck it there."

The object was the size of his fist, a swollen mushroom covered in the same pallid, leathery skin they had seen on the eye-spiders and the exploding pustules in the power chamber. Peyton had sealed it in a clear jar of water and taken it back to the central bridge. Now he, Dredd, Quint and Bane were clustered around it, watching as it pulsed softly.

Quint had activated a table-map. The table had bright biolumes under the surface, for illuminating maps and charts from below. It also did a very good job of illuminating the thing in the jar.

"Every few minutes," Peyton continued, "it… Hold on, here goes."

As they watched, the mushroom drew back into itself, then gave a stronger pulse. Holes in its wider end dilated, allowing black dust to spill out into the water.

There was already a coating of similar dust on the bottom of the jar.

"Spores," said Peyton, straightening up. "Microscopic and tougher than Justice Department boots. It's been releasing them into the water supply since before D-shift was attacked."

"But the filters," Quint began. "Why didn't they–"

"If it had just put germs in the water, the filters would have killed them. The boiler would have made them safe before they got to distribution. But spores, some of them, can survive almost anything: trips through interstellar space, being cooked in volcanoes, and worse."

Bane looked puzzled. "So the spores get into the water, and into the bottles. People drink the water and get sick. But why?"

"Area denial," said Peyton simply. At Dredd's questioning glance, he continued. "Remember I said that the Warchild units had a number of mission profiles? I reckon this batch was set for area denial. Get into enemy territory and make it uninhabitable. It killed enough people to hide its intentions, ate enough of them to provide itself with biomass for the booby traps and the spiders and this, and then waited for the population to start dying off." He stepped back and folded his arms. "The plague and the Warchild are one and the same problem."

"Drokk," Quint snarled. "Unless we can cure this spore-plague, your monster has killed us all."

"I wish Hellermann was here," Peyton said, then noticed that the others were looking at him very hard. "No, what I mean is, we need her expertise. She'd know how this thing works."

"Wouldn't tell us, though, would she?" Vix was still slumped in her chair on the other side of the bridge. "She'd rather watch us all die."

Peyton had to admit that was true. He turned to Dredd. "Sir? I'd like to request a change of assignment."

"Wouldn't we all?" said Vix. Peyton narrowed his eyes in her direction then turned back to Dredd. "I'm no street Judge, sir, and face to face with the Warchild I'd be worse than useless. But this might be something I can help with. Request transfer to the *Venturer* so I can work on a cure."

"Peyton," whispered Bane. "That's suicide. It's obviously gone beyond something you catch from bad water. You'd get it too."

"Maybe. But hell, there's nothing like a tight deadline to sharpen the mind, is there?"

Dredd didn't like losing Peyton, but the man was right. There was far more he could do for the case on the *Venturer* than chasing after the Warchild.

Bane had helped him collect as much equipment as he could from the Judges' medikits, leaving just enough painkillers and bandages for Vix. There would be other equipment on the *Venturer*, Quint had told him. As *Sargasso*'s newest hospital it had already been fitted out with the best the cityship had to offer.

Dredd watched him go from the long windows, with Bane guiding him. Quint was studying a control board next to him. "Looks like you're on your own, Dredd."

"I work best that way." He waited for Vix to make a snide comment, but when he glanced over at her, she'd fallen asleep. "What can you tell me about the *Kraken*'s sump outlets?"

Quint was still studying his board. "Wait a moment, Dredd." The skipper walked to another board, one that looked like a comms set. He lifted a microphone on the end of a coiled cable. "Stern lookout, what have you got bearing one-seven-five?"

There was a hiss of static. "Ah, hard to tell, skipper. Lot of gunk in that direction. The screws are kicking up some real drek."

Quint made a face. "Keep looking."

Dredd watched him walk back to the board he had been working before. "What's the problem?"

"I'm not sure. Take a look at this and tell me what you see."

Dredd studied the monitor screen set into the control board. It looked like a broad-scan sensor array: feeds from deep sonar, surface radar, and even high-intensity laser-return sets all patched into one integrated system.

The monitor screen was largely blank, save for a few motes scattered around. But there was a hazy line dogging the lower edge. "Looks like a laser return."

"That's what I thought." Quint tapped commands into the board, cycling the screen through a number of different modes. Only one showed the ghostly line. "Yeah, laser all right. But why aren't we getting a return from anything else?"

"Stealth?" suggested Dredd. As he said it, Quint's eye went wide.

He raced back to the comms set. "Stern lookout, bearing one-seven-five! Switch off all electronic assist and use your eyes! What do you see?"

The silence was longer this time. "We have a sighting, skipper, mark one-seven-five. Another cityship at extreme visual range. It must be stealth-clad along the bow, that's why we didn't catch it."

"Stealth-clad? Grud…" Quint turned to stare out of the bridge's rear ports then went to a side door and shoved it open. Dredd saw him step out onto an observation deck and followed.

"What now, Quint?"

In answer, Quint stretched out a massive arm and pointed. "There. See it?"

On the stern horizon, past the fountains of spray kicked up by the drive screws, was a low, flat cloud of dark vapour. "Another city?"

"Another city. One with stealth plating, heading right for us."

Not all cityships, Bane told Dredd later, made their living by salvage and fishing. Some preferred quicker, riskier profits. Among the twenty or so cityships that plied the Black Atlantic, at least two were known pirates.

Instead of scavenger vessels, they had fleets of attack

ships. Usually they would concentrate their efforts on single vessels, using suites of sophisticated sensors to detect them at long range, then creep in masked by stealth plates. The attack ships had such plates too. Bane knew this from bitter experience. She had almost lost the Warchild casket to a stealth-clad pirate. "Wish I had now," she sighed.

"You and me both," said Dredd. They were on one of the upper balconies, using Bane's binocs to watch the other cityship's approach. "How often do they attack another city?"

"Not once in my lifetime. But they're coming in fast. Quint says they'll be on us in about ten hours."

The other cityship had been identified as the *Abraxis*. It was smaller than *Sargasso*, but significantly faster. Quint had ordered the harbour barges to close their doors, and skipper's men had been stationed at the city's edges, ready to repel boarders. Heavy weapons were being prepared, but such things were rare on the open ocean. *Sargasso* had access to a few dozen twin-linked spit guns, a few ship-to-ship missiles, maybe even a torpedo or two. But nothing that could even dent an entire cityship.

"Dredd?" Vix had appeared at the balcony hatch. She was still pale and hanging onto the wall for support, but there was a familiar set to her jaw and she had her helmet back on. Despite being almost eviscerated only a short time ago, she was back on the case. Buell would have been proud. "You better come and listen to this."

Dredd and Bane followed her back onto the bridge. Vix had taken over one of the sensor workstations, and she led them there before dropping heavily back into its seat.

"The Sargassans have been trying to hail the *Abraxis* for an hour," she said, gloved fingers tapping at the workstation's keyboard. "No reply, of course. They're persistent, I'll give them that, but to be quite honest they couldn't run a listening post to save their lives."

"And you could?" Bane muttered. Vix grinned.

"It's my job. Now this is the interesting part. *Sargasso* did get a reply, but no one heard it. Before anyone saw the *Abraxis*, we got this."

She tapped a final key, and a long, wavering squawk of static erupted from the speakers. Dredd saw Bane wincing.

The static finished. "Well," Dredd growled. "Very enlightening."

Vix tapped more keys. "Okay, maybe I'm more used to this kind of thing. This is all the filters I have here – try now."

This time, there was a voice embedded in the static. It said one word.

"*Everyone.*"

Another hour went by, during which time Dredd learned that the *Kraken*'s sump outlets could have deposited the Warchild in any one of fifteen different spots, all of them in easy reach of either the open sea or a way back to the city-ship. Once again, he was reduced to waiting for someone to see spiders. In the meantime, the *Abraxis* drew ever closer, but neither modified its course or sent any further transmissions.

Eventually, Vix took Dredd aside. "Sir, I've got a very bad feeling about this."

"When have you ever had a good one?"

"Captain Bane told me that there was at least one more casket out at sea when she picked her one up. We know that Hellermann's first batch consisted of ten Warchild units. What if the stealth ship that attacked Bane picked one up or more than one? They might all be on the same timer and they'd all have the same programming."

"So why aim *Abraxis* right at *Sargasso* and put their foot down?"

She shook her head. "I don't know. But maybe the *Abraxis* is unable to alter course. If they can't, maybe we should."

"They have. Quint slammed the *Sargasso* hard to port as soon as the *Abraxis* was confirmed. But with something this size, it's gonna be twenty hours before it even starts to turn away."

Vix sagged. "Twenty hours… Grud. What can we do?"

"I'm working on that," Dredd told her. "And in spite of my better judgement, I'll need your help."

16. ALWAYS AND EVERYONE

Peyton had been given a little office on board the *Venturer*. He had turned it as quickly as possible into a disease control laboratory, equipped with everything Quint had been able to find for him. He had microscopes, a spectrogram, bio-scanners and bacterial growth chambers. He had a small hot zone box, pressure sealed and with two heavy rubberised gloves poking into it from the front face. He had a computer. He had several competent, dedicated nurses, even if a couple of them did have more eyes than usual.

What he didn't have was a clue. People were dying around him and right now he didn't have the faintest notion of what to do about it.

Peyton put his notepad aside and rubbed his eyes. He'd only been working on the *Venturer* for a few hours, but he was already exhausted. There were six hundred patients aboard – the full capacity. When he had arrived there had been six hundred, then twenty minutes later there had been four hundred and seventy, plus one hundred and thirty corpses. Now there were six hundred again.

He could imagine this process continuing until there was no one left on *Sargasso* at all.

The disease killed everyone it touched. It was one of the very few infections with a one hundred per cent kill-rate.

There was a tap on the door. As he lifted his head, the door opened and one of the nurses looked in. "Judge Peyton? There's been another wave."

"How many this time?"

"Ninety-six," she said quietly, and drew the door closed behind her. Peyton groaned. The time between the waves of deaths seemed impossible to predict. They might come an hour apart, or a minute. But no one on the *Venturer* died alone.

In a while, skipper's men wearing breath-masks would come in and take the bodies away, while more would bring the new arrivals. It was like a murderous production line. Bring out the dead, take in the living, and wait for them to die.

Judge Peyton sat back and wondered if was going to be any more use here than he would facing an angry Warchild.

The hardest part was not going out into the ship to help the sick. That had been his first reaction upon reaching the *Venturer*, to don a mask and gown and help the nurses treat the fevers and the pains. Peyton had joined the Justice Department out of a desire to serve the people of Mega-City One, to help those in need, protect those who could not protect themselves. Here, on this great floating city-state, he was surrounded by people he couldn't help. He was watching them die right in front of him.

Victims of the disease rapidly became horribly lethargic, barely able to move. They were breathless, suffered terrible muscle pains and shivered constantly. Their skin, especially over the major blood vessels, became a sprawl of angry red rashes. They were feverish, coughing and terrified.

Then, very suddenly, they died.

And he didn't know why.

The stern lookout was set high above the deck. Unusually for the *Sargasso* it had been purpose-built – a tall, cantilevered tower topped by a plastiglass dome the size of a pat-wagon.

Dredd was able to get Vix into the lookout by means of a walkway leading from the central bridge. The walkway was narrow and flimsy, shuddering in the breeze and floored in the same open mesh that the Sargassans used whenever they had to build a platform over a long drop. Still, she never would have made it into the lookout by its other accessway; that was a ladder with more than two hundred rungs.

Quint had told the lookout operator to stand down while Vix was in the pod on Dredd's recommendation. Not that Vix needed to be alone to do her job, but if she were up there with anyone from the *Sargasso*'s crew she would probably end up provoking him into a fist fight.

Dredd watched as Vix settled herself into the lookout seat. The seat was on a rail that ran across the pod, port to starboard. She slid herself back and forward a few times, experimentally, making sure she was in easy reach of the various telescopes, binocs and scanners that were set into the pod's sternward side.

"Whee," she said flatly.

"This isn't a game, Vix," Dredd said. "You're supposed to be the big surveillance expert, so start surveilling."

Vix rolled along to the big telescope in the centre of the pod. There was a video camera attached to the eyepiece, with a feed cable running back to a monitor screen. Vix tried to focus it for about four seconds before losing patience and tearing the camera away. The monitor screen showed a momentary whirl of colour, then the olive-green top of Dredd's boot.

"That's better," muttered Vix, peering directly into the eyepiece. "No resolution on that piece of drek worth mentioning."

"Never mind that. What do you see?"

Vix was silent for a long moment. "I've got the *Abraxis*," she murmured after a time. "Bridge, upper deck, top structures. A lot of armour. Stealth plates over almost everything. No crew, though."

"They hiding?"

"A hundred thousand people?" Vix frowned, increasing the magnification. "Maybe they're all concealed, but it would be quite a... Hold on, I've got someone. Ah."

"Is 'ah' an SJS term I'm not yet aware of?"

In reply, Vix rolled the chair away and gestured at the eyepiece. Dredd leaned down and peered through it.

Vix had focussed the telescope on the bridge of the *Abraxis*. The scope was extremely powerful; all Dredd could see of the pirate cityship was a section of front window. There was someone sitting behind the window, looking out, headphones covering his ears. Probably a comms operator of some kind, thought Dredd.

Then he noticed that the man's face was paper white, scattered with dull scarlet rashes. The jaw hung slackly open and the eyes were rolled back, staring up at nothing.

"*Everyone*," hissed Dredd. "What, everyone's dead?"

"Dead, dying, what's the difference?" Vix sat back in disgust. "There's no one there to attack *Sargasso*. The place is a floating ghost town."

"No one to alter course, either..." Dredd knew what he had to do. If *Sargasso* couldn't move out of the way, then *Abraxis* would have to change course instead. Quint had told Dredd that *Sargasso* would take twenty hours to make any noticeable course change, but *Abraxis* was only one-tenth the size and built for speed.

It could work. But he'd need a boat and someone to watch his back.

"Vix. How would you like to stay up here for a while?"

The boat Quint found for him was called *Seawasp*, and it was the fastest vessel *Sargasso* had to offer. It looked like a rich man's plaything; little more than a slender, powder-blue polycarbonate hull five metres long, with a needle-sharp prow and a blunt, flared stern housing twin aquajet drives. A shallow windshield angled back towards a single bucket seat and a control board that seemed to consist entirely of throttles.

The whole thing looked flimsy and feathery, as though a good kick in the right place would send it to the bottom.

Bane was there to send him off. She'd taken him down to the harbour where *Seawasp* bobbed lightly among the scavengers and fishing smacks. "It's only used for observation, normally," she told him. "Scooting around the hulls, making sure everything's okay. Not much good for anything else."

"Will it get me to *Abraxis*?" Dredd was settling into the bucket seat and testing the controls. "Don't want to get halfway there and run out of juice."

"You've got plenty." She gave the hull a farewell slap. "Just try not to hit anything. The hull would shatter."

"Comforting." He thumbed the start key and heard the drives growl throatily behind him. Quint had already opened one of the harbour doors partway.

With Dredd's gloved hands on the throttles, the *Seawasp* nosed carefully around the massive door and out into the open sea. The sun was well up now and glinting off the sluggish, oily surface of the Atlantic. Ahead of him, Dredd could see the angular grey bulk of the *Abraxis*. It looked like a dark island, studded with sensor masts and weapons mounts. Even from this distance he could see that the pirate city had its harbours facing forwards, so that the attack vessels could go straight into action.

Like *Sargasso*, *Abraxis* was surrounded by a cloud of spray churned up by its titan engines.

Dredd eased the throttles forward. *Seawasp* slowly built up speed, nosing easily through the water. Then, quite without warning, the vessel leapt forwards.

Dredd found himself howling through the water at close to Lawmaster speeds. The rich idiot who had designed the vessel must had set a point on the throttle tracks that kicked in some kind of overdrive; no doubt to impress other rich idiots who might be watching. Dredd gripped the twin throttle bars hard, playing one against the other to keep *Seawasp* on track. Every wave on the ocean made the boat skip violently to one side or the other.

He dropped his helmet mike. "Dredd to Vix."

"I've got you, Dredd. Nice boat."

"Cut the chatter and keep watching, Vix. I'll need your eyes on me all the way." If Dredd's gut feeling about the *Abraxis* proved right, he'd need eyes in the back of his head for this trip. Vix, sitting up there in the stern lookout with her telescopes aimed right at him, would be those eyes.

He could have taken someone with him – Bane, maybe – but if he was walking into the lion's den he'd rather do it alone. Better to put himself voluntarily under SJS surveillance than to chaperone a civilian around. It was going to be tough enough guarding his own skin.

He pushed the throttles as far forward as they could go and aimed *Seawasp* at the *Abraxis*, piloting the little boat by feel as a mountain of grey steel grew beyond the prow.

While Dredd was skimming the black waves towards *Abraxis*, Judge Peyton was, against all the odds, making progress. Through a series of tests, biopsies and lucky guesses he now had a breakdown of how the disease functioned. He should have done autopsies, he knew, but there was no way he could bring himself to open up a corpse. The biopsies were hard enough. Peyton's training was in DNA resequencing and the largest part of a human being he usually handled was a fragment of genome. His knowledge of medicine was rudimentary, to say the least.

This, he'd decided, had to be the most radical cross-training programme in Justice Department history.

He had made his breakthroughs by ignoring the physiology of the victims, about which he knew very little, and instead concentrating on the spores that caused it. The DNA they contained was quite simple and easy to sequence. It was also encrypted, but since Peyton himself had worked on the encryption algorithms on the Warchild project, he could take that apart as easily as he could strip a Lawgiver.

His first clue had been the way the patients died in waves.

He had seen it with his own eyes. The nurses had been tending a small girl with silvery hair and two forearms emerging from each elbow. He had just taken a blood sample from the girl and been watching the nurses when the girl had suddenly convulsed on the bed and died. There was no hope for her: no heroic battle to keep her organs free from oxygen starvation, no electrical restarting of the heart. She was instantly, utterly dead.

Her nervous system, he later found out, had chemically broken down.

When the nurses had turned to check on the girl's brother and sister who were brought in at the same time, they were dead too.

His second clue was the noise they made when they died. A long, airy groan, as though their tiny lungs were being squeezed empty. He had heard that noise before when Judge Adams had died.

After that, it really hadn't taken him long to chart the processes of the disease. And what he had been able to discover both impressed and appalled him. It seemed that the Warchild plague, as he couldn't help but call it, was the kind of disease that could never have evolved on its own. It was too ordered, to specific to be natural. Only a human being could be so perverse as to create such a thing.

It began with the spores.

Infinitesimal and almost indestructible, the spores remained dormant in the water supply until ingested. The only evidence that a bottle of water contained the spores was a faint, but noticeable, aftertaste, probably caused by a chemical released by the tiny motes as they began to self-activate.

Their catalyst was human saliva. Peyton surmised that any mutant on the ship whose body chemistry was sufficiently modified might escape becoming a disease carrier, since the chemicals sought by the spores were quite specific. But that wasn't the end of the story, not by a long way.

The spores were not in themselves, even dangerous.

However, each one was a tiny factory. Once a spore had encountered the saliva-borne chemical triggers, it would open like a flower, attaching itself to whatever tissue it could find. Many would be washed through the host's system, but a few would lodge. They would then begin producing bacteria.

Once loose in the bloodstream, the bacteria would swarm and multiply at a ferocious rate. The human immune system did not affect them in the slightest – they had been designed very specifically to deal with it. Once in the bloodstream, they caused an allergic reaction, hence the rashes of red dots following infested blood vessels. They were also adept at spreading to new hosts, finding their way into the lungs and moving to new victims through droplet contact. A single sneeze could release a hundred million of them into the atmosphere.

The bacteria would spread through the victim's bloodstream until it had almost reached saturation point, making it difficult for the host to take up oxygen, and causing listlessness and shivering. Then, after a certain level of bacterial infection had occurred, they simply died. Every bacterium committed cellular suicide in a sudden, catastrophic cascade.

When they died, their last act was to release a tiny amount of toxin, very much like that in the Warchild's poisoned needles. The victim didn't have a chance. In seconds, the myelin sheath surrounding every nerve cell in their bodies would suffer total and complete breakdown.

So Peyton knew how the disease worked. But he still didn't have the faintest idea of how to cure it. The spores were difficult to harm and they would begin releasing their bacterial load after being in the host's system for only a few minutes.

He had to target the bacteria. But if he found a cure, something that killed the bacteria themselves, their deaths would also release the neurotoxin, crippling or killing the host.

"As a wise man once said," he muttered to himself, "you don't dare kill it."

He was still in the office, every microscope in use and the computer humming. He had stopped the growth chamber as he didn't need any more bacteria. Every time he had started to grow some they had multiplied at insane speeds, then broken down into a puddle of lethal poison.

It was getting hot in the office. Peyton turned to set the aircon a little higher, and then stopped. As he had reached for the control the sleeve of his uniform had ridden up a little.

Peyton swallowed hard, then pulled his sleeve up. The arm beneath was white with a scattering of crimson dots.

His deadline had just become a lot tighter.

Dredd took *Seawasp* around to the starboard side of *Abraxis*, skimming around the pirate city's perimeter with the throttles wide open the boat heeled over at a massive angle, almost on its side. He had to fight the controls as he went through the enormous wake at the stern – the cityship's huge engines were ripping the water into a frenzy; creating a thundering grey storm of spray and lethal undercurrents.

Vix immediately told him he was out of sight, which was exactly what he didn'e want to hear. He needed the SJS-Judge to be watching him constantly.

After he was out of the other side, he slowed *Seawasp* down and began to look for a way to board. The harbours, he had noticed on the way in, all had their doors closed. No way in there, and besides, it would make the journey to the bridge longer.

Here, close to the cityship's massive hulls, *Seawasp* had another advantage over larger vessels. The little vessel could skate right over currents that would drag a scavenger clear under the surface.

He tooled *Seawasp* around the port side of the city, hunting for a way to get on board. After a minute or two he saw it – a long service ladder stretching down to a tiny, sea level platform. He nosed *Seawasp* in and triggered the mooring clamps.

Cables hissed from the vessel's starboard flank, each tipped with a magnetic projectile. The clamps slapped onto the pirate city's hull, locking tightly, and then the cable drums in *Seawasp*'s shell began to reel in. In a few seconds, the little craft was securely moored next to the platform.

The hull next to him was a grey cliff of steel, stretching up out of sight.

Dredd clambered up onto the mesh and began to climb the ladder. "Vix, I'm aboard. Have you still got me?"

"I have. Climbing up an extremely tall ladder. You look like a bug on a drekhouse wall."

"Vix..."

"I'm checking the top of the ladder. There's a platform over the gunwales. You'll have to step up onto that, then down onto the deck. No one about, as before."

"Acknowledged." Dredd took the last few rungs of the ladder more slowly, unholstering his Lawgiver as he reached the top. As Vix had reported there was no one in sight. Dredd leapt up onto the platform and then dropped to the deck, standing in a narrow area between the gunwales and an angled wall of stealth-plates.

The cityship was silent, save the distant bellow of the engines. Then Dredd heard another sound – a weird, directionless droning that he couldn't immediately identify. Other than that, nothing. He moved away from the gunwale and onto the open deck.

As he rounded one of the protective stealth-plates, he discovered what the droning sound was.

"Dredd?" Vix's voice was hissing in his helmet comm. "Dredd, I can't quite see you, but I can see smoke coming up. What is that?"

"It's not smoke," Dredd told her. "It's flies."

Abraxis was swarming with untold millions of flies. Clouds of them hung over the deck, swirling in great sheets and swarms around the hab-stacks and towers. Gantrywork that Dredd had taken to be painted black became abruptly metallic again as he approached, as the insects covering them leapt away. They were blocking out the sun.

"Looks like they got their Warchild casket open early," he muttered. "These people have been dead a while..."

There were corpses everywhere, lying where they had fallen and coated in a thick, living blanket of voracious insects. Most of the population of *Abraxis* must have stayed below decks to die, but Dredd could still see a couple of thousand, just from where he was standing.

He was accomplishing nothing here. The bridge he had seen through Vix's telescope was a few hundred metres ahead and to his right. He began to make his way through the reeking corpses towards it. As he walked, flies billowed into the air whenever he put his boot down. The cityship was a nightmare.

Vix was silent for a while. Watching Dredd through the telescope, she must have been able to see the carnage too. Dredd was doubly glad he hadn't taken Bane along – she couldn't have handled this.

Finally, as Dredd was reaching the outer levels of the bridge, Vix spoke. "What do you think, were they trying to find help? They set course for *Sargasso* hoping someone there could help them?"

"Reckon." Dredd skirted around a pile of bodies and found an open hatchway into the bridge tower. "I'm going in."

"Get to the main command area as fast as you can. I'll be able to see you from there."

There was a stairway up the centre of the tower. Dredd climbed it quickly, ignoring the rooms full of twisted bodies to either side, and found his way to the main bridge.

The dead comms operator was still there. There weren't nearly as many flies inside the bridge as there were on deck, but a few still buzzed out of the man's mouth as Dredd approached. "I'm here. So is our friend."

"I've got you."

The entire forward edge of the bridge was a massive bank of control boards. Dredd walked from left to right, quickly scanning the boards and memorising their positions. Within seconds he'd worked out which ones were for weapons control, which for sensors and communications.

"I've got navigation." A large, complex board towards the right of the bridge housed the directional controls. Much of it was taken up with a single monitor screen, showing the pirate city's course in a series of animated maps and charts.

He was hoping there would be a single control, something that he could operate easily and then be away. But nothing was ever that simple. The navigation board looked as though it was mainly a signalling device, issuing orders to secondary computers in the core drives and the other sternward ships.

He began tapping at the keyboard, trying to open up a command chain. A window appeared on the monitor, overlaid over the maps. Standard enough for an antique.

Dredd typed fast, setting up a linked chain of navigation commands. He'd have liked to slam *Abraxis* to starboard and watch the cityship come apart at the seams, but the navigation computer was too clever for that. It knew exactly how much lateral stress the huge, fluid structure of the cityship could take, and wouldn't allow Dredd to go outside those boundaries.

He had to settle for a more gentle path, easing away to starboard in a wide, hundred kilometre curve. *Abraxis* would get awfully close to *Sargasso*, but as long as the bigger cityship maintained its speed there would be no collision.

He keyed the execution command. The window closed and the monitor showed a new map.

"Damned antiquated systems," he growled. It would have been far easier with a modern ship where he could have just called up the central computer and told it where to go.

"Dredd?" That was Vix.

"I'm done here. On my way."

"Dredd, don't go out through the port door. I just saw part of the wall move."

Dredd brought his Lawgiver up. The Warchild that had killed all on *Abraxis* was less than ten metres away from him. "Keep it in sight."

He began edging towards the starboard exit. Like *Sargasso*, *Abraxis* had a bridge that was roughly symmetrical, so there was another door on the opposite side. Dredd backed towards it, keeping his Lawgiver trained on the port door.

The hatch was just behind him now. He turned smoothly, kicked it open and a blade of white bone whickered down through the air towards his head.

Dredd moved aside, feeling an impact as the blade took a few centimetres off his shoulder armour. The Warchild's other blade whipped around at gut level, but Dredd was already wise to that trick, snapping himself out of the way and countering with a solid kick to the Warchild's side.

The bioweapon went over, correcting in midair and leaping up onto the nearest control board. Its camouflage shimmered.

"Dredd! Six o'clock!"

At Vix's alarm, Dredd whipped about and put a three-shot burst of execution rounds into another Warchild's chest. He heard it shriek and saw it go down, its camouflage flashing crazily. Then the first one was on him again, blades whirling. One went diagonally through the dead comms operator's skull, shearing most of his head off. Another sliced into a control board, sending up a spray of brilliant sparks.

Dredd hurled himself away. There was no way to block those blades – from the way they went through metal and bone with such ease, they must have been edged with monomolecular fibres. He heard a blade sing through the air again and the comms operator's chair fell away in two pieces. The corpse did too.

"The one you blasted, Dredd. It's getting up!"

"Drokk!" He brought the Lawgiver around and the injured Warchild's blade took it in half, clear through the magazine. Shell casings scattered across the deck.

Dredd flung the rest of the weapon aside. One of these creeps he could have handled, but two was pushing it. Time to bug out.

He slid his daystick from its belt loop and dived at the wounded Warchild. It flailed at him, but the heart shots, while not killing it, had damaged its balance. He added to its woes by slamming the daystick into the back of its opened skull as he went past.

The control boards were in front of him. He jumped, his hand coming down hard on the nearest board, propelling him up and sideways. The soles of his boots hit the big front window together.

The window – decades-old plastiglass scored through by years of Black Atlantic spray, shattered out of its frame. Dredd sailed on through, turning in midair to come down feet first. He heard Vix scream his name.

It was fifteen metres from the bridge to the deck.

Dredd had aimed his jump perfectly, coming down in a pile of *Abraxis* corpses. He felt bones shattering under his boots, insect-chewed flesh tearing away, and he instantly was surrounded by a droning, blinding cloud of flies. But the rotting bodies had given him enough of a cushion to survive the fall without his thighbones being driven up through his pelvis.

He slid down the stack of carcasses, rolled, and then jumped to his feet, batting the last of the flies away. He ran.

Behind him, up on the bridge, he could hear the Warchild units screaming.

"Vix!" he snapped, leaping another pile of corpses. "Update!"

"They're not following! Grud, Dredd, I can't believe you did that!"

"Sometimes we must call on the citizens to help us, Judge Vix." He reached the stealth-plates and ducked back around them, hunting for the ladder.

"Even if they're dead."

17. ELEKTRA DESCENDING

Councillor Atia Borla had worn a breath-mask ever since the meeting in Quint's office. Every time she went up onto the bridge of her ship, she could see the boxy superstructure of the *Pride of Macao* just a few hulls forward. The constant breeze caused by *Sargasso*'s passage through the ocean must have been blowing gouts of infection clear back into the *Elektra Maru*.

The *Elektra* was a big vessel, a factory ship two hundred metres from bow to stern. In its day it had sailed the Atlantic's coastal waters, the robots in its multiple decks turning out cheap goods by the thousand. The goods might not have been very well made and the robots poorly maintained, but that didn't matter. The captain of the *Elektra* had been careful to shut down construction every time he strayed into anyone's territorial waters.

Now the robots were gone and the factory units broken up for scrap. *Elektra* had gone out of business when Mega-City One extended its territorial margin; the journey from the dockside markets out to the legal limit was now no longer cost-effective, and that was the end of the *Elektra Maru*'s trading days. Her captain – Borla's father – had died a broken man.

Now his dream, his home, was about to be wiped out by plague, all because Mako Quint didn't have the guts to deal with it.

Borla stood on the bridge of the *Elektra* and glared out across the deck. Last night a few of her people had gone across to the *Macao* and tried to close the vents off. They hadn't gone under her orders, or even with her blessing. But she hadn't exactly told them not to do it, either.

Quint's men had put paid to that plan, however. Now most of her security details were in the brig and Borla had a shipful of angry, frightened citizens to deal with. *Elektra* was one of the food production units in *Sargasso*, her empty factories now dedicated to the gutting of fish and the growing of algae. The workers who produced the food lived on board, in container-habs on deck and converted staterooms below. *Elektra Maru* had a population of over five thousand and, like many vessels in *Sargasso*, was almost a self-contained community.

Not, in Borla's opinion, quite self-contained enough.

There was a knock at the bridge hatch. Borla had made it clear she didn't want to be disturbed, but it opened anyway. Fennet, one of the security men who hadn't been arrested, put his bullet-shaped head around. "Councillor?"

"What is it, Fennet?" She motioned him to come in, and noticed that as he did so he was careful to look outside, both ways, and close the door behind him.

"Councillor, we got a problem." Fennet was keeping his voice low. "I was talking with, well, a guy I know from *The Samarkand*. He knows someone who sends the skipper's reports up to centre bridge."

"Let me guess," Borla interrupted. "Some of the reports happen to fall open before they get onto Quint's desk."

"Gravity's a funny thing."

Borla gave him a grim half-smile, but then remembered he wouldn't be able to see it through the breath-mask. "Okay, what did your friend have to tell you?"

Fennet reached into his coat pocket and tugged out a folded sheet of paper. "This didn't come cheap," he warned her. "But it makes good reading."

Borla took the paper and unfolded it, flattening the creases with the heel of her hand. The text on the page was quite dense and the copy not very good. But it only took Borla a minute or two to realise what it meant.

"Dear grud," she whispered. "It's already off. He lied to us."

Fennet nodded. "When you were in there, he already had this on his desk."

Borla took a deep breath. "Right," she said, after a few seconds. "The decision's been made for us. Break out the demolition charges and let me know when they've been distributed."

"You're going ahead?" Fennet, for all his bull-headed-ness and thuggish reputation, was starting to look worried. "What about the skipper?"

"He'll never know until it's a done deal." Borla reached out and slapped him on the shoulder. "Hey, don't fall apart on me now! If we do this right, all our problems will be over in a couple of hours."

Fennet left, shaking his head. Borla wondered if he was really the right man for the job in such troubled times, but she didn't really have that much of a choice. Still, he could always be replaced once the deed was done.

She turned back to the view from the window and began to contemplate blasting a ship clear out of the city.

Bane was on the bridge with Quint when Judge Vix came back across the walkway. They watched her approach, walking carefully on the swaying mesh and supporting herself with both hands on the railings.

Bane opened the hatch for her. "How are you feeling, skull-head?" she asked.

"Enriched," Vix replied, her voice a disinterested monotone. "I find life at sea so invigorating."

Bane threw Quint a knowing glance and turned back to the long window.

"Dredd's done the job," Vix continued. "He's on his way back and should be here in a few minutes. He's taken *Abraxis* on a starboard tack. It'll be close, but they should skate right past if we continue as we are."

"Well," said Quint, "some good news at last."

"Not for the *Abraxis*." Vix moved across the bridge, found a chair and eased down into it, wincing. "He said you'll need to stock up on bug spray."

Bane remembered the explosive shell knocking a splintered hole through *Golgotha*'s gunwales and found it difficult to feel sorry for the pirate city. *Abraxis* had been responsible for many atrocities in the past; when they attacked a vessel, the crew were normally killed in the battle or put over the side. Occasionally they set them adrift in lifeboats. On *Sargasso*, that was called exile, and was the worst punishment that could be meted out. On the *Abraxis*, it was called mercy.

"That's what you get for stealing my salvage, drokkers," she whispered.

"Which just leaves us the Warchild problem," Vix said quietly. She was looking out of one of the side ports. "And the plague."

"Peyton's working on that," said Quint. "Can't say I've much faith in Mega-City Judges, but that one seems all right. He may come up with something."

To Bane's surprise, Vix didn't offer any disparaging comments about that at all. "And the Warchild?" she said.

Quint was checking the navigation board, watching the operator key in the pirate city's projected course change. "I thought that was your job."

Vix gave a bitter laugh. "My job was to keep Hellermann alive, to learn what she knew about the Warchild so we could protect ourselves if there were any more." She shifted uncomfortably in the chair, still gazing out of the porthole. "Which I completely failed to do."

"What'll happen when you get back?" asked Bane, wondering why she was interested.

"If," said Vix, her voice still flat and dead. "*If* I get back. Well, maybe my boss won't have me accidentally assassinated. But I doubt it. Lot of activity on that ship, Quint."

Quint didn't look up. "Which ship?"

"*Elektra Maru.*"

Curious, Bane walked across and joined Vix at the porthole. The *Elektra Maru* was portside of the bridge, and a
few hulls sternwards. As Bane looked down on it, she
could see figures scurrying about the deck, moving from
structure to structure.

"They're up to something," muttered Vix. She straightened a little; this had caught her interest, Bane could see.
"You can tell by the way they're moving."

"Skipper?" Bane beckoned Quint over. "She's right, sir.
You should have a look at this."

Quint's size meant that he couldn't use the same porthole as the two women, so he went to the next one along.
He watched for about half a minute then turned and went
quickly back to the comms board.

Bane saw him pull the microphone from the board so
violently it almost came off. "Councillor Borla!" he roared.

There was a pause, and a hiss of static. Finally a
woman's voice, hard and clipped, sounded over the speakers.

"Don't try to stop us, Quint. We're capable of defending
ourselves!"

"Borla, this is insanity!"

"Don't lecture me on insanity, skipper!" the voice
snarled. "You kept the facts from us! The plague was
already off the *Macao* when we were in your office, and
you've done nothing to stop it."

"That's not true and you know it. We've got people
working on a cure right now, but this is not the answer!
Borla, you know what will happen!"

"What will happen is that we won't be around to watch
you die of plague, Skipper Quint!"

The line went dead. Quint stayed where he was for a
moment, breathing hard. Then he turned to his comms
officer.

"Get me Dredd."

● ● ●

Dredd was only a few minutes away from the *Sargasso* when the call came in. After the cityship's customary hiss of interference – the ancient comms system tracking down his frequency, he had learned – Quint's booming voice emerged over his helmet speakers. "Dredd, we've got a situation."

"Now there's a switch."

"One of the sternward vessels is trying to blast free by blowing her links and backing out of the city."

"Let me guess: they reckon they'll be better off on their own." Dredd had heard that story before, too. Religious maniacs leading their followers into the Cursed Earth for a "better life." Whole blocks trying to declare independence. It always ended in disaster, no matter how it was played.

"They're more likely to tear the city apart. Dredd, I've got Jennig and all the skipper's men I can muster on their way, but I'd like you there as well."

"Voice of authority?"

"Element of surprise."

Dredd could think of worse things to be. "I'm on my way. Quint, I need to speak with Vix."

There was a moment's pause. "Sir, this isn't our fight."

"It will be if those idiots break *Sargasso* in half. Do you have access to Larson's Lawgiver?"

"I can get it."

"Disable the SD charge and send it down with Bane to meet me at the harbour. Mine suffered a failure."

As *Seawasp* jetted back into *Sargasso*'s harbour, alert sirens began to howl out across the cityship. Dredd took the little boat in fast, flipped it around and slammed it against the side of the dock.

Bane was waiting for him, carrying something heavy wrapped in a piece of tarpaulin. "Special delivery."

Dredd took it from her and unwrapped the package. Larson's Lawgiver nestled inside, indicators already glowing on the ammo select. "I'd stand back," Dredd grated.

"Wouldn't put it entirely beyond Vix to not disable the SD as much as she could…"

Thankfully, the SJS-Judge had followed his orders properly – the gun didn't blow his hand off. He wouldn't be able to use the voice-select until he had properly reset the on-board computer. To be honest, he didn't like using another Judge's gun, but he figured the *Elektra Maru* situation might be slightly beyond a boot knife and a daystick.

Bane showed him the quickest way up. Once he was on the deck it was easy to find his way to the *Elektra Maru*. He just followed the sound of the gunfire.

The crew of the rogue ship had obviously stashed some weapons away and were using them to keep the skipper's men back while they planted their charges. Dredd was interested to see that most of the gunfire was being aimed high, as if those firing were trying to keep casualties to a minimum. It was a laudable sentiment, and one encountered all too seldom back in the Meg, but it would mean nothing if the *Elektra* tore free and left *Sargasso* in tatters behind it.

Philo Jennig was on the *Mystere*, the vessel directly starboard of the *Elektra*. Dredd spotted him taking cover behind a vent funnel, and slid to a halt next to him. "Skipper said you might need some back-up."

Jennig shook his head. "No offence, Dredd, but this is beyond back-up. We haven't got the men."

"Maybe I can appeal to their better judgement."

Dredd broke cover and sprinted towards the edge of the deck. There was a group of the *Elektra*'s crew there, mostly wearing the blue coveralls of food workers. They were planting demolition charges around a structure there – one of the giant linking braces that held their ship to the next. Dredd could see other groups doing the same, working around the bridges and walkways. Some of the upper level ramps and walkways had already been severed.

This had gone far enough. He dropped his helmet mike and set the volume to maximum.

"*Elektra Maru*," he bellowed.

All activity aboard the food ship ceased, as Dredd's amplified tones blasted out across the deck.

"*Elektra Maru*, I am the Law! Drop those demo charges and step away. If you do not comply, there will be trouble!"

For a moment, it almost looked as if it would work. Several of the blue-clad workers did exactly as they were told, setting their charges down and moving back.

Others among them, however, were not so sensible. Dredd saw one man raise a half-empty bottle of spirit and fling it over the deck at him. "You can't shoot us all, Judge!"

Dredd snapped a round through the man's kneecap and watched him sprawl, howling. "Want a bet?"

But the spell had already been broken. A low murmur of anger was already rippling along the vessel. And out of the corner of his eye, Dredd saw something raised towards him.

He tried to bring the Lawgiver around, but it was already too late.

There was a snapping explosion and a hiss of cable. He saw the missile for a split second before it hit, just enough time to twist out of the way, but it had opened at the tip into a wide dish. It took him in the right arm, knocked him back with massive force and slammed him into a hab wall. It stuck.

The missile was a magnetic harpoon, a larger version of the docking projectiles on *Seawasp*. Dredd's arm was crushed against the hab wall as the magoon tried to reach the metal. His armoured elbow-pad had saved his bones from being shattered, but he was trapped and he couldn't get his Lawgiver around.

The magoon hummed with power. Its batteries could keep him there for a week.

Dredd dropped his free hand down to his boot and pulled the knife free. The broad, serrated edge slipped into a seam between two panels on the magoon's shaft, and with a savage twist Dredd had the thing open. He raised the knife and stabbed it down into a maze of exposed wiring.

There was a fizzing whine and the magoon fell away. Dredd whipped the Lawgiver around and put a bullet through a man who was aiming a second one at him, then headshot another who was arming a charge. "Jennig!" he roared, racing towards the *Elektra*. "Open fire! Drive them away from those charges!"

Elektra Maru's deck began to come apart, kicking up in clouds of splinters as spit gun fire raked across it. Blue-clad workers fell back, dead or injured or blinded by splinters, it no longer mattered.

He had to keep those charges from being set off.

Up on the *Elektra*'s bridge, Atia Borla could see the Mega-City Judge belting across the *Mystere* towards her ship. Dredd jumped, leaping the gap between the two vessels, landing easily on the deck. Her workers were already scattering.

If she didn't act now, everything would be ruined. She'd be in the brig when the plague came for her.

Before having the demo charges handed out, she'd switched them all to remote control. She hoped to set them all off when they were all in place and everyone was under cover, but that wasn't to be. She hoped history would forgive her for the sacrifices she was about to make.

The remote had a cover protecting the single button. She flipped the cover up and pressed the key.

Brilliant flashes erupted around the *Elektra Maru*.

A couple went off on the deck, where her people had dropped the explosives, and sent great clouds of splinters into the air. The rest detonated where they had been set, making bridges fly apart and the great braces near the prow shatter and collapse in on themselves. In a single second, nearly every link between the *Elektra Maru* and her neighbour ships turned to fire and whirling shrapnel.

One of the braces hadn't had its charges set properly. Dredd had shot the men there.

The deck was covered in dead and injured mutants, those shot by the skippers men and the many, many more who had been too close to the exploding demo charges. But the ship was free.

"Back us out," she told her helmsman. "Nudge the stern-ward vessels aside. If they've any wits at all they'll let us go."

With a grumble of long unused engines, the *Elektra Maru* began to rip its way out of the cityship.

Dredd had been close to a charge when it had gone off. The blast had rolled him across the deck and slammed him into the gunwales. His head felt as though someone had hammered it flat and his right arm would need some work when he got back to the Meg. He hoped the Speed-Heal machines were up and running.

He struggled up and opened his right hand, letting the Lawgiver drop into his left. Most of his targets were already down. The deck of the *Elektra Maru* was on fire in a dozen places, the ancient wood burning through and churning black smoke into the air.

The ship was moving.

Dredd could feel it dragging backwards, tearing the last of its links free. A mesh bridge snapped like stretched rubber only a few metres from him, and went whistling back to slam into *Mystere*. The engines were thundering, kicking spray high over the deck, and the whole vessel was beginning to shudder under his boots.

There was an awful sound from near the bow, a deafening shriek of stressed metal. He spun to see that one of the braces hadn't been blown apart and was gradually ripping its way free of the *Maru's* hull. It was twisting backwards on its huge bolts, the girders bending with long, agonised metallic moans.

Deck timbers shattered and spun across the deck.

Dredd started to head towards the bridge. There was a chance he could stop this if he could bring these lethal idiots to heel.

• • •

Borla watched Dredd running towards her. "Lock the bridge doors!"

The helmsman was cursing steadily, working the ships throttles. The days when the bridge merely signalled the speed commands to the engine room had been long gone before *Elektra*'s keel had been laid down, but even with sail-by-wire, the ship was massively slow to react.

The remaining brace was still holding. It was forcing *Elektra* over at an angle.

"Helmsman!" Borla yelled. "Full power, or we'll never break away!"

"She'll go into the ships sternward! They'll never move in time!"

She ran over to him and shoved the throttle back herself. "Full reverse!"

Behind Dredd, the last brace exploded.

The entire ship seemed to shift sideways. He looked back and saw the brace twisting apart, the great square base slamming up out of its mounts. The whole assembly seemed to teeter in the air for a long second, and then it crumpled down through *Elektra*'s gunwales and into the space between the ships.

Seconds later, *Elektra Maru*'s hull ground sickeningly against that of the *Waterloo Sunset*, on the portside. The deck tilted violently, sending Dredd sprawling towards the gunwales again.

The *Elektra Maru* was heeling over between the two ships. The helmsman was hauling on the throttles and manhandling the rudders for all he was worth, but it wasn't doing any good. "Cross-current!" he screamed. "It's got the prow!"

Borla was hanging onto a control throne to avoid being slung clear across the bridge. She could feel the ship sliding out from under her. The huge, complex shape of the city-ship had always set up lethal currents for kilometres around, but as long as it stayed as one, the relatively fluid structure of its multiple hulls settled into a stable system.

But the *Elektra* was breaking that system.

Without warning, the current changed direction. The ship tilted massively to starboard and the bow tore into *Mystere*'s flank.

The current was shaking *Elektra Maru* from side to side like a dog shaking a rat. As soon as Dredd felt the ringing impact against the *Mystere* die away, the *Elektra*'s bow was already heading towards the *Waterloo Sunset*.

He got back onto his feet and hung onto the gunwale. The ship was tilted over at almost forty-five degrees. It had moved back out of formation by nearly a quarter of its length, and that was bringing it into contact with the ships behind. Its stern was hammering into their bows.

The ship was lost. Dredd was no sailor, but he could feel it through his boots. *Elektra Maru* was coming apart and there wasn't a gruddamned thing he could do about it.

Borla was on the deck of the bridge. The last impact had flung her from the seat and against the wall.

The bridge was in chaos. Half the crew were still at their boards, trying everything they could to slow the vessel's destruction, the other half were screaming and banging at the locked doors. The helmsman had slumped across the throttles; the last impact had been enough to fling his head fatally against the controls.

Borla got to her feet. She felt the ship swaying, wallowing, but suddenly the violent side-to-side rocking had ceased.

Maybe the *Elektra* was clear, she thought wildly. Then a groan echoed throughout the vessel, from prow to stern, almost as if the ship knew it was dying.

The bow had been destroyed by the repeated slamming against the nearest ships and seawater was rushing into the forward compartments. Hundreds of people must have already drowned, if they hadn't been crushed by the impacts.

The *Elektra Maru* groaned again, and dipped forwards.

That was when the two ships at the back hit it square in the stern, and drove underneath her.

When the ships collided, Dredd was already on the *Mystere*. He'd jumped across and only just been able to grab a railing on the other ship. It was Philo Jennig who'd pulled him up.

The noise of the collision was incredible, awful. Jennig was staring at the *Elektra Maru* in utter horror. Even Dredd heard himself cursing in shock.

The *Elektra Maru* was going up on her bow.

The two ships behind had slammed into its stern with crushing force, but they had been lower in the deck than the *Elektra*. Their forward momentum had driven them clear under the stricken vessel's stern.

Elektra's shattered bow had gone completely into the Black Atlantic, and stopped almost dead. Dredd watched as the whole vast length of the ship, shedding crewmen and debris and tonnes of noisome black water, went tilting up over his head.

He saw the propellers still spinning as the ship reached vertical. Then the superstructure ripped free and began to fall, tearing a path down through the deck.

The ship twisted in place, propellers still whirling, sheets of flame billowing from the drives. Then it began to tilt over the rest of the way.

It went over like a felled tree, gaining momentum as it did, thousands of tonnes of steel and wood and screaming, dying mutants soaring sideways and slamming, with ear-splitting force, into the deck of the *Mystere*.

18. FALLOUT

Peyton was still on the *Venturer* when the *Elektra Maru* came down. He wasn't in the office any more, as there was nothing more he could do there. He'd moved himself into the small cot room that adjoined the office and taken up residence on the bunk.

He was running out of time.

The disease had progressed swiftly in his system. Already he was a mass of rashes and he felt as though he were choking, as though the life were already being squeezed out of his lungs.

Eight minutes previously he had injected himself with the contents of a gas pressure syringe. The drug was the product of a short, extremely hasty burst of work in a completely new direction. Peyton would have preferred to work for longer on it, but he wasn't sure how much longer he had. Anyway, the lack of oxygen to his brain was affecting his thought processes.

He lay on his back, shivering violently, feeling waves of pain wash down him from the top of his head to the soles of his feet. He was hoping that the nurse wouldn't come in before the bacteria went into cascade suicide. He simply didn't have the strength to explain to anyone what he'd done.

As he lay there, he felt a strange sensation. At first he wondered if it was something to do with the disease, but he quickly realised that there was something physical going on. A vibration had run through the *Venturer*'s hull as though it had been shoved, hard.

There was another. Peyton tried to sit up, to call for someone to tell him what was going on, but he was too weak.
There was too much bacteria in his system.

More thumps, faster. And a noise, distant through the *Venturer*'s walls. Screaming. The other patients were screaming.

Something terrible was happening to the cityship. Peyton
knew that with a sudden, terrified clarity, just as the neurotoxin washed into his bloodstream, swallowing him in a
flare of agonised darkness.

The Old Man was close to the *Elektra Maru* when it fell. He
was on the same side of the cityship, and maybe three-
quarters of the way along its length. He couldn't have said
which ship he was on at the time, and he didn't really care.
It was the people on them that mattered, not the words
etched into pieces of their hull plating.

He had been making a final pilgrimage through the city.
Like Peyton, he would have liked to have spent more time
doing it, but simply didn't know how much time he had.
That was always the way with the most important things,
he told himself. They always got left until last. But if they
got done first, they wouldn't have been important. It was a
puzzle he no longer had time to solve.

The people he'd met along the way had been glad to see
him. Many had offered him gifts, and asked him to sit with
them and tell them what was going to happen. Most had
just shaken his bony hands and wept, and told him that
they were glad they had seen him, this one last time.

A lot of people aboard *Sargasso* believed they were going
to die.

He had not taken the gifts, and anyone expecting his
usual cryptic answers had been disappointed too. He had
tried to reassure people wherever he went, and he believed
that, quite often, it had worked.

While most of *Sargasso*'s component vessels were very
densely populated, there would always be parts of it that
were not. The Old Man sometimes walked through ships

with no one on them at all, or with just a few work crews who would wave at him and carry on. Very rarely he was challenged, but only because the places he was about to go were not safe. It had never been difficult to simply take another route.

It had been on one of these seemingly random detours when he had found the Warchild.

That, of course, had been the other reason for his pilgrimage. He had been following the ripples left by the Warchild in the background of his mind.

The weapon hadn't moved for a long time, since just after it had been damaged. The Old Man hadn't known exactly where it was, or when he'd find it. He just knew he would. Sometimes, things came to him that way.

He had stopped to drink some water as it ran down the pipes in the hull-space of a giant chem-tanker. The water had been sweet and cool, and as the Old Man let his heavy head fall back to swallow it, he had seen the Warchild crouched in the gantry above him.

"Aha," he whispered. "There you are. I've been looking for you."

The Warchild didn't move. It was still badly damaged, with its arm wrecked and what looked like a catalogue of other injuries. It looked to the Old Man as if the weapon had fallen from somewhere very high. Its eyes were open, but it saw nothing. It simply didn't have any eyelids.

The Old Man didn't move either, He stood, looking up at the nightmare of exposed bone and white-leather flesh above him, and just watched. In his mind, his odd, mutant mind, the patterns it formed gradually fell away, layer by layer. It was as if the Warchild became a blueprint in his brain, a diagram. A complex artefact whose secrets were as open to him as a road map.

It took a long time.

Finally, the Old Man blinked and allowed a smile to creep over his face. "Well," he thought. "Somebody really did the number on you, didn't they?"

He had discovered something very interesting about the Warchild.

That was when the *Elektra Maru* fell over.

He had felt the impacts of the ship slamming against its neighbours, but only vaguely, like the grumbles of a distant storm. But when the *Elektra* twisted on her broken bow and toppled over into the *Mystere*, a great wave had crashed outwards from the collision. It hammered into the ship the Old Man and the Warchild were on, and sent it banging hard into the next vessel along.

The hull-space rang like a titanic gong, and suddenly the Old Man was being showered with kilos of ancient rust. He had to steady himself against the wall to avoid being shaken off his feet, and the rust-storm made him duck his head and close his eyes to avoid being blinded.

When he opened them again, the Warchild was standing in front of him.

It hadn't attacked and hadn't tried to camouflage itself, although the mimetic cells in its skin were sending subtle patterns across its body in a self-test routine. Its rough ball of a head tilted this way and that, as if slowly shaking itself awake. As the Old Man watched, its remaining arm-blade extended, hinging out and forwards until it extended a metre in front of its hand, almost touching the floor.

Without warning, it erupted into motion. The arm whipped out, too fast to follow.

The Old Man stepped aside and the tip of the blade whined past his face.

The cityship was still shaking. Noises filtered through the metal of the ship's hull.

The Warchild had taken a few steps back, confused. Its thoughts – no, its algorithms and programs – were still in turmoil. It simply couldn't understand why the target in front of it had not been subdued. It tried again, its blade darting out, but finding nothing but air.

Unluckily for the Old Man, the third attack coincided with the explosion caused by the *Elektra Maru*, now a twisted and broken wreck, slamming back through the two smaller ships behind it and crashing into the *Kraken*.

The wave this caused slammed into the ship on which the Warchild and the Old Man fought. The Warchild skidded forwards and the Old Man, knocked off his footing by the impact, spread his arms to catch it. It was a kind of reflex.

For a moment, they embraced like wounded brothers. Then the Warchild withdrew its blade from the Old Man's chest.

"Oh," he said, watching as it scrambled away. "That wasn't exactly what I'd planned…"

Gethsemane Bane was on the central bridge when the *Elektra Maru* took out the *Kraken*. She was there with Quint and Judge Vix, watching in utter horror as the destruction played out below her.

The fall of the food ship onto the *Mystere* had been enough to fling them all off their feet. Bane had seen it come down, had stayed with her eyes fixed on it as the superstructure had torn free of its mountings and ripped its way down the vertical deck. She had resolved not to see it strike the *Mystere*, to look away as the ships connected so she wouldn't have the image of their destruction embedded permanently in her mind. But when the moment came, she couldn't turn away. Couldn't even close her eyes. So she saw it all: the food ship slamming into the *Mystere* with such force that a great sheet of deck simply folded up around it, crushing dozens of habs and sending others spinning and whirling into the air, trailing pieces of gantry, bits of deck and occupants. Hundreds must have died in that second.

Then the wave hit. The massive wave had been sent skating through the hulls by the death of the *Elektra*. It had sent the *Putin* sideways about ten metres and tilted it over several degrees. That didn't make too much of a difference on deck, but on the bridge everyone who wasn't strapped down hit the floor and rolled.

Quint was on his feet first, already hauling himself back to the comms board as the ship tilted back the other way in the swell. He was yelling commands into the microphone, trying desperately to minimise the damage. Judge Vix had hit the deck and stayed there, on her back, breathing hard. Bane looked across at her and saw fresh blood soaking into her bandages.

She reached up to the rim of the porthole and pulled herself upright. Outside, the wreckage of the *Elektra* was being dragged back along the deck of the *Mystere* by the current, scouring it clean of structure. Bane could see tiny figures running like insects in every direction, and watched in horror as hundreds of them were caught by the *Elektra* and swept away.

Judge Dredd must have been one of those figures, if he had even lived that long.

The deck was shuddering under her feet, convulsions rippling through the *Sargasso*'s structure as the waves punched outwards from the collision point. She had to hold on tight to the rim of the port so as not to be thrown aside.

Finally, the *Elektra* came away from the *Mystere*. The part of it that had been in the water finally succumbed to drag and current, and pulled the rest away down into the Atlantic. Bane saw it topple sideways, taking a tangle of structures with it from the *Mystere*, and thump down into the water. A fountain of grey spume erupted upwards as it hit and went under.

"It's gone," she whispered. "It went under the water. It's gone."

"Ow," said Vix, very quietly.

Bane couldn't turn away from the porthole. Something hadn't happened yet, but her shocked brain couldn't work out what it was. When something goes into the water, she thought wildly, it sinks. If it's got air in it, it floats. But if it's heavy and it's got air in it, first it sinks, then it–

The *Elektra* came up again.

Like a drowning man reaching up into life and air one last time, the *Elektra Maru* roared back up to the surface. Its shattered bow speared upwards between the two ships that had battered its stern, as if in revenge, and then it was flung over again by the current. It tore a ragged gap between the two smaller vessels, sending their habs sprawling into the sea and finally, just before the ocean took it forever, it crunched into the nose of the *Kraken*.

The *Kraken* held a fusion torus. Bane was looking right at it when the magnetic containment field, holding a ring of sun-hot plasma in check, failed.

Judge Dredd was not on the *Mystere* when the *Elektra Maru* shattered its deck. Neither was Philo Jennig.

Both men had their own particular insight into what was about to happen when the food ship started to rise over their heads. Jennig had been a sailor all his life, he told Dredd later, and had never set foot on dry land. He had seen ships sink before and knew the way they died. He had known that this disaster, while doubtless the biggest he had ever witnessed, was going to play out in the same manner.

Judge Dredd, on the other hand, was not a sailor. But he had seen enough things come apart in his time.

As the *Elektra* began to tilt both men had been in full retreat, sprinting across the *Mystere*'s deck and yelling at anyone who would listen to do the same. A lot of Sargassans followed suit on reflex – had they seen these two men, the respected skipper's man and the feared lawman from the Mega-City, making a stand on the *Mystere*, they would have done the same and died with them. By knowing when to back out, Dredd and Jennig saved countless lives.

Dredd had his back to the *Kraken* when the fusion torus failed, which probably spared his bionic eyes some maintenance. Fusion reactors that suffer catastrophic failure do not explode. The plasma reaction they sustain is so volatile that as soon as the magnetic field begins to waver it simply breaks down. That breakdown could sometimes be lethal. When the *Kraken*'s reactor was struck by the *Elektra Maru*, its shattered magnets released, for an instant of time too small to measure, a horizontal tongue of plasma as hot as the surface of a star. It flashed out to port, impossibly bright, carving a glowing track ten metres high through the *Kraken*'s hull from bow to stern. The flash melted the hull of the next ship along, too, and dozens of mutants were rendered blind by the flare.

Sargasso got off lightly. Had the plasma lashed out into the water – if the *Kraken* had been heeled over, say – the steam explosion would have been enough to take the entire city out of the water.

As soon as they saw the flash and heard the screams, Dredd and the deputy realised just what had happened. At that time, though, it was only Jennig who realised the full implications.

Councillor Atia Borla, far from taking her people to safety across the sea, had instead doomed the cityship *Sargasso* to collide with *Abraxis*.

The immediate destruction had ended by the time Judge Peyton had woken up.

He lay still for a time, wondering what had happened to him. Realisation only came slowly, along with sensation. It was a minute or two before he could even see.

After a time he was able to sit up. He could still hear screams and shouting from outside the office, but he couldn't face that yet. He felt as though he'd been run over by a Mo-Pad.

He was, however, alive. Against all the odds.

The gas-syringe was still lying on the floor where he'd dropped it. He hadn't remembered that, but when he looked at it he knew that by the time he'd injected himself, he was so weak with the infection that he hadn't even been able to put it back on the desk.

He rolled up his sleeve. His skin was still corpse-white, but the rashes were fading. With the bacteria dead in his bloodstream the allergic reaction to their presence was dying too.

"Grud," he whispered, "I'm gonna get stuff named after me..."

He hauled himself up, staggered to the door and called for a nurse.

When Dredd got to the central bridge the place was in complete mayhem. Skipper Quint was running up and down the line of control boards, roaring orders as he went. Vix was lying in the corner with her bandages soaked in blood. It looked as though every operator was doing at least three things at once. Luckily, several of them had enough arms for it.

Bane had been darting about with a fire extinguisher, putting out small fires in the bridge's wiring. As Dredd stepped through the hatch she almost dropped it in surprise.

"Drokk! Where did you spring from?" She set the extinguisher down and ran over to him. "Are you okay?"

"Arm's broken," he snapped. "But it'll keep. What's the situation?"

"Not good." Quint stopped by a nearby control board and stabbed at several keys. The response he saw on the monitor made him growl under his breath. "We're having to shut down the rest of the core drives."

Dredd gave Bane a questioning glance. "*Sargasso*'s too fluid to survive the stress," she told him. "If the other drives keep going, *Kraken* will start to fall back. That'll have the whole quadrant pulling backwards on the rest of *Sargasso* and eventually we'll come apart."

"Got to be a phased shutdown," said Quint. "Take everything in stages, compensate for the currents and the damage. It'll take a while."

Dredd nodded. "How's Vix?"

"Unconscious," said Bane. "She fell really hard when the wave hit us. Dredd?"

"Hm?"

"I know you did everything you could."

Dredd scowled. "Not enough. Quint, how's this mess going to alter our course?"

Quint had obviously reached a point in the process where he had to stop and wait for a while. "If it was just an engine shutdown, we wouldn't have a problem. Under regular circumstances it takes a day to even start slowing down."

He gestured out of the long window. "But all this? We've got new crosscurrents, pieces of debris still attached and dragging us back, hulls taking on water and slowing the whole system. We're even losing hulls from the outer edges. We've had to send out scavenger ships to pick up survivors. It's chaotic." The skipper folded his arms and turned to Dredd. "Our best guess? *Abraxis* will hit us in about three hours."

"Then we haven't got long," Dredd replied. "Quint, start getting your best crews together. I'll need you and anyone relevant down in the council chamber in thirty minutes. That means keep the council out."

"What are you going to do?" Bane asked, her eyes wide. "Abandon ship?"

He shook his head. "We're going to sink the *Abraxis*."

19. THE RETURN OF METHUSELAH

The council chamber filled up quickly. By the time Mako Quint had brought in all the captains and skipper's men he needed, there was barely anywhere to sit.

Dredd preferred to stand. He took a position in front of the benches and waited for everyone to settle. Although time was short, he needed them all with him on this. Going in hard would accomplish nothing.

He'd taken a moment to splint up his broken arm. It was a temporary repair, but it would get him through the day.

It was Quint who spoke first. "I'll get straight to the point. Since the *Elektra Maru* went down we've had to initiate a phased shutdown of all engines, just to avoid *Sargasso* being torn to pieces. We've got a handle on that now, and given enough time we'll start off again with a redistributed drive load." He looked across at Dredd.

"Problem is, you don't have that time," Dredd grated. "*Abraxis* is on a new heading, but you know how long it takes these crates to turn around. It'll hit you in three hours."

Unlike Dredd's previous time in the council chamber, there was no immediate outbursts from the men and women on the benches – a few sharp intakes of breath, but little more. This, Dredd reflected, was the correct way to run a community. People capable of making the decisions, making them for those who weren't.

"We have a choice," said Quint. "We can break the *Sargasso*, take everyone we can to the outermost hulls and blow their links. We could get maybe thirty per cent of the population away on those vessels, and then move the others to the forward hulls. There's a chance *Abraxis* would be slowed enough by the first impacts to not drive straight through."

Bane, who had a place on the benches with the other captains, raised a hand. "Aren't there more Warchild units on the *Abraxis*?"

"Two," Dredd agreed. "At least. So the second choice is to sink the *Abraxis*."

That did ellicit more of a response. There were shouts of disbelief, and worse. The idea of sinking a cityship, even a pirate vessel full of corpses, was anathema to men and women who had spent their whole lives trying to keep one afloat.

"What about the Warchild on *Sargasso*?" one man yelled above the din. "And the plague?" Dredd fixed him with a glare.

"The *Abraxis* will kill you a lot faster than the plague will," he snarled. "As for the Warchild, leave it to me. That creep's going down, and I'm taking it there."

"I've seen your Warchild," said a voice behind him.

He turned. There, standing by the hatchway, was a very Old Man. His skin was dark, like ancient oak, and his hair was pure white. He wore a dingy pair of safari shorts and a fish-skin shirt, and dozens of totems were strung around his scrawny neck. He was so old, he looked like a skeleton draped in brown leather.

Everyone in the room, barring Dredd himself, gasped.

Gethsemane Bane jumped down from her place at the bench and ran across the room. She threw her arms around the new arrival. "Old Man! They said you were missing!"

"Guess I've been found," he smiled.

Bane smiled at Dredd. "This is our Old Man," she said. "He's our, well… He tells us things. He's like a teacher."

"More like a shaman," said Quint. "Although sometimes I think he's the only one with any wits on this city."

"We've met," said Judge Dredd.

Bane blinked at him. "Excuse me?"

"We certainly have," the old man grinned. "How long has it been, Dredd? Since you picked me up by the scruff of the neck and threw me out of your city?"

Suddenly, the council chamber was very silent.

"Twenty-two years," replied Dredd. "I never forget a case."

"A case?" Bane was aghast. "You *judged* him?"

"His name," Dredd told her, "is Meredith Caine, aka Methuselah. A mutant noted for his extreme persistence in staying alive. And certain empathic abilities."

"That's not exactly true–"

"Whatever you call them, Caine, you used them to con a lot of people out of a lot of money." He turned to Bane. "Your shaman was at the centre of a citywide cult. It took us three months to shut him down. Psi Division couldn't prove his psionic powers, but his mutant DNA was enough to convict him."

The Old Man drew himself up. "You sentenced me to exile!"

"You were judged according to the Law!" thundered Dredd. "There were thirteen suicides among your cult followers. People leaping off city blocks because they thought your magic would bring them eternal life!"

Caine lowered his head. "I know," he said. "I did those things, and I'm sorry. I heard the screams of those thirteen people, even from outside the city walls. They've stayed with me forever."

"And this is where you've been hiding out?"

"Dredd!" Bane rounded on him, still staying protectively near the Old Man. "Whatever he did in the past, that's nothing to do with us now. The Old Man's been the heart of this cityship for over twenty years. He's been more like blood to me than any real relative."

"Speaking of blood," Dredd pointed at Caine's shirt. "Cut yourself?"

"I said I'd seen your Warchild," the Old Man replied. "Trouble is, it saw me at the same time." He lifted his shirt.

A rough bandage had been tied around his chest, and blood was soaking through it. "We had a little 'disagreement'."

Instantly the Old Man was surrounded. Bane grabbed a spare chair from the side of the room and eased the Old Man down into it. Someone else was keeping pressure on the wound, yet another man shouted for a medikit.

Caine seemed quite irritated by the attention. "For grud's sake," he snapped, brushing their hands away, "don't you have more important things to be doing?"

Quint gritted his teeth. "I have to agree," he said. "Despite our feelings for this–" he threw Dredd a vicious glance, "*man* – we have to decide."

"No!" Caine shouted. "No! Gethsemane Bane, you said yourself – what's in the past is in the past. None of that matters now. What matters is that Dredd's plan has to succeed!"

"But–"

"Follow him!" The Old Man's skinny finger was pointed at Dredd. "Follow the lawman, if you want *Sargasso* to survive. Don't fret about the plague, that's already been dealt with. Just get in your ships and go!"

For the next hour, *Sargasso*'s harbours thundered with activity. Every serviceable vessel, barring those that were out picking up survivors of the *Elektra Maru* disaster, was being loaded with demolition charges.

According to Bane, the charges were normally used for blasting massive pieces of salvage to a more manageable size. Dredd could only hope that they would be enough to fatally damage the *Abraxis*. In the plan's favour, it had only taken one rogue ship to threaten the entire survival of *Sargasso*. Big enough holes in all the right places should put paid to the pirate city, too.

Just in case, Dredd had convinced Quint to prepare a surprise. But he still didn't know if it would work.

There would have been no profit in telling Captain Bane that, however. She was with him on the quayside, helping her crew load demo charges onto the *Golgotha*. Dredd was putting as many as feasible onto *Seawasp*.

"I still can't believe you judged him," she growled.

"He committed a crime. While his acolytes were leaping from tweenblock plazas, he was buying himself a pleasure skimmer."

"He's not like that now."

"Nothing's to say a perp can't be reformed, Bane. I just don't have much faith in the process." He picked up another case of charges and set it onto *Seawasp*'s floor. The vessel sank a little lower into the water. "Looks like that's about it. Are you done?"

"Almost." Bane handed another case to one of her crew, a young redheaded man with far too many elbows in each arm. She leaned on the gunwale and looked down at him. "Is this really going to work?"

"We have a chance."

She looked away and hugged herself. "A chance. What's your stake in this, Dredd? Why are you even here? *Sargasso*'s not your city."

"No," he said. "But the mess it's in came from mine. That makes it my job to clear it up."

Seawasp was out of the harbour first, going not much faster than a scavenger with all the demo charges weighing it down. Dredd took the little vessel out and then waited while the flotilla began to form up behind him. Up ahead, partially enveloped in a vast cloud of spray and flies, *Abraxis* looked like a mountain of grimy metal sliding across the sea towards him.

He opened his helmet comms and patched into *Sargasso*'s central bridge. "Quint, we're forming up. Should be under way in ten."

"That doesn't give you long to do the job, Dredd."

"Never mind that. Have you got the present ready?"

"All set to be unwrapped. By the way, I've someone here who needs a word."

Dredd felt his teeth grinding together. "Put her on."

"Vix here, Dredd. Going fishing?"

"Yeah, real pleasure cruise," he snapped. "How are you doing?"

"I'll live. It doesn't hurt as long as I don't breathe."

He couldn't help but shrug. "So don't breathe."

"Ha," she said flatly. "My report to Judge Buell is going to be a real doozy, you know that? Anyway, I've just got confirmation from Judge Peyton. He beat the plague, just like your Old Man said."

"I'm impressed."

"I hate to admit it, but so am I. Seems the disease's final stage kills with a dose of neurotoxin. Same stuff as in the needles. Peyton came up with an antitoxin, not a cure as such. The disease cures itself, but the antitoxin stops you dying before the bacteria do."

Behind him, the scavengers were in formation. He looked to starboard and saw Bane wave at him from the bridge of the *Golgotha*. "Guess that means the SJS gets something useful out of this after all. A defence against the Warchild poison."

"Dredd? If I hadn't seen your Psi-Division reports, I'd say you were reading my mind. Vix out."

Dredd let the mic snap back up out of sight and raised his right hand high. In response, the sirens on every vessel behind him – over forty little ships, from scavengers and fishing smacks to repair platforms with spare aquajets bolted to their blunt sterns – ripped out across the water. It was a mournful noise, but edged with anger, in the way some of the captains were hammering the controls. A stuttering, vengeful howl.

It was time to go and sink a city.

20. AREA DENIAL

The flotilla moved out on Dredd's command.

Bane was at the helm of the *Golgotha*, and it felt good to be back. Dray was handling the navigation board, while Angle and Can-Rat – his ribs still tightly bound – were down on deck, readying the demo charges.

The only empty station was down in the engine room. *Golgotha* would be able to make the party without Orca's tinkering, but it would miss him. Bane missed him already. There was, however, an unspoken rule already being enforced aboard the scavenger, and that was not to mention the loss.

"Grud," Dray whispered. "D'you hear that?"

Bane frowned. "I don't hear anything." In reply, Dray just nodded and gestured to stern.

Of course, Bane thought. The *Sargasso*'s engines weren't running. Every other time she'd left the harbour the noise of the core drives had been a roar, almost deafening. Spray had soaked the decks, made the windshield run with grubby, foamy water. Now there was nothing past the sound of *Golgotha*'s engines and those of the other ships around it. Just a sluggish wake of rolling swells, tipping them back and forth as they left *Sargasso* behind.

There were two formations, one from each harbour. As it turned out, most of the port formation were scavenger vessels, because they tended to congregate in the port barge. The starboard crowd were more varied, with a lot of fishing vessels, maintenance sleds, and repair barges. And Judge Dredd, wallowing along in front in his little powder-blue speedboat. Bane hoped that, far above her head, some kind of spy satellite was looking down on them all and taking picture after picture. Because the world deserved to see this. It was a sight not to be missed.

Out past Dredd, the *Abraxis* loomed out of a cloud of oily spray; a dead thing, but still moving, bringing its corpses and its flies and its ravening monsters to crush her home. Bane found her hands tightening on the controls.

"Not on my watch, you bastich," she whispered, and eased the throttles forward, just a little.

It was going to be tough, she knew that. The currents around a cityship's hulls were something to be feared, the reason every vessel coming in to dock at *Sargasso*'s harbours went in wide. Bane was hoping that *Abraxis* would throw out less of a swell, but if she'd had the slightest doubt that what they were going to do wasn't lethally dangerous she would have been fooling herself.

The two formations were closing up, stretching into long lines of vessels and closing in towards the *Abraxis* like the claws of a spit-crab. Up on *Golgotha*'s deck, Can-Rat was helping Angle strap himself to one of the starboard cranes.

Bane glanced across at Dray. "Can you take her for a second? I'll be back before the swell hits."

She darted out of the hatch, not even bothering to throw on her slicker, and clattered down the steps. When she reached the crane Angle gave her a lazy mock salute. "Captain on deck!"

"Yeah, yeah." She slipped behind him and helped Can-Rat tighten the straps until Angle wheezed. "Hey, a guy's got to breathe!"

"Breathe yes, fall off the damn crane, no." She looked ahead. *Abraxis* filled half the horizon. "This is it. Remember, throw them on – the magnets will be enough to hold them. If we start rolling towards *Abraxis* we'll swing the crane back out of the way. Get ready for a rough ride."

He grinned. "The rougher the better, captain. You know that."

"Ah, you wish." She waved him away. "Canny, you okay with this?"

Can-Rat, sensibly, had also lashed himself to the crane with a long cable. He'd be able to get all over the deck if he needed to, but a freak wave wouldn't be able to wash him overboard. "Yes, captain. Well, I've no choice, have I?"

She almost slapped his shoulder, then remembered his broken ribs and held back. "That's the spirit," she grinned then paused. "You don't, kind of, feel anything's going to, you know…"

Can-Rat shook his head. "Maybe if I was less terrified."

Bane couldn't ask for more than that. "Don't throw too hard," she yelled at Angle, then turned and ran back to the bridge.

Dray was waiting to hand the controls over. "Here we go."

Dredd's boat was level with the first hull in *Abraxis*.

He was ignoring it, powering on past. Amazing how he could operate the throttles with a broken ulna, but she'd always heard Mega-City Judges were built tough. Peyton had tested cures on himself while he was dying of Warchild plague. Vix had taken a monomolecular sword across the ribs and still had the energy to be suspicious, sarcastic and unpleasant.

Golgotha was fourth in line now the formation had closed up. Bane was watching the ships in front, seeing how they reacted to the swells and crosscurrents. Dredd's boat wasn't worth watching, it was too light, but the *Valentino* was next along and that had almost the same tonnage as *Golgotha*.

"Okay Dray, get him up." At Bane's command, Dray began to work the crane's controls. Can-Rat had already switched them from deck operation to the bridge. Bane watched as Angle was hoisted up and out over the side.

He had a demo charge in his hand and two more of the head-sized devices dangling from his belt.

She saw him swing his arms up and hurl the charge forward. It hit the nearest hull-side and attached itself there. "Yes! First blood!"

Golgotha was trying to get away from her. Bane was watching the *Valentino*, trying to keep her eyes off what Angle was doing. The other scavenger was heeling violently to port, and then abruptly it swung around and to starboard. The captain brought it swiftly back to heel, and when *Golgotha* passed over the same spot Bane was ready for the change.

Angle had thrown all three charges he had with him. Dray brought him back to the deck for a reload.

Behind her, a fishing smack was taken too far by a cross-current. Bane heard the screams first then looked back to see the ship sliding sideways along the hull line. Seconds later it went over, shattering as she watched. The next scavenger in line rode right over it and only just avoided having the bottom of its hull torn open.

Bane felt the ship slide horribly sideways, quite without warning. She cursed her lack of attention and hauled on the controls, dragging *Golgotha* back on course. On the deck, Can-Rat sprawled as the vessel went over at forty degrees, but scampered back to his feet and went back to handing charges to Angle.

Suddenly, in a moment of awful clarity, she realised the plan wasn't going to work.

All the charges were going onto the outer vessels of the pirate city. When they went off, *Abraxis* would shed those hulls like a slick-eel's old skin. But there still wouldn't be enough drag to stop the cityship before it collided with *Sargasso*. If anything, they were going to make *Abraxis* faster. Sleeker.

She opened the comm. "Dredd!"

"I'm busy, Bane."

"Dredd, this isn't going to fly! We're just going to take the outer hulls off!"

"I was beginning to think that myself. Okay, Bane, change of plan. We're going for the core drives."

Bane felt herself go cold. "We're *what*?"

Dredd's plan was simplicity itself. If you wanted a simple way of getting killed.

Send as many ships as possible into the *Abraxis*, into the narrow channels between the hulls. Negotiate those channels until they reached the core drives. Plaster the noses of the drives with as many charges as possible, in order to knock out the fusion cores. At worst, if any ship got that far, it could stop the main engines of *Abraxis* and give the *Sargasso* maybe enough breathing room to get out of the way. At best, they might even cause a steam explosion.

But that meant steering bulky, wallowing scavenger vessels between linked hulls hundreds of metres long, each one sailing only a few metres apart and riding on cross-currents that were stable only when compared to the nightmare undertows at the outer hulls.

It was suicide.

And it was their only chance.

Most of the vessels would never get between the pirate city's hulls in the first place. Those that could assembled along the port side. *Golgotha*, as long as all the cranes were retracted, could just about make it.

Bane's stomach had turned into a small, hard knot the size of her fist. She couldn't even swallow properly. "C'mon, Dredd," she croaked. "Let's get it over with."

Almost as if he'd heard her, Dredd stood up in *Seawasp* and raised his hand.

"Here we go," said Dray quietly. "Nice working with you."

Bane didn't answer, just eased *Golgotha* forwards. Dredd was still alongside *Abraxis*, powering towards the stern. Suddenly, in a sheet of spray, he slung the little boat to starboard, disappearing between two enormous hulls.

The *Valentino* tried to go the same way, but its captain had judged the crossing a moment too late.

The scavenger almost made it. Then the starboard gunwales clipped the huge angular bow of the next hull in line. The impact caught the *Valentino* and battered it around, robbing it of speed. Suddenly, it couldn't get out of the way in time.

The pirate hull rode it down as if it wasn't there. Splinters of wood and plasteen spun across the space between the hulls. As Bane watched, bits of the *Valentino* began to surface alongside the *Abraxis* – a mast, half the bridge, part of the helmsman.

She looked away then took a deep breath, focussing every mutant sense she had, and slammed the *Golgotha* forwards. The next gap along leapt towards her and she hauled *Golgotha* over as it came past. Walls of metal raced past on either side and abruptly she was in darkness. The pirate city's deck was above her.

The second hull slammed into *Golgotha*'s stern and slung it around. Bane fought the throttles until the engines howled and brought the scavenger back into line.

Abraxis was still moving past her, but this time on either side and above. She turned all the searchlights on.

Bane let out a deep breath and waited. Another gap was coming up. Dredd wasn't in sight – he must have either gone further in or been ridden down by the cityship. Bane rolled her head around on her neck, trying to get the tension kinks out of her shoulders, then slammed the rudders over again.

This time she made it without even touching the sides.

"There!" Dray was pointing through the windshield. Several hulls ahead, something vast and round-nosed could be seen. Daylight, hazy in the spray, shone beyond it. If she wasn't looking right at a core drive, Bane would never see anything that looked more like one.

There was another massive impact on *Golgotha*'s stern. Bane couldn't help looking around just as a brilliant explosion lit up the underside of *Abraxis*'s hulls in every direction. Bane winced, remembering the pain of seeing the *Kraken*'s fusion torus go up. Only her extra eyelids had saved her from permanent blindness.

Out of the cloud of flame, the entire forward end of the *Melchior* spun out into the channel. The water shuddered and leapt under *Golgotha*. Bane had to drag hard on the rudders to avoid being slapped against the nearest hull by the shockwave.

Melchior had been struck by a hull and one of the demo charges on board had gone off.

Bane opened a general comms channel. "*Golgotha* to all vessels. Don't anyone else try to get in – we've got a core-drive in sight. If taking out one doesn't do the job, nothing will."

Dray was staring at her. "Cap'n, do you really think–"

"If this all goes to hell, maybe some of them can make it to shore." That was all she had to say on the matter. Her next action was to throttle *Golgotha* forwards.

When they got to the core drive, Dredd was already there. He was throwing demo charges up as high as he could, but they were heavy, and he was working with a broken arm. Bane told Dray to take Angle up as high as the crane would go.

She watched the lad going up, keeping *Golgotha* as steady as she could. The swell was awful and she was having to sail backwards to keep up with *Abraxis*. She wondered how far they were from *Sargasso*.

Angle had his arms full of charges. With his long, flexible limbs wrapped around as many as he could carry, he was still able to flick them underarm towards the core drive, even though the crane was swinging in every direction. *Golgotha* was wallowing badly and the motion was being transferred up the crane and being amplified by the height. With every swell, Angle was being sent ten metres forward and back.

He was throwing the charges when he was closest to the hull, and readying another on the backswing.

Bane saw him throw the last charge and wave wildly to be brought back down. She opened her mouth to ask Dray to do it when she saw part of the sky move oddly, high up between the pirate city's decks.

In happier times, she would have told herself that it was a drop of water running down the windshield, nothing more. Now, she knew exactly what it was. "Dredd! Warchild!"

As she yelled, it dropped down onto the deck.

Its camouflage shivered out, leaving it a white nightmare of armour and extended arm-blades. It saw Can-Rat and darted towards him. Bane heard herself scream.

Maybe Can-Rat's legendary ability to see trouble coming had returned, or maybe he was just lucky. Whatever the reason, he ducked once under the Warchild's blade and then, as it was whipping back for another blow, hurled himself over the gunwales.

Bane saw the cable go taut. She also saw a hands-length of Can-Rat's tail flopping on the deck.

Momentarily robbed of its target, the Warchild paused. Bane looked about wildly, trying to find Dredd. *Seawasp* had disappeared.

There was a heavy thump at the stern. Bane yelped. Hadn't Dredd told her that at least two Warchild units were loose on *Abraxis*? She turned to look, trying to see out of the stern ports, and then the windshield shattered.

The Warchild on the deck had put a blade clear through it.

Bane shrieked and dropped to the deck. The blade was slicing left and right, trying to decapitate her from outside. Dray cursed and fell aside, blood welling up from a thin line across his face. He'd taken the tip of the blade from jawline to nose.

Abruptly, the Warchild fell away. Something came down after it, something big and black and carrying a Lawgiver in its left hand.

Dredd had been on the roof.

Bane scrambled up and saw him fire at the Warchild – instead of a single bullet, the Lawgiver fired out about half a dozen, three of which caught the bioweapon across the chest. It staggered back, its skin flashing a wild pattern, its blades flailing.

Can-Rat was clambering back onto the deck.

The Warchild saw him and launched itself forwards. Dredd's gun flashed out another bullet, this time one that sizzled as it left a trail of fire through the air. It hit the Warchild in the head.

The bioweapon erupted into flames. The incendiary shell had turned it into a column of fire, lighting up the front of the core drive like a signal flare. The Warchild whirled away, howling. Dredd followed it and kicked it unceremoniously off the deck.

Bane snarled a wordless cry of fury and slammed the throttles open. *Golgotha* surged forwards over the stricken bioweapon and into the channel alongside the core drive. She felt a scrabbling as the Warchild went under the hull, still trying to rip its way in, then the propellers lurched and slowed. A second later, they spun back up.

Bane looked astern for just a moment and saw pieces of Warchild, still on fire, bobbing to the surface. Then the core drive was past them and they were into its wake.

The churning water took the scavenger and hurled it around, full circle, then sent it skating across a wild series of eddies. Bane whipped the rudders hard left, then hard right. She felt one of them come off. The ship went up on its stern, and then crashed back down in a blinding fountain of spray. With the windshield gone, Bane caught most of it in the face. Then they were clear.

Bane spat out foul Black Atlantic water, blinking it out of her eyes. *Golgotha* was still rotating slowly, but it was clear of the cityship's wake by a hundred metres or more.

By some miracle, they were free. Bane steadied the ship, stopping the rotation with the remaining rudder. As the vessel settled back to a straight course, the bridge hatch opened and Dredd ducked through. "Nice driving."

"Nice shooting." She had *Golgotha* on a wide course around the cityship. She could already see that it was frighteningly close to *Sargasso*. Dredd saw it too. Bane saw a tiny microphone drop down from his helmet.

"Dredd to all vessels. Get clear, we're blowing the charges in sixty seconds."

The ship was level with the multiple bows of *Abraxis*, drawing gradually past. Dredd gave the other vessels a time check on thirty, and then changed comm channel. "Quint?"

"I'm here. Glad to see some of you made it."

Bane wondered how many had, but she didn't ask.

"It's time," Dredd snarled. "Hit the button."

The charges went off.

Bane was looking back at *Abraxis* when the hulls blew. Everyone was. She saw a line of flickers race around the outer hull, each one sending out a great spray of metal and fire. *Abraxis* seemed to shiver from end to end. The deck turned hazy black as every feasting fly darted into the air.

Then the core drive blew, sending a brilliant flash of light erupting from the stern. Most of it was blocked by the cityship's vast bulk, but beams of it, for a tiny fraction of a second, strobed out from between the hulls like searchlights.

The outer hulls were starting to take on water. Great jagged holes had been torn into them. Many were on fire and smoke began to twist into the air. Bane saw one of the vessels begin to slide over sideways, ripping free of the deck above in a shower of debris and corpses.

A billowing cloud of flame spurted up from behind the cityship's bridge, surrounded by a wavefront of fragmented metal. There had been no steam explosion, but the dying fusion reaction must have caught a fuel store. In seconds, the whole rear section of *Abraxis* was ablaze.

It still wasn't going to be enough.

Dredd saw it too and cursed under his breath. He opened the comms again. "Quint? Time to deliver the present."

"Present?" asked Bane. "What present? Who's getting a–"

Something lashed out from *Sargasso*'s stern. Bane saw it carve a track through the water, impossibly fast, past the *Golgotha* and into the centre forward hull of *Abraxis*.

The hull lifted out of the water. When it came back down, the entire forward half of it was tumbling back in pieces. A shattering roar rippled out across the water, a disc of shockwave, and Bane felt it roll *Golgotha* hard as it struck.

The destroyed hull was digging down into the water. Its stern was up, like the *Elektra*'s had been, tearing upwards through the deck. Behind it, stealth-clad towers of habs were tumbling over like toys.

Abraxis was dying.

They'd done it.

21. GRUDSPEED

It would take hours for *Abraxis* to die. The cityship, small though it was compared with a leviathan like *Sargasso*, was still far too vast to go down all in one go. Bane estimated that it would be a day, maybe more, before it would finally slip beneath the surface.

By the time they got back to the harbour, the rest of the flotilla were already in. Out of more than forty ships, only eighteen returned. *Golgotha* was now one of only seven scavengers. Any real feelings of triumph were torn from her by the sight of all those empty berths in the port harbour.

Quint was on the quayside waiting for them to come in. He looked stricken. The loss of all those ships, all those crews, had taken its toll on him.

Skipper of a cityship had never been an easy job, but this was more than anyone should bear.

Bane helped Can-Rat and Angle down the gangplank first. Can-Rat had rebroken a number of his ribs on the way over *Golgotha*'s side, and the end of his tail was lost forever. Angle, after being whipped about on the end of a crane for the whole trip, had finally succumbed to the worst bout of seasickness Bane had ever seen strike anyone.

She had bandaged Dray's face on the way in. She sent him down next: as captain, she should be last off.

Dredd was waiting for her on deck. "Pretty fancy sailing," he said.

"Thanks." She knew it was as close to a compliment she was ever going to get from the man. "But it's not over, is it? The Warchild's still aboard, and we don't know where."

"Caine knows where."

It took her a few moments to realise that he was talking about the Old Man.

After the ships were all docked, Dredd went to find Mako Quint.

The skipper was on the bridge. Dredd found him standing at the long forward window, looking out over the undamaged portions of the cityship. He looked old.

As Dredd approached, the man glanced around. "We killed a city," he said, his voice flat and dead. "No one's ever killed a cityship before."

"It happens." Dredd folded his arms. "Better them than you."

"I've been doing this job too long. You know something? Back when I started as skipper, I would have looked at *Abraxis* and thought, wow, that's going to keep us in salvage forever. Now I can't even bring myself to look at it."

"That's command, Quint. You're in charge of people, and people die. That's the job." Dredd nodded sternwards. "Think on this: if you hadn't salvaged a hellfire torpedo all those years back, you wouldn't be standing here."

Quint was silent for a long time before he gave a bitter chuckle. "Well, if those Sovs will keep leaving bits of submarine lying about…"

"You came up with the goods, Quint. No one on this city will say you didn't."

"And you, Judge Dredd? For a Mega-City man, you're not a half-bad sailor."

"I'll keep the day job, thank. In the meantime, I need a word with your shaman."

The Old Man was up high, on top of one of the hab stacks. Dredd had to climb three ladders to get to him.

He was sitting cross-legged on the top hab, looking out at the *Abraxis*. The cityship was halfway gone, with several hulls almost vertical in the water, tearing their way gradually free and sinking below the oily waves. The process would continue for a while yet, but all the time it did the two cityships would be moving further apart.

"Judge Dredd," said Caine, not looking round. "Come to say hello?"

"I've come to find out where you saw the Warchild, Old Man." Dredd stood next to him, his boots planted firmly on the hab roof. A tangy and acidic breeze whipped up at him. "Which ship?"

"I don't know." Caine pointed vaguely forwards. "Some-where over there. But it's not important."

"I'll be the judge of that."

The Old Man looked up at him, squinting into the day-light. "You know how I work, Dredd? How I do what I do?"

"Some mutant ability, that's all I need to know. More than that, I couldn't care less."

Caine ignored him. "Patterns, Dredd. That's what it's all about. Everything makes patterns: you, me, the Warchild, this city, your city... Look deep enough, and you'll see the signs. You can find out anything about anything, if you can read the patterns right."

"And you can fool a lot of people out of their money if you get the mumbo-jumbo right, eh, Methuselah?"

Caine roared with laughter. "Yes, that too. But I found out something about your Warchild when we met. Something quite important."

"Okay, I'll bite." Dredd leaned close to Caine's face. "Impress me."

"It's dying."

There was a pause. "Go on."

The Old Man shrugged. "What more can I say? It has massive internal injuries, shrapnel wounds. Only one arm. From what I could see, it looked as though someone had dropped it from a great height. Or dropped something heavy on it." He sniffed. "Possibly both."

"I wonder." Dredd straightened, looking out over the city. "It can self-repair. We know that from Hellermann."

"Grud rest her damaged little soul. Only to a limited degree, and if it can ingest enough biomass. But past a certain point, the energy levels required for it to regenerate its structure are greater than it can gain, no matter how much it eats." The Old Man smiled a secret smile. "Hellermann would have told you that, I think."

"So it's dying. How long will it take?"

Caine gave a shrug. "Longer than I will."

"You look all right to me."

"Well," Caine shifted a little on the deck. "A man's heart should beat, don't you think? Mine hasn't since the Warchild put his claw through me. I rather miss the sound of it."

"Are you telling me you've been walking around for half a day without a heartbeat?"

The man nodded. "Ask your Judge Peyton, he seems rather good." Then he stretched and sighed. "No, there's no time. It's goodbye, I'm afraid."

Dredd was suddenly unsure of what he was seeing here. "Caine–"

"Do something for me, Judge. Tell Gethsemane Bane that one day, she'll skipper this city." Then he gave Dredd a mischievous sideways grin. "On second thoughts, don't. Better to find out that kind of thing on your own, hmm?"

And he closed his eyes.

There were a lot of bodies to bury on *Sargasso*, and not much time to do it. Lying in state wasn't a good idea when there were Black Atlantic insects around, hungry for a meal and a place to start a family. Most of the dead would be weighted and dropped into the water en masse.

But the Old Man was different. As Bane had once told Judge Dredd, in his way he had been the heart of the city.

The funeral took place in the harbour, and was simple enough. Bane herself had wrapped the tiny, frail body in tarpaulin, and weighted it with chain. Then six skipper's men, Philo Jennig among them, had brought out a long crate. Bane lifted the body into it.

Before they closed the lid, they put some bottles of liquor in there with him, the ones with the charms around the neck. Just in case.

Gethsemane Bane was rather surprised to find herself still dry-eyed. She had thought when the Old Man finally passed on, that she would cry an ocean. Effectively he was her last remaining family. But after hearing about his past she realised that she couldn't shed him any tears. Not because of any evil he might have done in the past – that had been over almost before she was born. No, it was because she knew that he had finally got what he wanted after all this time.

He had peace. And a few good bottles of booze.

They took the body to the quayside. The harbour pool was open to the sea and away from the worst of the stern wake by necessity. Anything dropped there would be under the waves before the turbulence touched it, and heading for bottom by the quickest, smoothest route there was.

Oddly, the Mega-City Judges were there, but standing a respectful distance away. Bane couldn't quite work out why and she wasn't about to ask. But she had a feeling that for them, if they were there when one fallen Sargassan was sent on his final journey, it would be as if they had watched them all go.

Land-folk. Bane shook her head, silently. She could never understand them.

The crate containing the Old Man was heavy with all that chain. Bane helped the skipper's men lift it to the edge of the quay and slide it forward. It disappeared beneath the surface without fuss and was swallowed by the inky water.

Bane watched it go and raised her head. Something had moved, up above the harbour doors.

It took her a second to see it. "Oh, drokk!"

The Warchild had found them.

It was crouched in the door mechanisms, up on the huge horizontal shaft that connected the two drive motors. Its camouflage pulsed feebly and Bane could see that its damaged arm was still a shrivelled, opened wreck.

The quayside was suddenly a mass of screams and people running for cover. Bane scampered back to where the Judges had spread out, aiming their Lawgivers: Dredd left-handed, Peyton clutching his tightly in both fists, Vix with her free hand across her middle. Bane got behind Dredd, as it was probably the safest place to be.

The Warchild seemed to notice the Judge. It cocked its head slightly to one side and jumped. It hit the quayside, hard, with both feet, then raised itself to full height. It stood, swaying. Its arm-blade was already extended.

Dredd stepped forwards, Lawgiver centred on the creature's forehead. "Your move, creep," he snarled.

The Warchild slowly raised its blade past attack position until it was vertical – almost in salute.

And then it leapt.

Dredd's Lawgiver thumped once. The shot took the Warchild in the face.

The creature slowed, and stumbled to a halt. It seemed to look at Dredd hard, one last time. Then it stepped off the quay.

Roughly seven thousand people had died when the *Elektra Maru* tore itself free of *Sargasso*. The exact number was impossible to know since so many had been washed overboard, smashed to atoms by the falling food ship and incinerated by the *Kraken*'s plasma flare. Their bodies would never be found. It would be months before all the missing were listed. If they ever were.

The plague had taken more than twelve hundred. The Warchild had killed at least twenty-one, not counting Hellermann and the dead Judges. Out of a population of nearly a million, the numbers were perhaps quite small. But they would remain part of *Sargasso*'s history for as long as the cityship roamed the Black Atlantic.

Bane never saw the Warchild again. Later, on the deck of the *Putin*, she told Dredd that there was no way it could have survived. "You shot it through the face, Dredd. It had no brains left. Besides, it went under so fast."

Dredd's lip twisted. "Your Old Man walked around for half a day without his heart beating. On this ship, anything's possible."

Ahead of them a great, lumpy-looking machine was resting on the deck, just ahead of the bridge. There were big eagles painted onto it – Justice Department symbols. It had extended a ramp several minutes earlier, and the bodies of Hellermann, Larson and Adams had been loaded on board.

The three remaining Judges had been there to watch it land and had waited for the bodies to go on. Once that was done, there was no longer a reason for them to stay.

Dredd turned to her. "That's my ride."

"I'd guessed that. Dredd?"

"Hmm?"

"You gonna make that assault charge stick?"

"I'll think about it. Given that it was Vix you hit hardest." With that, he strode away, up the ramp and into the machine. Peyton gave her a rueful grin.

"That's kinda like 'Thanks' in Dredd-speak," he told her. "Take care, captain."

Vix was looking at her. She could tell, even though the skull-emblazoned helmet hid most of the woman's face. "What?"

The SJS Judge shook her head. "Nothing," she replied quietly. "Stay out of trouble, mu–"

She stopped. "Bane," she said finally, and followed the other two up the ramp.

Bane watched her go. Suddenly, she found herself grinning. She leapt up and down, waving madly. "Bye, Vix!" she called. "Hope your boss doesn't have you killed!"

Vix paused for a second at the top of the ramp. She didn't turn around, but she did wince visibly, almost as if imagining a blade in the back of her neck. Then she strode forward and was gone.

The machine turned on its drives, heavy turbines whining into life and sending spray whipping up off the deck. Massive landing struts folded back into its base. The machine drifted up, closing its ramp as it went, and then it tipped to one side and hurtled away.

In seconds it was a dot. Bane watched it for a long time.

Then she walked away, back across the teeming decks of the *Sargasso*, towards the harbour. There was fuel to be bought and paid for, damage to the gunwales and the cranes, and a windshield to be fixed.

Salvage didn't just scoop itself out of the water.

Gethsemane Bane had a lot to do. She grinned, and increased her pace, arms swinging as she headed back to her ship.

EPILOGUE

Gosnold Seamount – one week later.

As he strapped himself into the cockpit of the seeker pod and locked down the hatch, Zheng Zhijian knew the honour of the *Chaoyang* rode entirely on his shoulders.

Captain Shao himself had come down from the bridge to see him off. It was a mark of great respect to Zheng to even see the captain face to face, let alone for the man to shake his hand. Zheng had only realised the true nature of the honour when Shao had leaned close to him during the handshake and whispered in his ear that, should he fail in his mission this time, he may as well try to point the seeker pod at Mega-City One and just keep going, because the bay door of the *Chaoyang* would not open for him again.

In other words, if the *Abraxis* wreck site did not turn up an intact bioweapon, Zheng was a dead man. The seeker pod was fantastically resilient, built to withstand the crushing pressures of the deepest ocean trenches, but the Black Atlantic had already begun to eat its way through the hull.

The bay sealed itself around him and filled rapidly with water. Zheng began to take the seeker pod through its pre-launch checks, tapping at the band of touchpads that ringed the observation dome. The little submarine seemed to be performing well, despite what the Atlantic had done to its outer casing.

The seeker pod was very small and Zheng had to pilot it lying on his belly. His head and hands were completely inside the synthetic-diamond dome at its prow, which gave him a superb view of his surroundings. It also helped offset the claustrophobia caused by being wrapped in a coffin-sized cylinder of metal at the bottom of the ocean, in pressures that would crush a man to a pulp in a second.

Zheng put such things out of his mind and keyed the release signal. He had work to do.

Below him, the bay door hinged open from the stern, forming a long ramp down into darkness. Zheng felt the pod drop and lurch as the holding clamps let it go, then he opened the twin throttles and sent the machine scooting down the ramp. For a second the flattened, manta-like bulk of *Chaoyang*'s belly scanned above him, then he was in open water.

According to Sino-Cit intelligence reports, the wreckage of the cityship *Abraxis* had come to rest across the Gosnold Seamount, an underwater mountain that rose to almost fifteen hundred metres below the surface. This was easily within the seeker pod's capabilities, but the *Chaoyang* could not go nearly so deep. Zheng had to take the pod down in steep dive for the first hour of his mission.

Although all Atlantic water was acidic and poisonous, the pollutants that turned it black tended to congregate at the surface. At two hundred metres down the *Chaoyang* had been drifting in water that was relatively clear. As Zheng dove deeper still, the water around him grew more and more transparent. There was no light, of course – he had to activate his flood lamps as soon as he had left the bay – but their cones seemed to stretch out forever in front of him.

At twelve hundred metres his sonar began to pick up the top of the Seamount. He keyed his comms unit. "Seeker One to *Chaoyang*. Come in"

"Base here, Zheng. Don't tell me you've found something."

Zheng made a face. "Don't get impatient, Li. I'm just reaching the peaks."

"Okay, Zheng. Next time I need to find a mountain, I'll send you to look for it."

Chaoyang had already tracked down the four Warchild caskets, all those that had not been picked up by scavengers. It hadn't been easy. Their broadcast frequencies had been supplied by Dr Hellermann before she had been arrested, but the Black Atlantic was a difficult place to search. On their second day out, they'd had to torpedo a megashark, and things hadn't got much better after that.

The first two cryopods had been on the surface, but by the time the *Chaoyang* had tracked down the other two the Atlantic's corrosive waters had broken through their seals, sending them to the bottom. The caskets and their contents had been designed to withstand a lot, but not the hammering weight of three thousand metres of acidic seawater. The caskets had been crumpled wrecks when Zheng had brought them aboard with the seeker pod, and their contents were so pulped that not even their DNA could be usefully extracted.

The pods on the surface were useless, too. Their countdown timers had reached zero and without other instructions they had simply opened, dumping their newborn contents into the sea. The area was known to be the feeding grounds of slick-eels and a particularly large variety of hellsquid, and so the retrieval of the bioweapons had been classed as "unlikely".

As pilot of the *Chaoyang*'s primary seeker pod, it had been Zheng who had brought each ruined, opened pod aboard in the machine's robot grabs. Thus, the dishonour of failure was his, four times over.

At sixteen hundred metres the pod's sensors began to pick up large amounts of metal. Zheng levelled the sub out and began to drift down horizontally, turning the machine on its axis as he did so.

Suddenly, a wall of metal scanned passed the dome.

Zheng yelped and hit the stops. When the pod was still he twisted the controls, turning the machine very slowly around. He brought it to rest with the flood lamps making twin discs of light on the hull of a chem-tanker.

The vast ship was resting almost vertically, its bow buried in the surface of the Seamount. Zheng brought the pod around until he was alongside the deck, then began to move down very slightly sideways, keeping the pools of light from his flood lamps steady on the side of the hull.

The further down he went, the more the wreckage of *Abraxis* rose up around him.

Within minutes he was surrounded by a forest of metal. He slowed his descent, letting the pod's sensors build up a model of the ruin around him. The cityship had come apart on its way to the seabed, the links between its component ships shearing and tearing free as the holed sections dragged their intact neighbours beneath the waves. By the time *Abraxis* hit the seamount, it had ceased to be a single, cohesive unit and had become a broad field of shattered metal ten kilometres across.

This, Zheng decided, was going to take a lot of searching.

Forty minutes later, one of his sensor readouts began to chime. He almost ignored it, as he was concentrating his attention on the pattern-recognition and DNA tracer systems. Zheng had gone down to the seamount hoping to find the body of one of the Warchild units lying intact, so it could be retrieved and dissected back in Sino-Cit. The motion sensor wasn't his primary concern.

Zheng frowned and studied the readout more closely. There was movement down here, that was certain. Not fast, and not coming towards him, which was a bonus. But the sensor had been programmed to screen out things like waving fronds of seaweed or objects drifting in the current. If the sensor was chiming, it meant that there was something alive on the Gosnold Seamount.

"Seeker One to *Chaoyang*. I'm getting movement down here. Going weapons-hot."

"Acknowledged, Zheng. Try not to blow yourself up."

Zheng made an obscene hand gesture towards the comm but kept his silence. If he'd activated his weapons array without informing the base ship he would have been in even more trouble.

It was probably just a slick-eel anyway, feeding on the corpses that had come down with *Abraxis*. And there were a lot of those. Zheng angled the seeker pod towards the source of movement, and throttled very gently forwards.

A hundred metres ahead of him, around a pile of fallen container-habs, lay the broken hull of a mid-sized freighter. The ship had twisted on the way down, its own weight breaking its back as it hit the Seamount, and the entire superstructure had torn free and was lying a short distance away. Zheng eased the pod towards the ragged, open base of the ship's tower.

His pattern and DNA sensors lit up with a triumphant buzzing.

Zheng found himself gaping. It took him a moment to get his jaw closed so he could talk coherently to the *Chaoyang*. "Li? I've found something."

"You're kidding. A dead Warchild?"

"Not exactly…"

The superstructure was on its side, its lower edge half-buried in sand and debris. The starboard wall was now a roof to an open chamber, and from this roof – in surprisingly neat rows – were dozens of translucent sacs.

Each sac was bigger than a crouching man, roughly egg-shaped and covered in leathery, transparent flesh. Each was sending out the distinctive DNA signature of the Warchild.

Zheng brought the pod close to one of the sacs. As his lights hit it, something within twitched fitfully. He saw limbs through the translucent wall, and teeth. "They reproduced," he gasped. "They laid eggs. I didn't think they could–"

There was a massive impact, and the pod crashed sideways.

Zheng screamed. The pod had been struck by something very powerful. For a second he thought he had been torpedoed, but then he heard noises through the hull: a terrible scraping, scratching noise, as if something was clawing the machine apart.

Zheng slammed the pod into full reverse, taking it clear out of the chamber and into open water. The scratching was still horribly loud. Suddenly, Zheng saw something slap down onto the dome.

It was a hand.

It was corpse-grey, with three long, clawed fingers and armoured joints. It began to tear at the dome. Impossibly, the talons started to leave score marks in the synthetic diamond.

Zheng gripped the controls and spun the pod on its axis, hard, but the hand wouldn't come free. Instead there was a series of blows to the pod's stern and the controls went abruptly dead.

The seabed, rocky and strewn with acid-eaten corpses, came up and hit the dome, blocking out the light.

On the *Chaoyang*'s bridge, Captain Shao listened to the screams for about half a minute. Then he opened up a small panel on the command board and pressed the button it concealed.

The screams ceased at once. The button, protected by a panel that would only open to Shao's fingerprints, had detonated a micro-fusion charge set just behind the seeker pod's pressure cabin. The explosion would have reduced Zheng and his machine to thumb-sized fragments instantaneously. His attacker too, but Shao didn't need that any more.

"Pilot Zheng Zhijian has bravely sacrificed himself for the good of *Chaoyang* and Sino-Cit," he announced. "Let his name forever be spoken with reverence and honour."

He turned to his first officer. "Mr Yun," he smiled. "Now that whining little failure is history, please prepare the cryotanks and send out the secondary pod to harvest those egg-sacs."

Yun saluted and left the bridge. Captain Shao went back to the monitor screen. It had been showing a view from the seeker pod's forward cameras, but since Shao had pressed the button, all it showed was static.

He rewound the playback, and froze the picture at the best frame of the sacs, lined up along the inside of a sunken freighter.

"Perfect," he whispered. "Perfect."

These new bioweapons would be even better than the consignment Sino-Cit had bought from Dr Hellerman. Tempered in the fires of combat and the lethal waters of the Black Atlantic, they would be tougher, faster, and more adaptable than before.

And they had evolved a new capability – they could reproduce. Before long, Sino-Cit would have a new army.

And when it did, the world would fear.

THE BIG MEG GLOSSARY

Atlantic Division: A cadre of Judges who scan the Black Atlantic for pirates, raiders and smugglers.

Atlantic Wall: The wall that divides the Black Atlantic from Mega-City One and protects the city from its polluted waters.

Black Atlantic: An apt description of the Atlantic Ocean whose waters are so heavily polluted that it is incredibly toxic and lethal to humans.

Block: Giant skyscrapers that make up most of Mega-City One. The inhabitants of blocks are known as blockers. Sometimes the pressures of living in such cramped high-rise conditions lead to block mania, which may spark a war.

Brit-Cit: British counterpart of Mega-City One.

Control: The nerve centre of Mega-City One, relaying information to Judges on the streets.

Cursed Earth: A vast radioactive wasteland that stretches across North America, populated by mutants, freaks and wild creatures.

Daystick: The Judge's favoured truncheon.

Dust Zone: An industrial sector of Mega-City One, dedicated to industry but off-limits to pedestrians and populated by acid pools.

Fattie: Thanks to food shortages after the Apocalypse War, excessive eating has become a valued craze, with the dedicated fattie weighing over a tonne.

Futsie: "Future shock", a mental breakdown of epic proportions, can spark some of The Big Meg's citizens to become irrationally violent such as going on a shooting spree.

Graveyard Shift: A term coined by the Judges for the late night/early morning period of duty.

Hondo-Cit: Japanese counterpart of Mega-City One.

Iso-Cube: The standard imprisonment for criminals, a huge block full of very small isolation cubes.

Lawgiver: The weapon of choice for the Judge, an automatic multi-shell gun whose ammunition ranges from armour piercing to ricochet rounds.

Lawmaster: The Judge's computer-controlled motorbike. Extremely powerful, intelligent and heavily armed.

Magoon: A large harpoon-style launcher.

Plascrete: Construction material for the Big Meg.

Power Tower: A controlled volcano, the Power Tower obtains red hot lava from beneath the Earth's crust to provide most of Mega-City One's energy supply.

SJS: The Special Judicial Squad act as the Judge's police; they seek out corruption and crime within the Law with extreme prejudice.

Skedway: A minor roadway; smaller than a megway but larger than an overzoom.

Smokatorium: A huge, block-sized building dedicated to legal tobacco smoking. To smoke tobacco outside the building is deemed illegal and can warrant a six-month sentence.

Statue of Judgement: Erected by public subscription in honour of the Law, the huge statue of a Judge dwarfs over the Statue of Liberty.

Synthi-caf: A refreshing drink that is similar to banned coffee, it has now deemed illegal due to its highly addictive properties and has been replaced by various forms of synthi-synthi-caf.

Tek-Judge: A technical and engineering specialist whose skills range from advanced forensic analysis to the repairing of vehicles, weapons, etc.

Titan: A small moon orbiting Saturn, used as a dedicated maximum-security prison for Mega-City One's most dangerous criminals.

Tri-D: Also known as holovision; there are over 312 channels in Mega-City One.